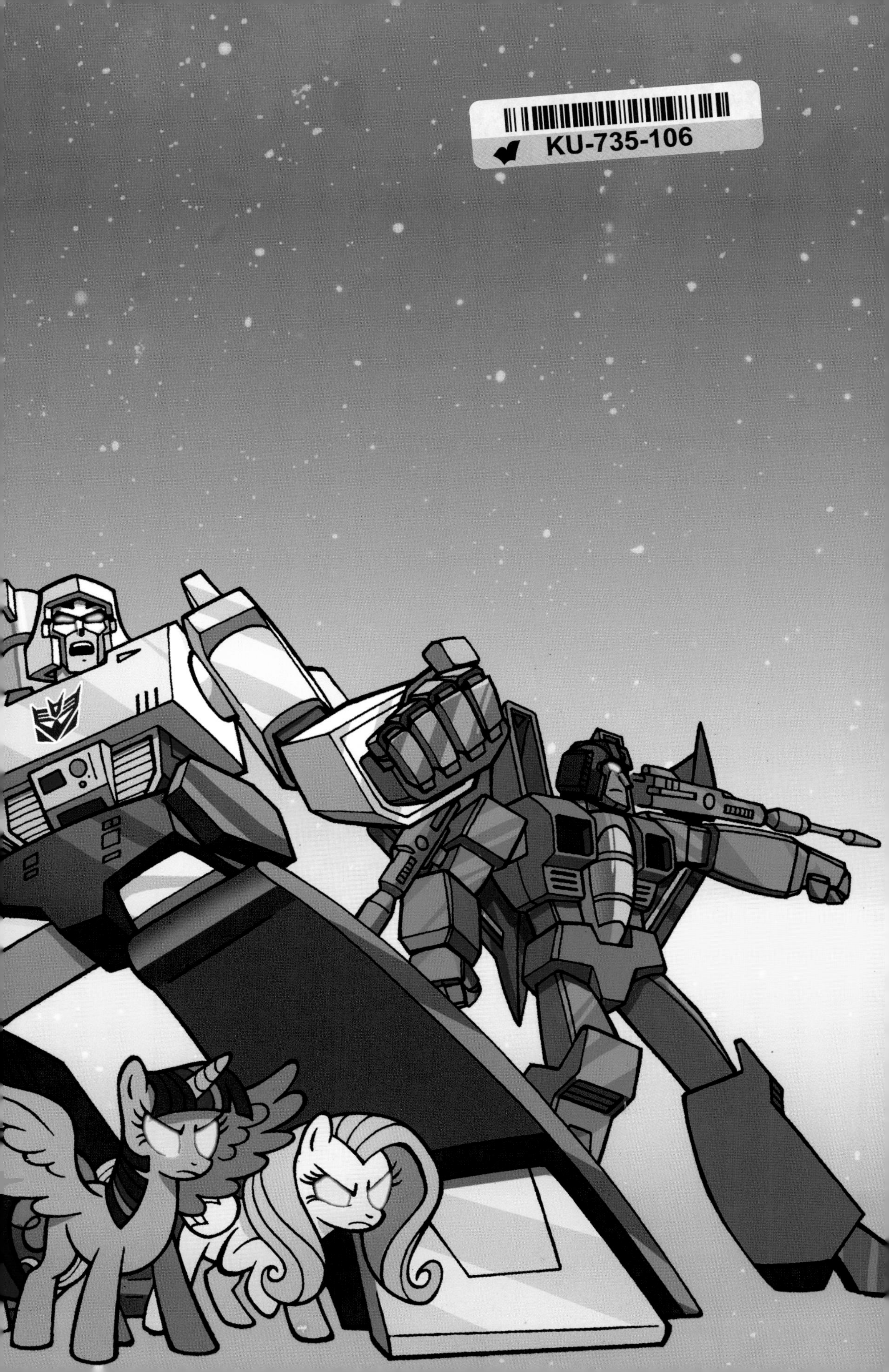

ROLL CALL *PONIES!*

THE MANE SIX
RAINBOW DASH, FLUTTERSHY, PINKIE PIE, TWILIGHT SPARKLE, RARITY, AND APPLEJACK!

AND SPIKE!

SOMBRA
FORMER RULER OF THE CRYSTAL EMPIRE

OCTAVIA AND VINYL SCRATCH
MUSICALLY INCLINED SUPERSTARS

THE WONDERBOLTS
HIGH FLYERS

HOLIDAY AND LOFTY
SCOOTALOO'S AUNTS, REAL TOUGH MOTHERS

THE YOUNG SIX
BEST FRIENDS AND YOUNG ADVENTURERS

SMOLDER
THE HEIGHTS-FLYING, FIRE-SPITTIN'-EST, TAKE-NO-GUFF-EST DRAGON OF THEM ALL!
(ALSO PART OF THE YOUNG SIX!)

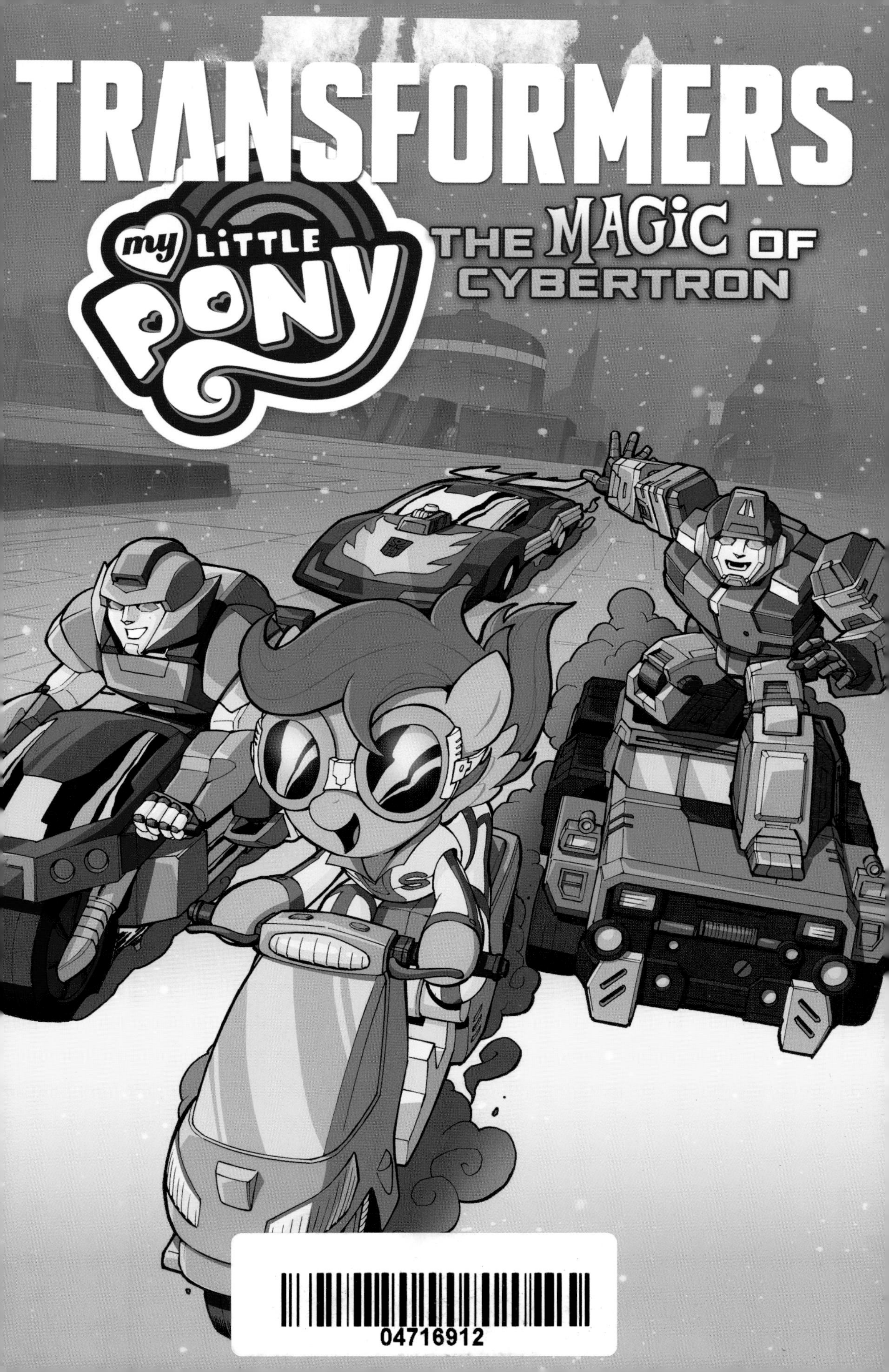
TRANSFORMERS
my LITTLE PONY
THE MAGIC OF CYBERTRON

Facebook: **facebook.com/idwpublishing**
Twitter: **@idwpublishing**
YouTube: **youtube.com/idwpublishing**
Instagram: **@idwpublishing**

Cover Art by
Tony Fleecs

Back Cover Art by
Evan Stanley

Series Edits by
Megan Brown

Series Consulting Editor
David Mariotte

Collection Edits by
Alonzo Simon
and **Zac Boone**

Collection Design by
Nathan Widick

Licensed By:

Special thanks to
Ed Lane,
Beth Artale,
Michael Kelly,
Bryony Latham,
Isabella Weiss,
Kelly Johnson
and Matt Clarke
for their invaluable assistance

ISBN: 978-1-68405-870-9   24 23 22 21   1 2 3 4

Nachie Marsham, Publisher
Blake Kobashigawa, VP of Sales
Tara McCrillis, VP Publishing Operations
John Barber, Editor-in-Chief
Mark Doyle, Editorial Director, Originals
Erika Turner, Executive Editor
Scott Dunbier, Director, Special Projects
Mark Irwin, Editorial Director, Consumer Products Mgr
Joe Hughes, Director, Talent Relations
Anna Morrow, Sr. Marketing Director
Alexandra Hargett, Book & Mass Market Sales Director
Keith Davidsen, Senior Manager, PR
Topher Alford, Sr Digital Marketing Manager
Shauna Monteforte, Sr. Director of Manufacturing Operations

Jamie Miller, Sr. Operations Manager
Nathan Widick, Sr. Art Director, Head of Design
Neil Uyetake, Sr. Art Director Design & Production
Shawn Lee, Art Director Design & Production
Jack Rivera, Art Director, Marketing

Ted Adams and Robbie Robbins, IDW Founders

For international rights, please contact
licensing@idwpublishing.com

ROLL CALL *ROBOTS!*

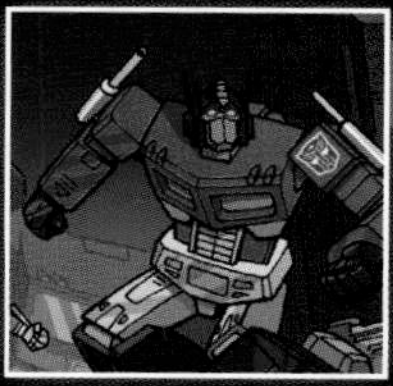

OPTIMUS PRIME
LEADER OF THE AUTOBOTS

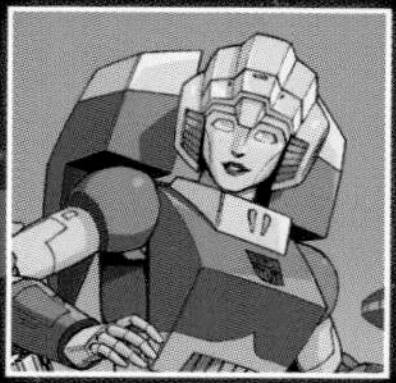

ARCEE
AUTOBOT

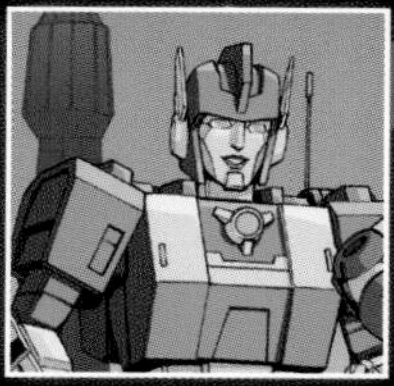

GREENLIGHT
AUTOBOT

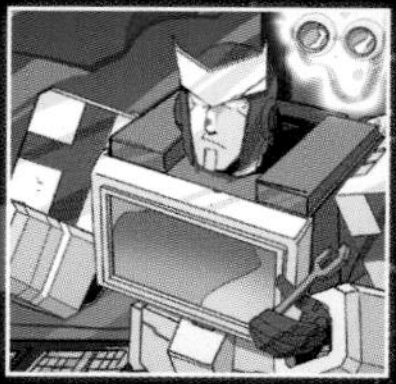

RATCHET
AUTOBOT

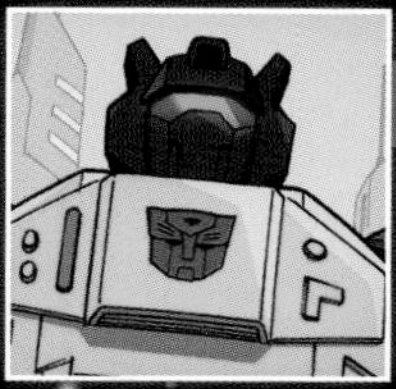

GRIMLOCK
DINOBOT

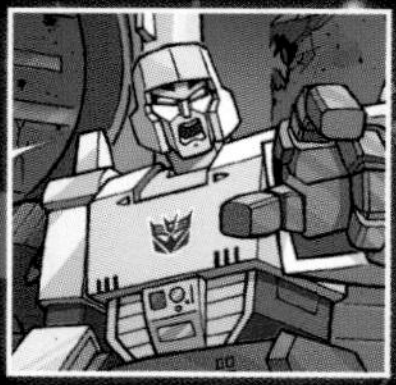

MEGATRON
WARLORD OF THE DECEPTICONS

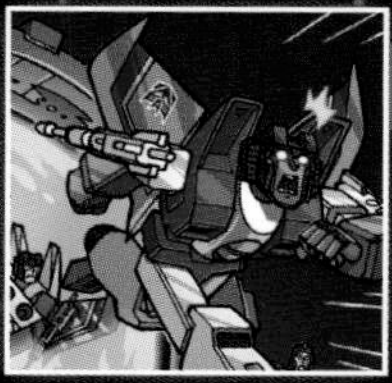

STARSCREAM
DECEPTICON

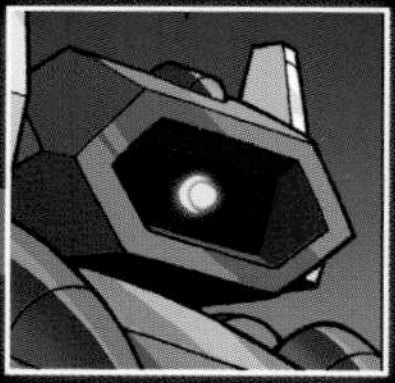

SHOCKWAVE
DECEPTICON

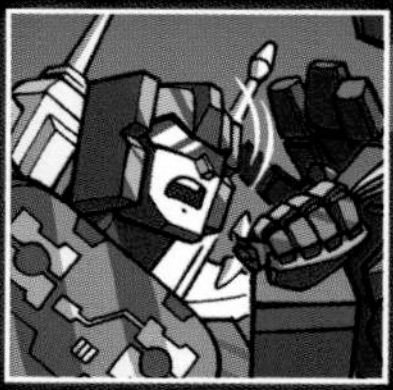

FRENZY
DECEPTICON

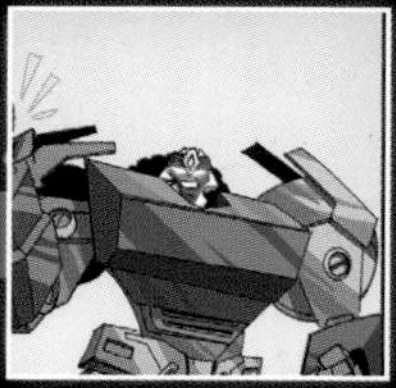

BREAKDOWN
DECEPTICON

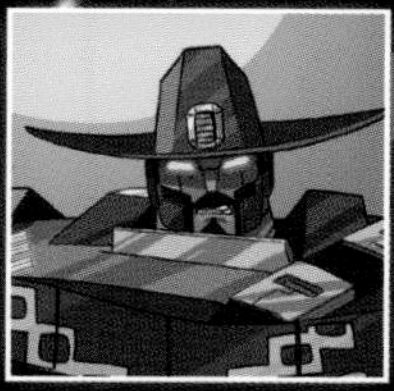

WILDWHEEL
FORMER AUTOBOT, CURRENT DECEPTICON

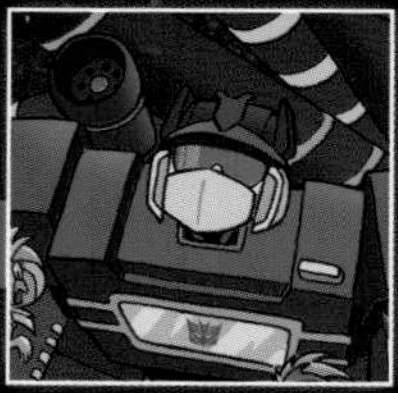

SOUNDWAVE
DECEPTICON

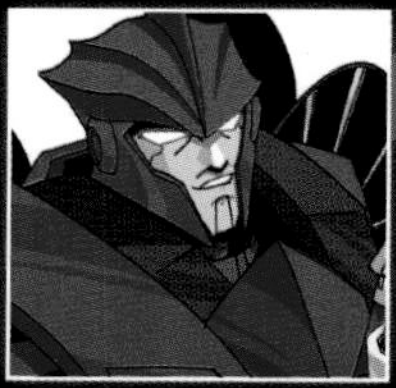

KNOCK OUT
DECEPTICON

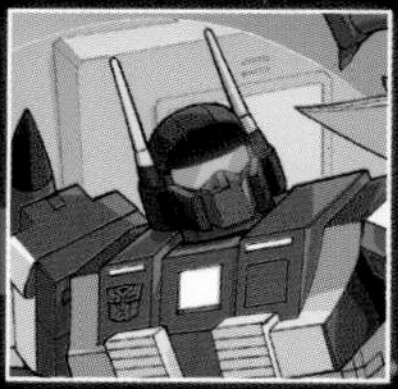

SUPERION
CYBERTRONIAN COMBINER

"THE MAGIC OF CYBERTRON"

WRITTEN BY **JAMES ASMUS**
ART BY **JACK LAWRENCE**
COLORS BY **LUIS ANTONIO DELGADO**
LETTERS BY **JAKE M. WOOD**

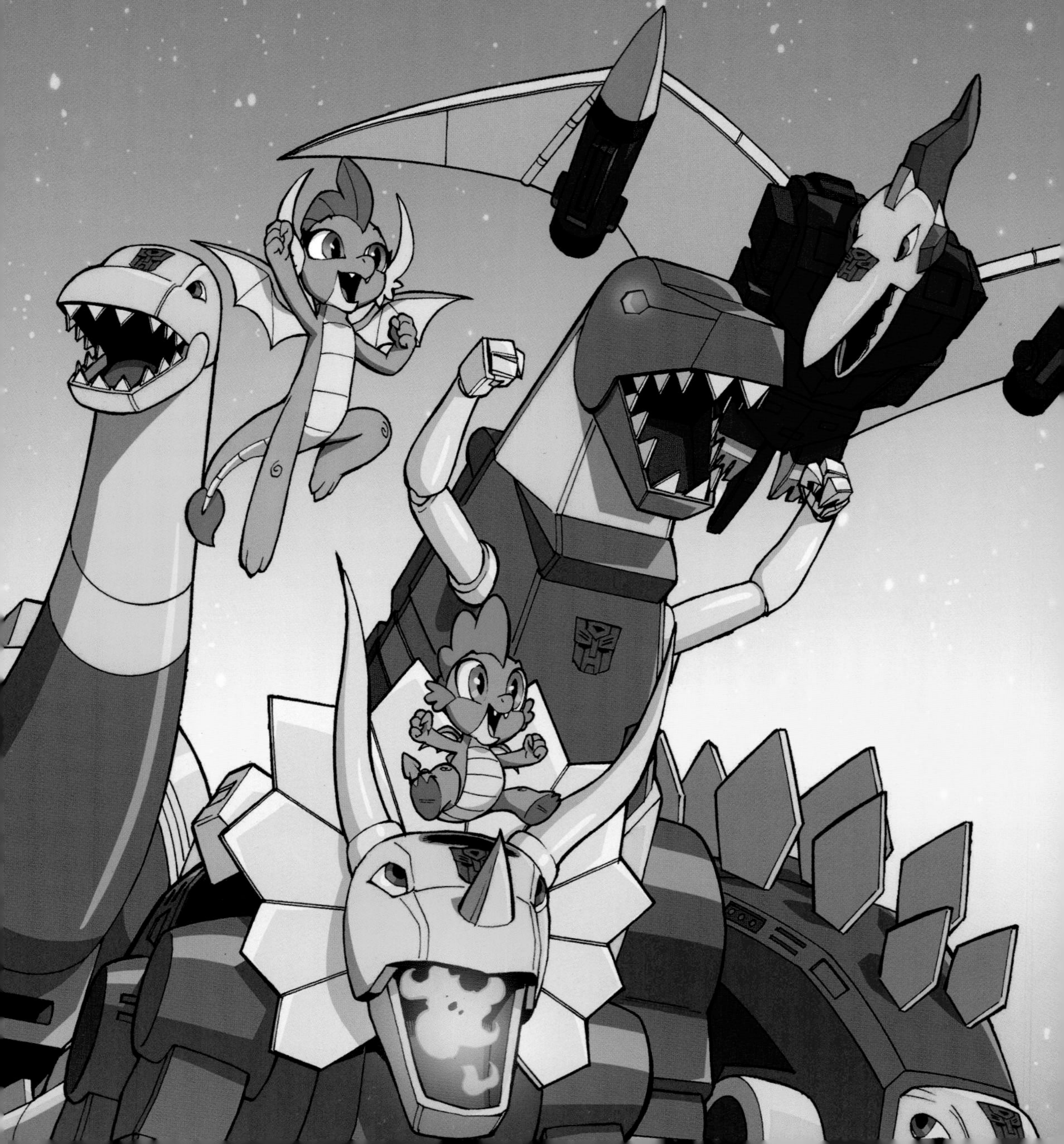

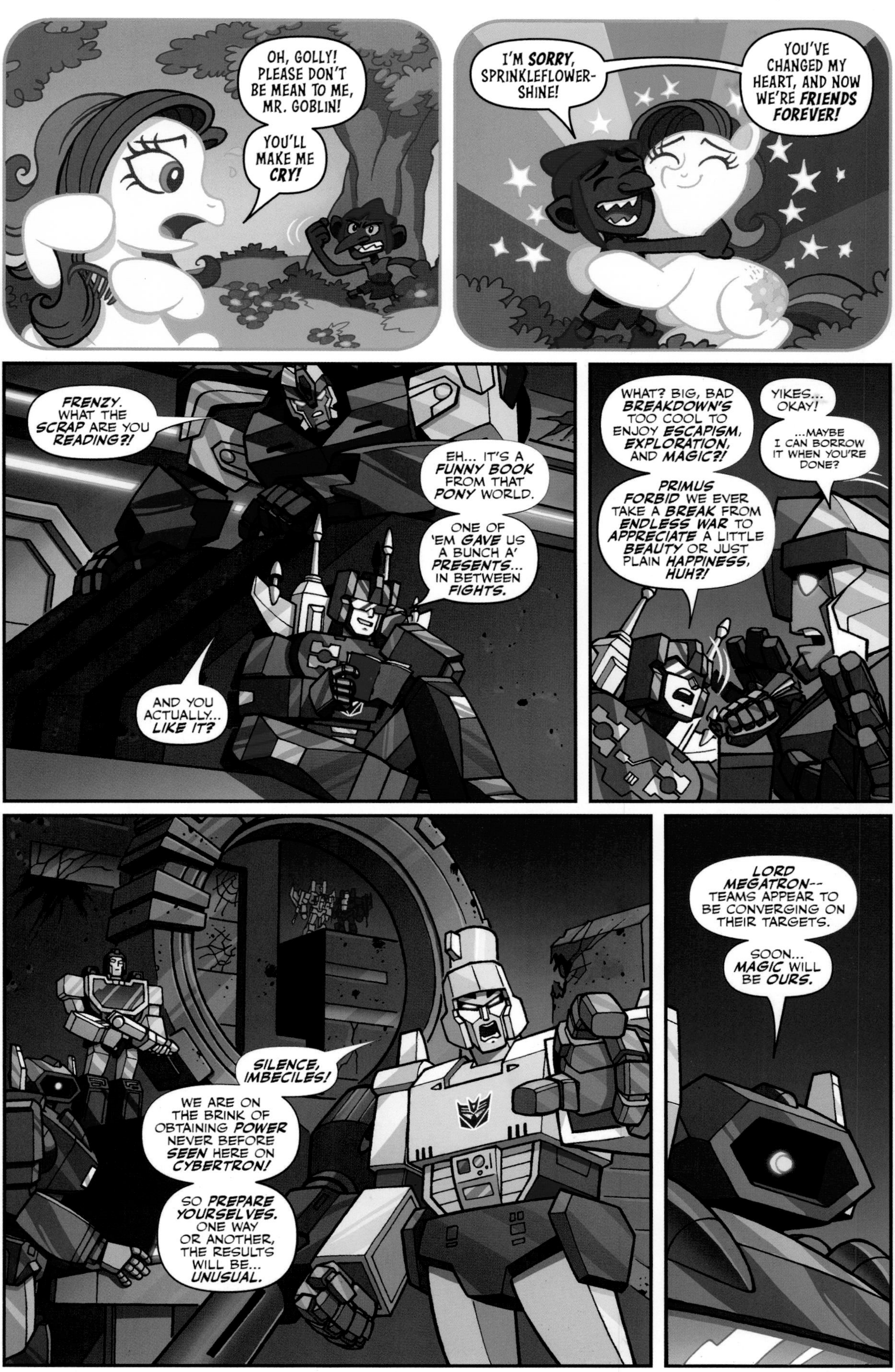
OH, GOLLY! PLEASE DON'T BE MEAN TO ME, MR. GOBLIN!
YOU'LL MAKE ME CRY!
I'M SORRY, SPRINKLEFLOWER-SHINE!
YOU'VE CHANGED MY HEART, AND NOW WE'RE FRIENDS FOREVER!
FRENZY. WHAT THE SCRAP ARE YOU READING?!
EH... IT'S A FUNNY BOOK FROM THAT PONY WORLD.
ONE OF 'EM GAVE US A BUNCH A' PRESENTS... IN BETWEEN FIGHTS.
AND YOU ACTUALLY... LIKE IT?
WHAT? BIG, BAD BREAKDOWN'S TOO COOL TO ENJOY ESCAPISM, EXPLORATION, AND MAGIC?!
PRIMUS FORBID WE EVER TAKE A BREAK FROM ENDLESS WAR TO APPRECIATE A LITTLE BEAUTY OR JUST PLAIN HAPPINESS, HUH?!
YIKES... OKAY!
...MAYBE I CAN BORROW IT WHEN YOU'RE DONE?
SILENCE, IMBECILES!
WE ARE ON THE BRINK OF OBTAINING POWER NEVER BEFORE SEEN HERE ON CYBERTRON!
SO PREPARE YOURSELVES. ONE WAY OR ANOTHER, THE RESULTS WILL BE... UNUSUAL.
LORD MEGATRON-- TEAMS APPEAR TO BE CONVERGING ON THEIR TARGETS.
SOON... MAGIC WILL BE OURS.

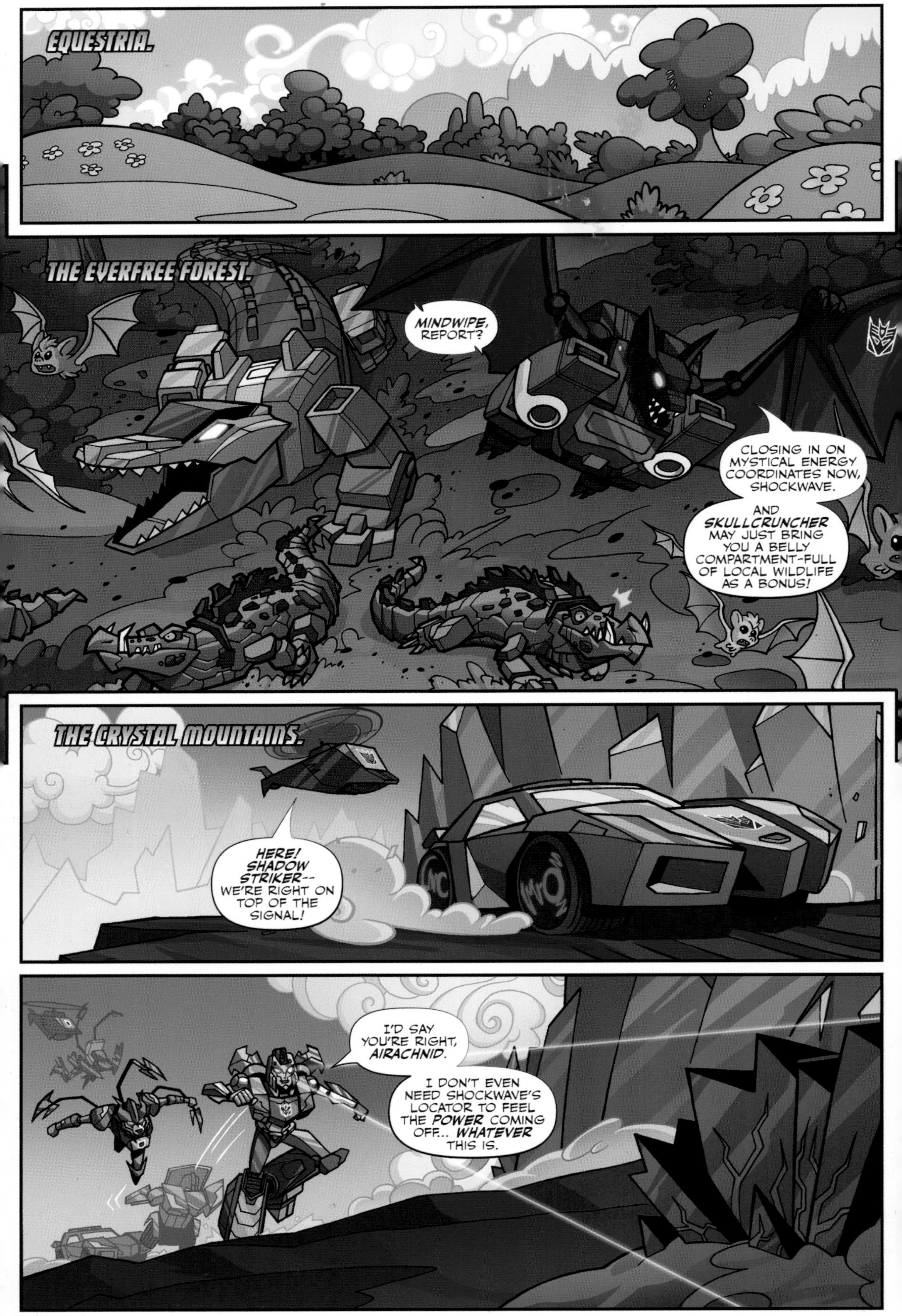
EQUESTRIA.
THE EVERFREE FOREST.
MINDWIPE, REPORT?
CLOSING IN ON MYSTICAL ENERGY COORDINATES NOW, SHOCKWAVE.
AND SKULLCRUNCHER MAY JUST BRING YOU A BELLY COMPARTMENT-FULL OF LOCAL WILDLIFE AS A BONUS!
THE CRYSTAL MOUNTAINS.
HERE! SHADOW STRIKER-- WE'RE RIGHT ON TOP OF THE SIGNAL!
I'D SAY YOU'RE RIGHT, AIRACHNID.
I DON'T EVEN NEED SHOCKWAVE'S LOCATOR TO FEEL THE POWER COMING OFF... WHATEVER THIS IS.

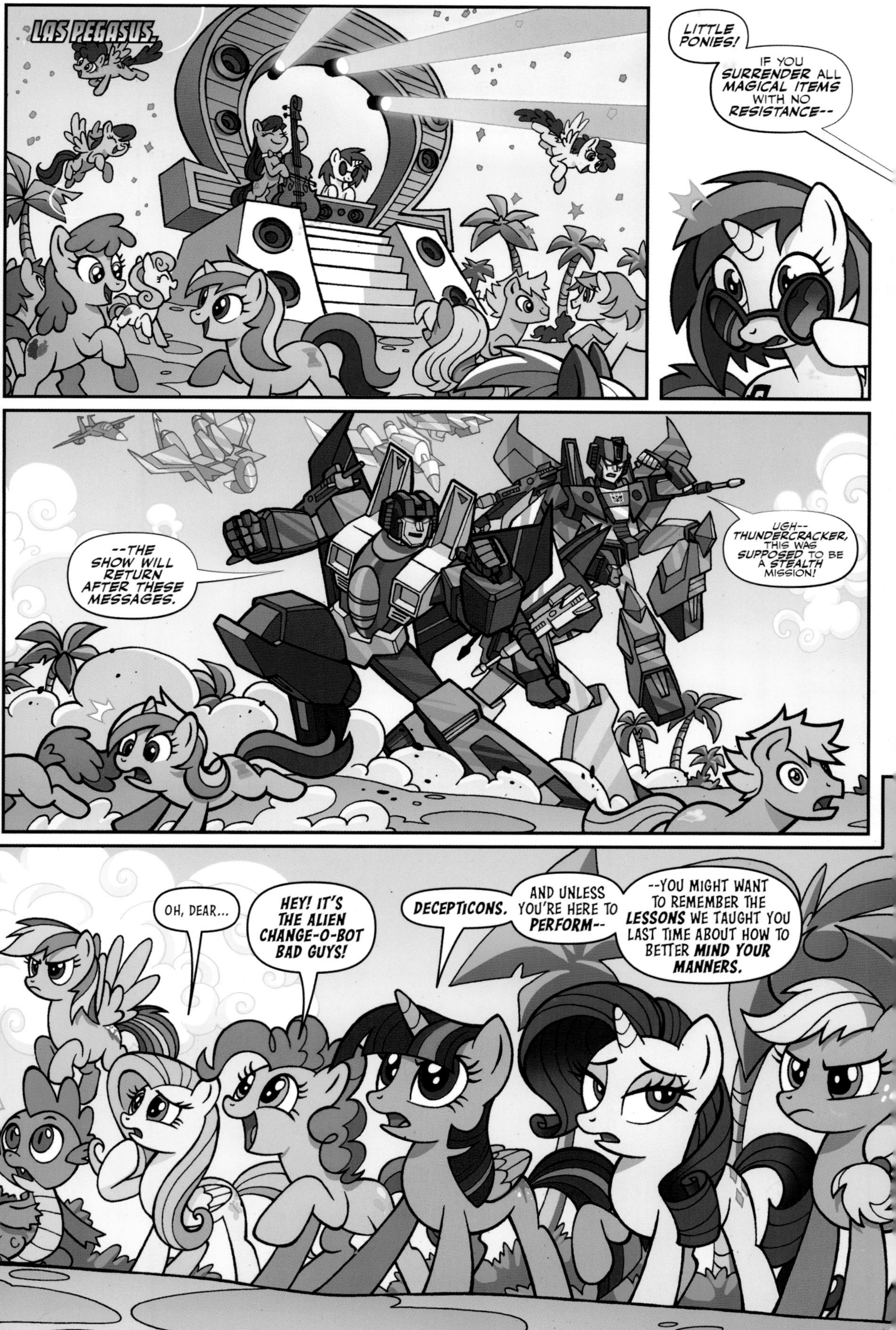
LAS PEGASUS.
LITTLE PONIES!
IF YOU SURRENDER ALL MAGICAL ITEMS WITH NO RESISTANCE--
--THE SHOW WILL RETURN AFTER THESE MESSAGES.
UGH-- THUNDERCRACKER, THIS WAS SUPPOSED TO BE A STEALTH MISSION!
OH, DEAR...
HEY! IT'S THE ALIEN CHANGE-O-BOT BAD GUYS!
DECEPTICONS.
AND UNLESS YOU'RE HERE TO PERFORM--
--YOU MIGHT WANT TO REMEMBER THE LESSONS WE TAUGHT YOU LAST TIME ABOUT HOW TO BETTER MIND YOUR MANNERS.

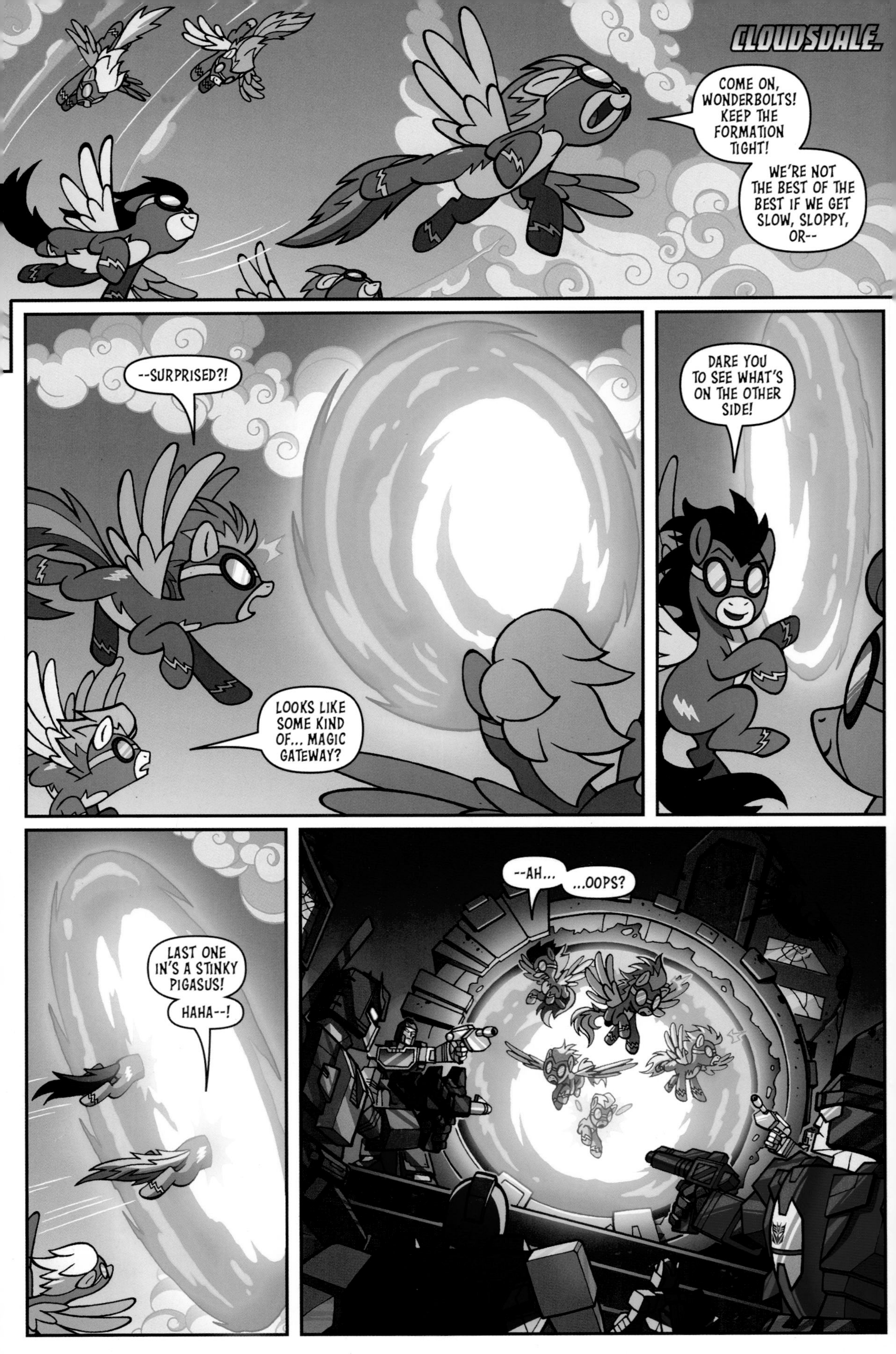
CLOUDSDALE.
COME ON, WONDERBOLTS! KEEP THE FORMATION TIGHT!
WE'RE NOT THE BEST OF THE BEST IF WE GET SLOW, SLOPPY, OR--
--SURPRISED?!
LOOKS LIKE SOME KIND OF... MAGIC GATEWAY?
DARE YOU TO SEE WHAT'S ON THE OTHER SIDE!
LAST ONE IN'S A STINKY PIGASUS!
HAHA--!
--AH...
...OOPS?

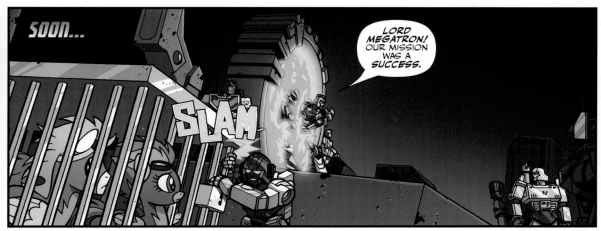

SOON...

LORD MEGATRON! OUR MISSION WAS A SUCCESS.

SLAM

I WILL BE THE JUDGE OF THAT, SHADOW STRIKER.

CLEAR THE WAY, FOOLS!

INCOMING!

OH, FOR PRIMUS' SAKE--!

YOU DIDN'T REALLY THINK YOU COULD OUT-FLY US, DID YOU?

DON'T BE TOO HARSH, RAINBOW DASH. WE DO ENCOURAGE EVERYPONY TO TRY THEIR BEST.

NOW LET'S SHOW THEM OURS.

CRCKRR.

WONDERBOLTS?

HOW'D *YOU* GET HERE?!

OH... RIGHT... FOLLOWING THROUGH THE PORTAL MEANT FOLLOWING THEM... TO *THEIR* WORLD...

OH, NO!

Y'KNOW, I FORGOT TO TELL YOU LAST TIME, BUT I *LOVE* YOUR MATCHING *CUTIE MARKS!*

DESTINY!

KRAKOOM

YOU CANNOT... DESTROY... *MY DESTINY!*

PRIME! ARE MY OPTICS HAYWIRE, OR--?

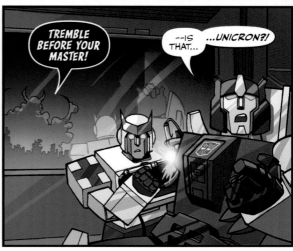

TREMBLE BEFORE YOUR *MASTER!*

--IS THAT...

...UNICRON?!

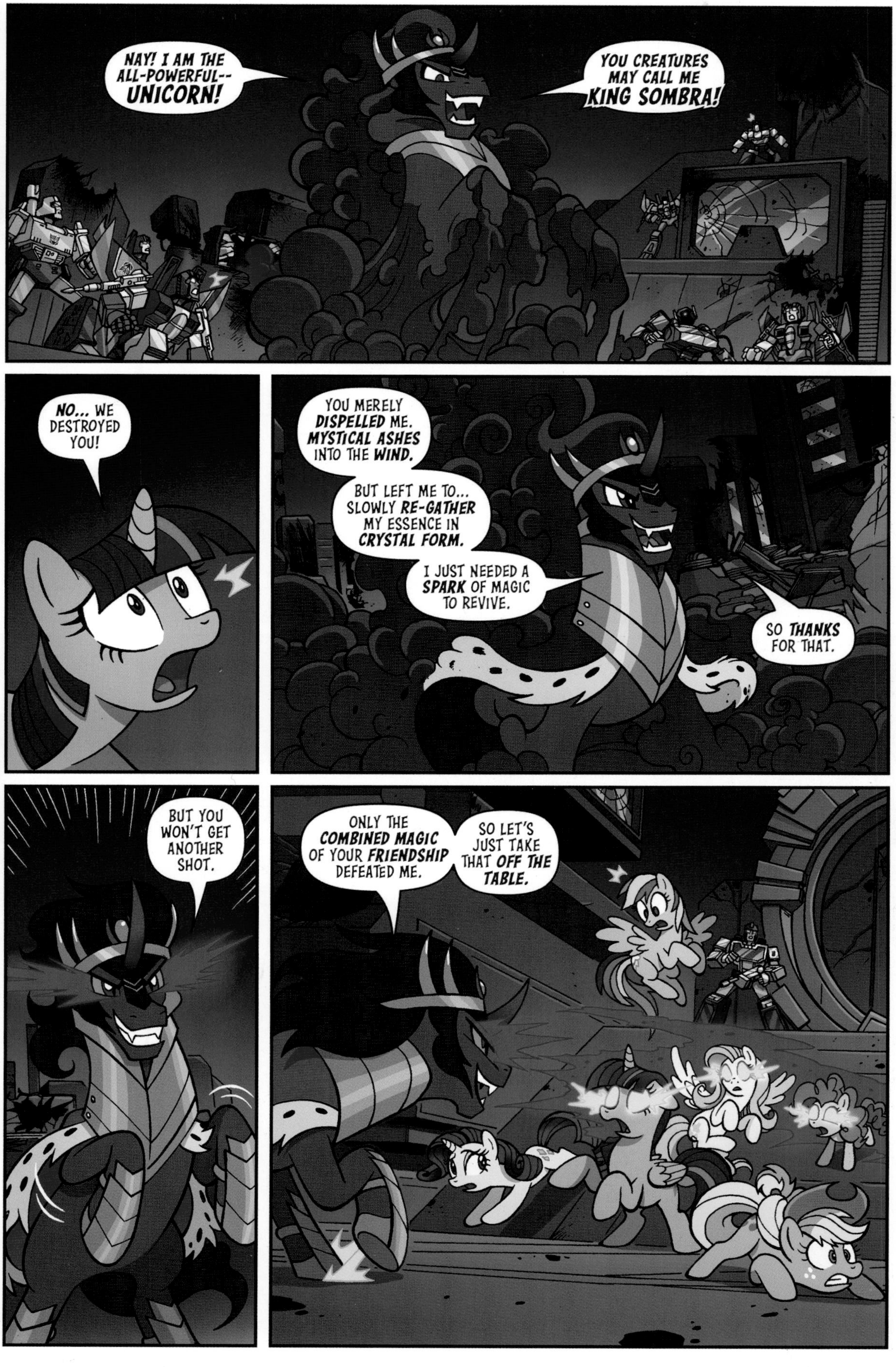
NAY! I AM THE ALL-POWERFUL-- UNICORN!
YOU CREATURES MAY CALL ME KING SOMBRA!
NO... WE DESTROYED YOU!
YOU MERELY DISPELLED ME. MYSTICAL ASHES INTO THE WIND.
BUT LEFT ME TO... SLOWLY RE-GATHER MY ESSENCE IN CRYSTAL FORM.
I JUST NEEDED A SPARK OF MAGIC TO REVIVE.
SO THANKS FOR THAT.
BUT YOU WON'T GET ANOTHER SHOT.
ONLY THE COMBINED MAGIC OF YOUR FRIENDSHIP DEFEATED ME.
SO LET'S JUST TAKE THAT OFF THE TABLE.

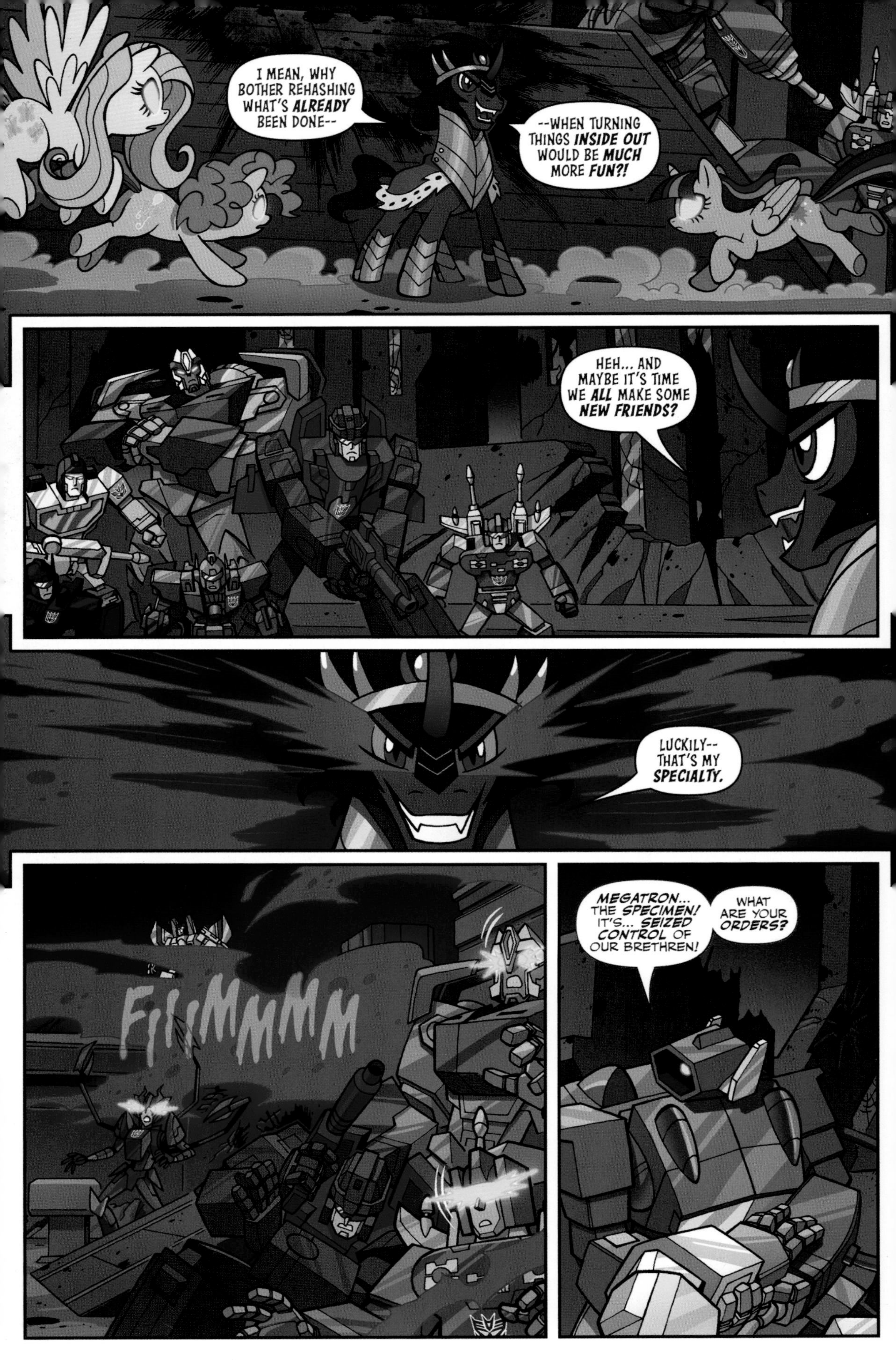
I MEAN, WHY BOTHER REHASHING WHAT'S ALREADY BEEN DONE--
--WHEN TURNING THINGS INSIDE OUT WOULD BE MUCH MORE FUN?!
HEH... AND MAYBE IT'S TIME WE ALL MAKE SOME NEW FRIENDS?
LUCKILY-- THAT'S MY SPECIALTY.
FIIIMMMM
MEGATRON... THE SPECIMEN! IT'S... SEIZED CONTROL OF OUR BRETHREN!
WHAT ARE YOUR ORDERS?

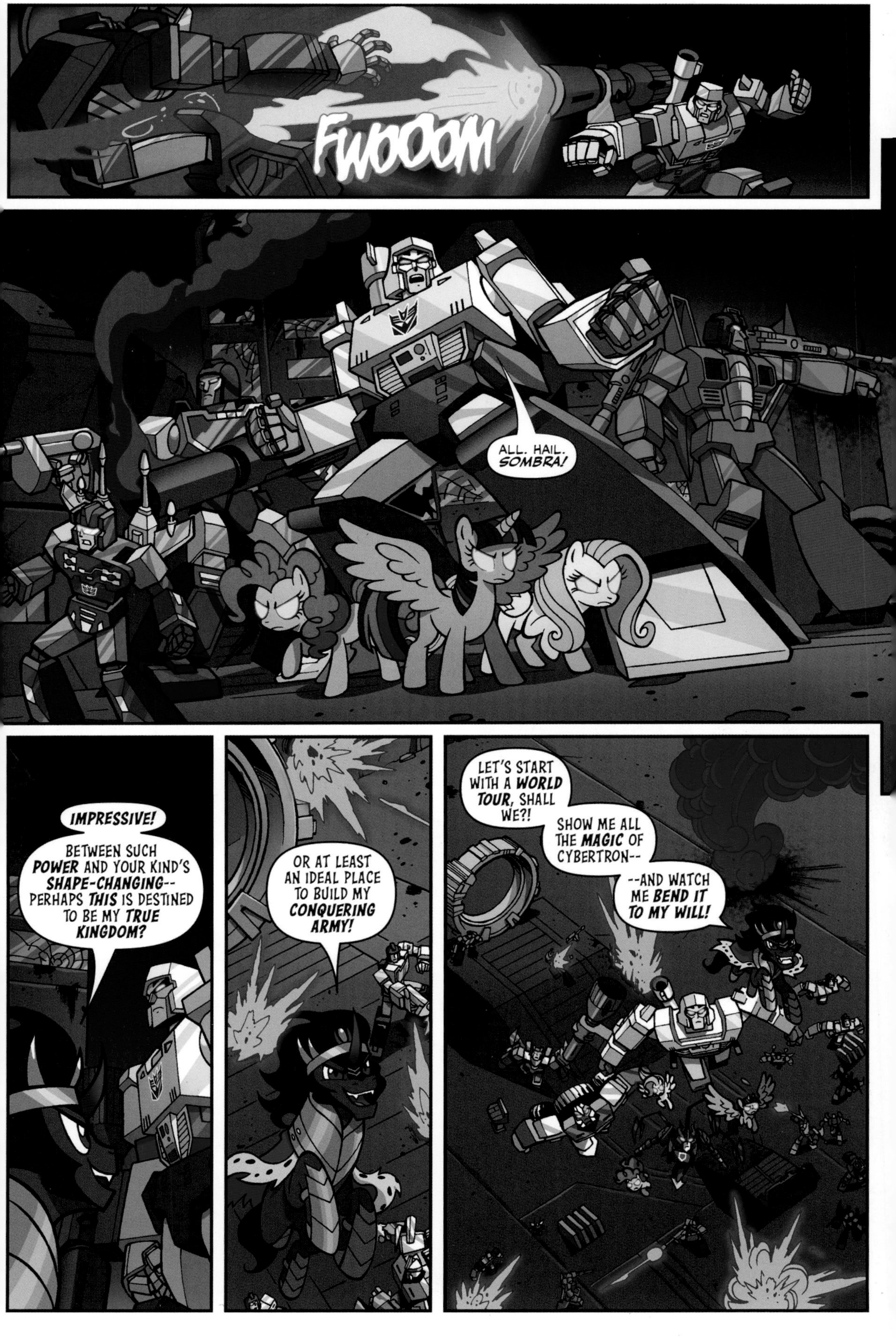
FWOOOM
ALL. HAIL. SOMBRA!
IMPRESSIVE!
BETWEEN SUCH POWER AND YOUR KIND'S SHAPE-CHANGING-- PERHAPS THIS IS DESTINED TO BE MY TRUE KINGDOM?
OR AT LEAST AN IDEAL PLACE TO BUILD MY CONQUERING ARMY!
LET'S START WITH A WORLD TOUR, SHALL WE?!
SHOW ME ALL THE MAGIC OF CYBERTRON--
--AND WATCH ME BEND IT TO MY WILL!

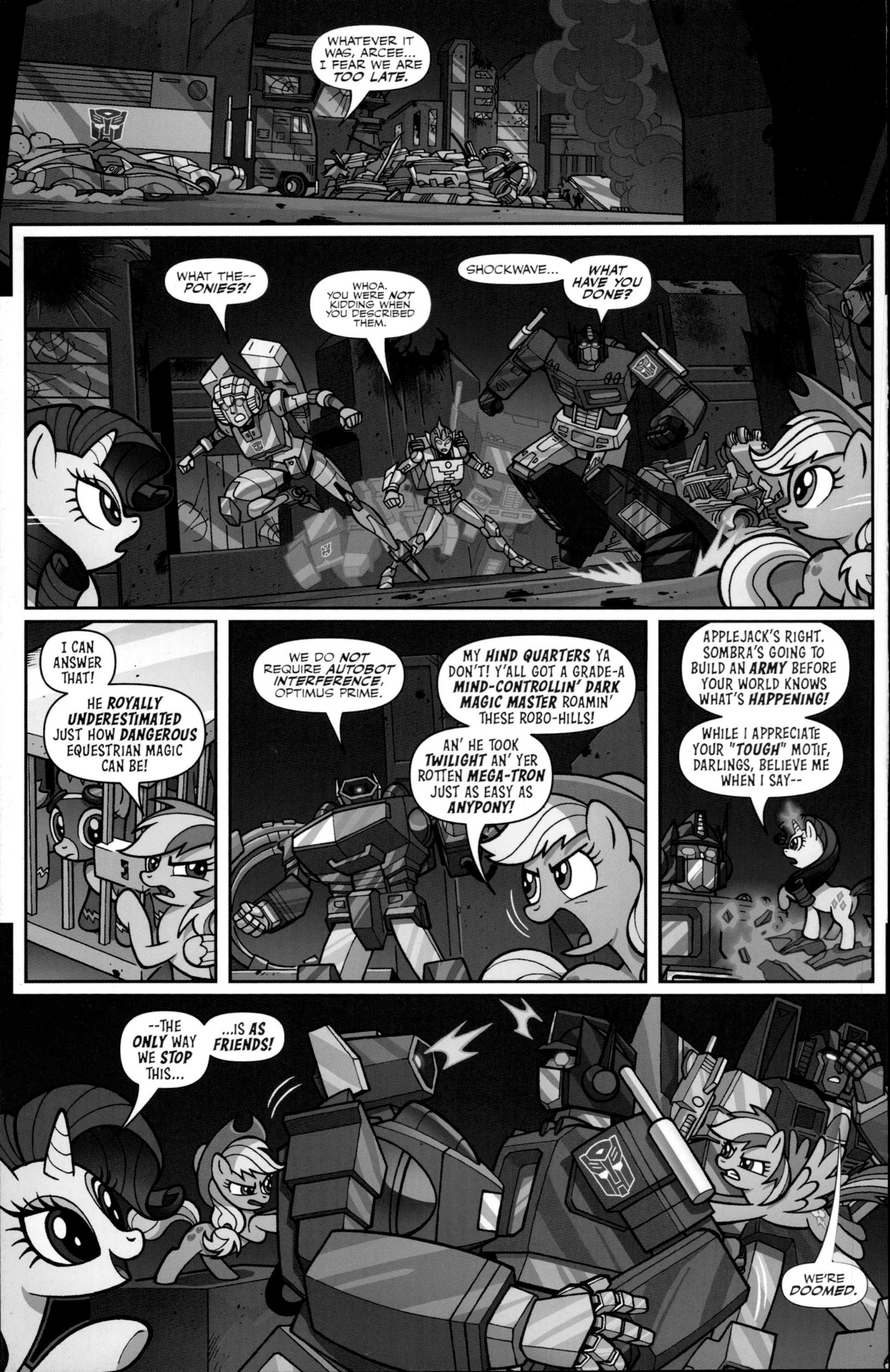
WHATEVER IT WAS, ARCEE... I FEAR WE ARE TOO LATE.
WHAT THE-- PONIES?!
WHOA. YOU WERE NOT KIDDING WHEN YOU DESCRIBED THEM.
SHOCKWAVE...
WHAT HAVE YOU DONE?
I CAN ANSWER THAT!
HE ROYALLY UNDERESTIMATED JUST HOW DANGEROUS EQUESTRIAN MAGIC CAN BE!
WE DO NOT REQUIRE AUTOBOT INTERFERENCE, OPTIMUS PRIME.
MY HIND QUARTERS YA DON'T! Y'ALL GOT A GRADE-A MIND-CONTROLLIN' DARK MAGIC MASTER ROAMIN' THESE ROBO-HILLS!
AN' HE TOOK TWILIGHT AN' YER ROTTEN MEGA-TRON JUST AS EASY AS ANYPONY!
APPLEJACK'S RIGHT. SOMBRA'S GOING TO BUILD AN ARMY BEFORE YOUR WORLD KNOWS WHAT'S HAPPENING!
WHILE I APPRECIATE YOUR "TOUGH" MOTIF, DARLINGS, BELIEVE ME WHEN I SAY--
--THE ONLY WAY WE STOP THIS...
...IS AS FRIENDS!
WE'RE DOOMED.

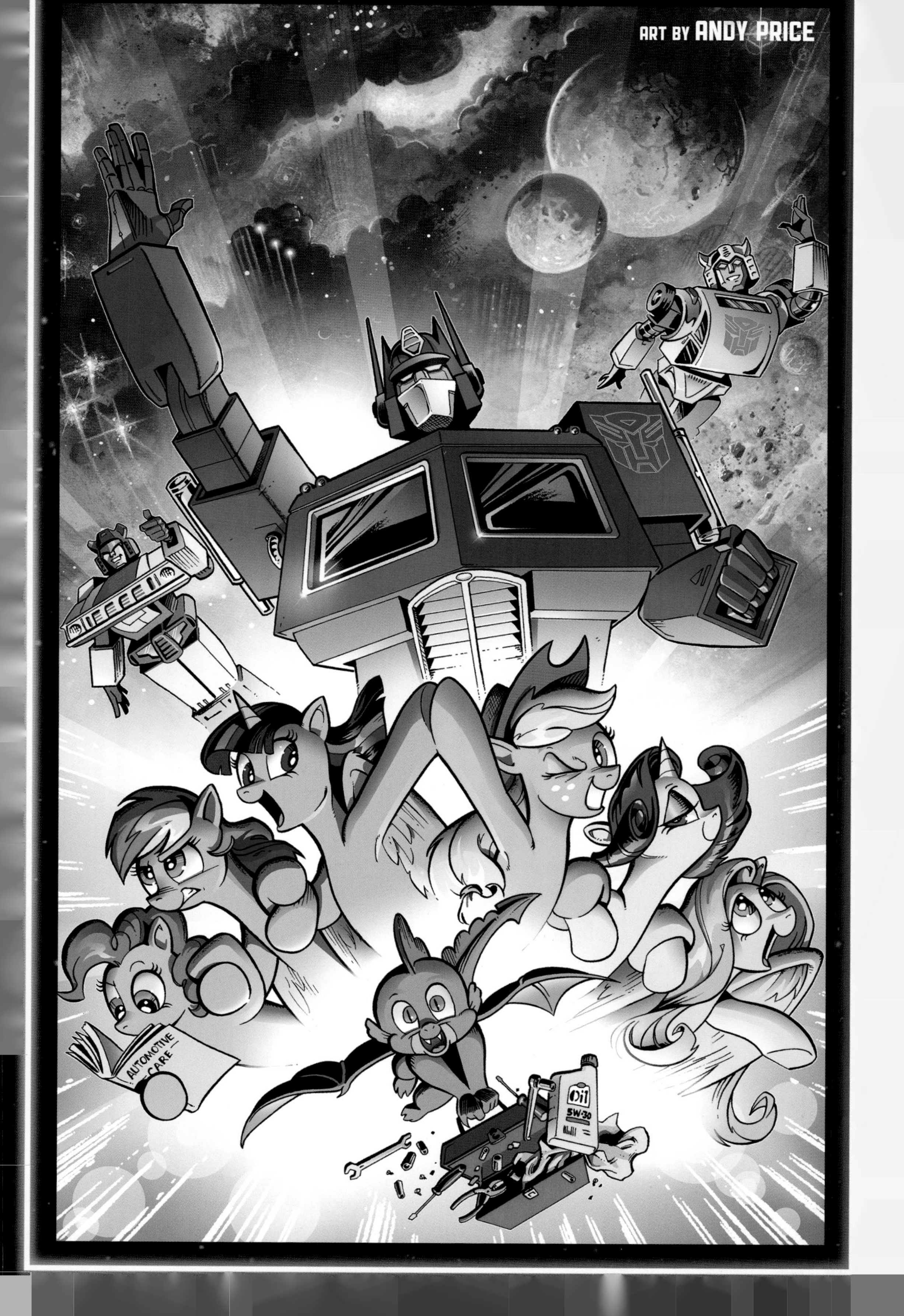
ART BY ANDY PRICE
AUTOMOTIVE CARE
Oil
5W-30

"A REAL MOTHER"

WRITTEN BY **SAM MAGGS**
ART BY **CASEY W. COLLER**
COLORS BY **JOANA LAFUENTE**
LETTERS BY **NEIL UYETAKE**

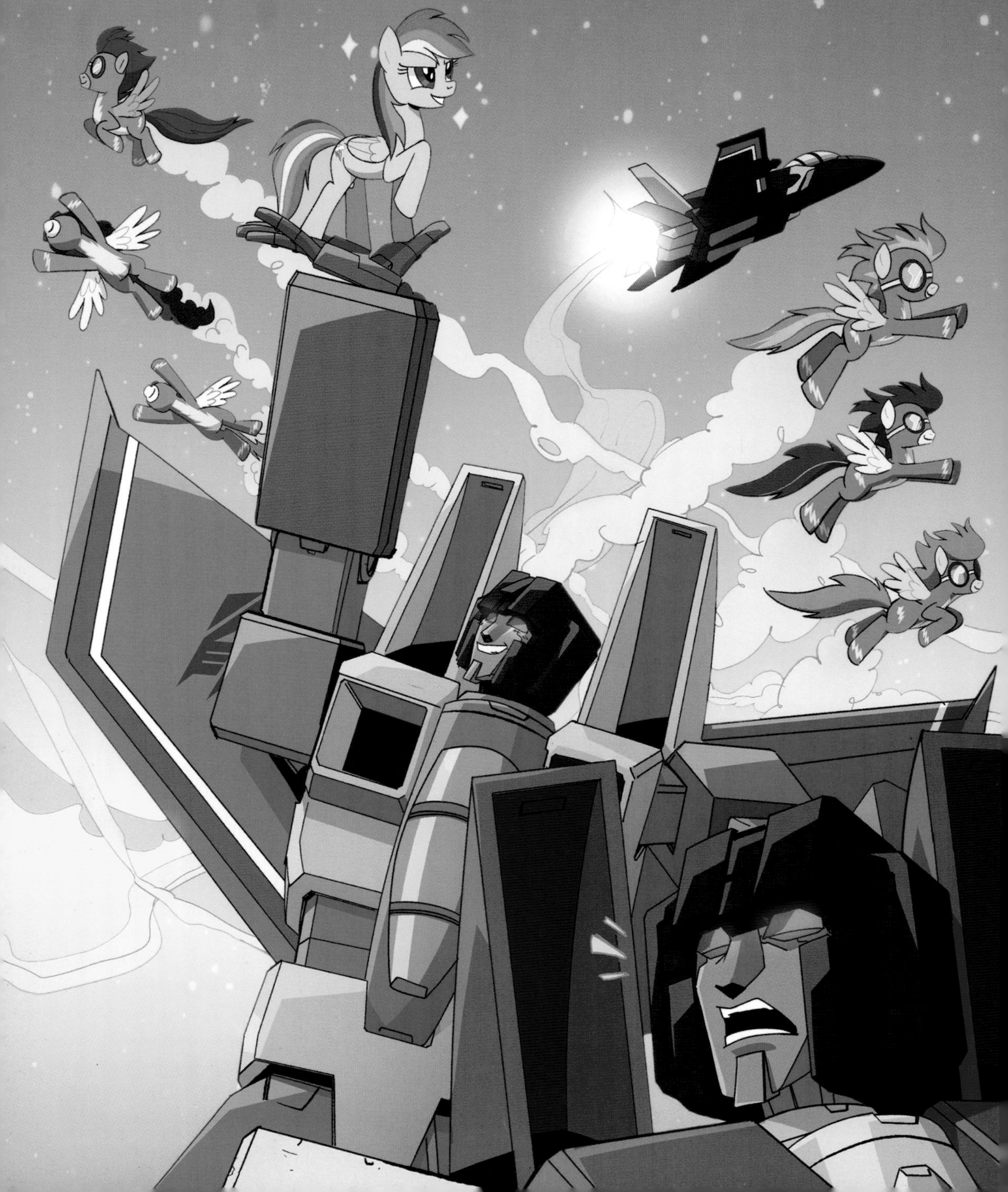

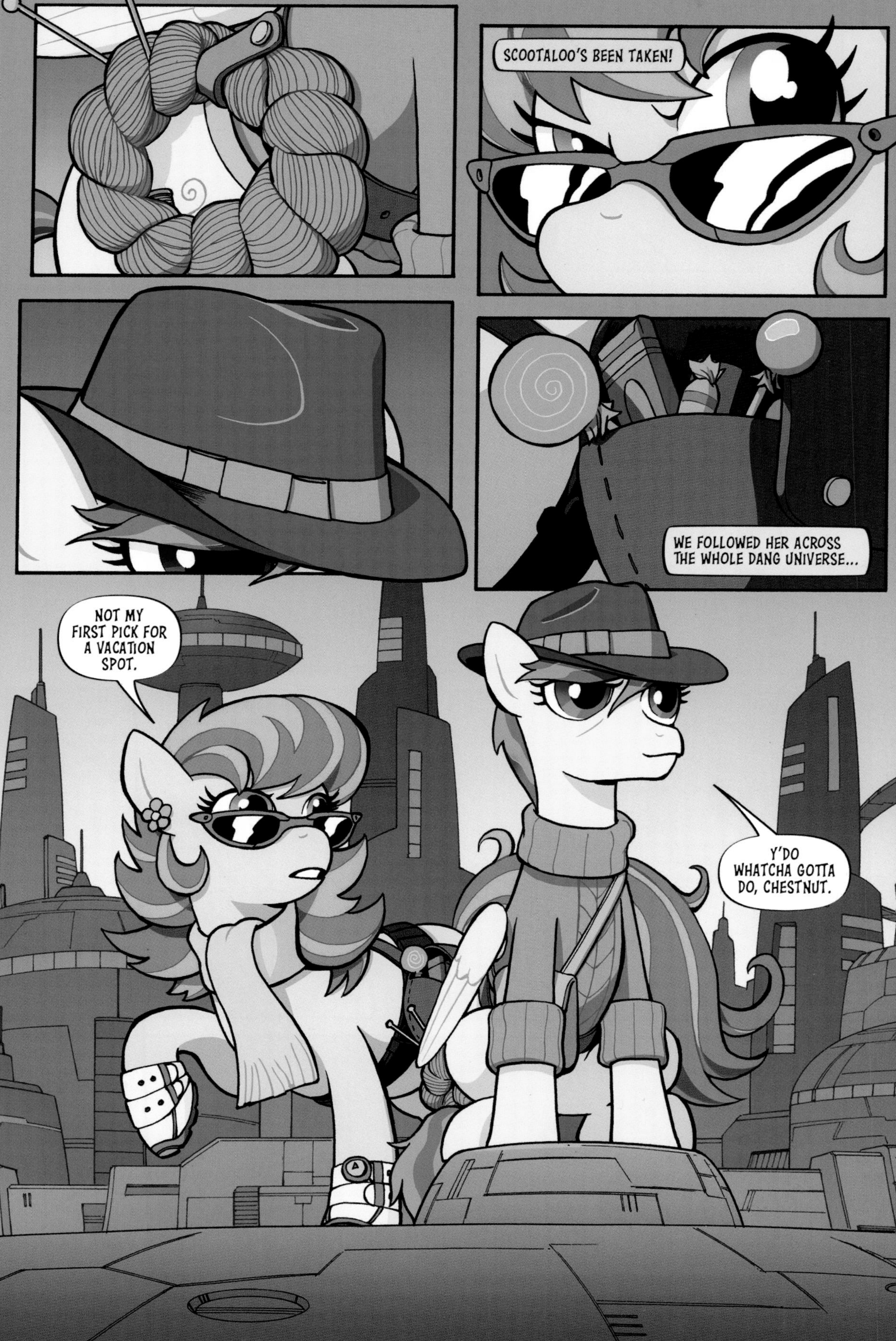
SCOOTALOO'S BEEN TAKEN!
WE FOLLOWED HER ACROSS THE WHOLE DANG UNIVERSE...
NOT MY FIRST PICK FOR A VACATION SPOT.
Y'DO WHATCHA GOTTA DO, CHESTNUT.

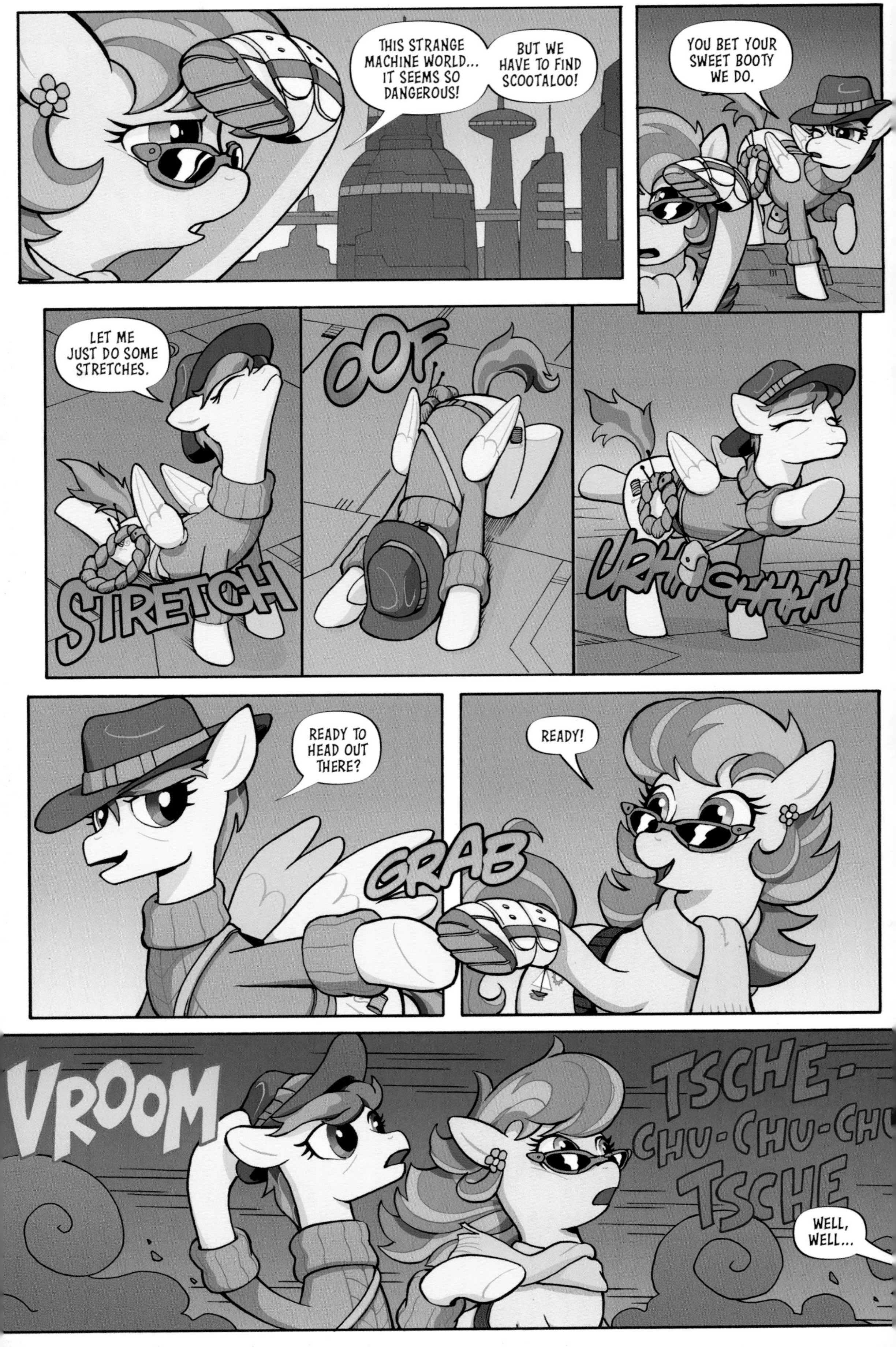
THIS STRANGE MACHINE WORLD... IT SEEMS SO DANGEROUS!
BUT WE HAVE TO FIND SCOOTALOO!
YOU BET YOUR SWEET BOOTY WE DO.
LET ME JUST DO SOME STRETCHES.
STRETCH
OOF
READY TO HEAD OUT THERE?
READY!
GRAB
VROOM
TSCHE-CHU-CHU-CHU
TSCHE
WELL, WELL...

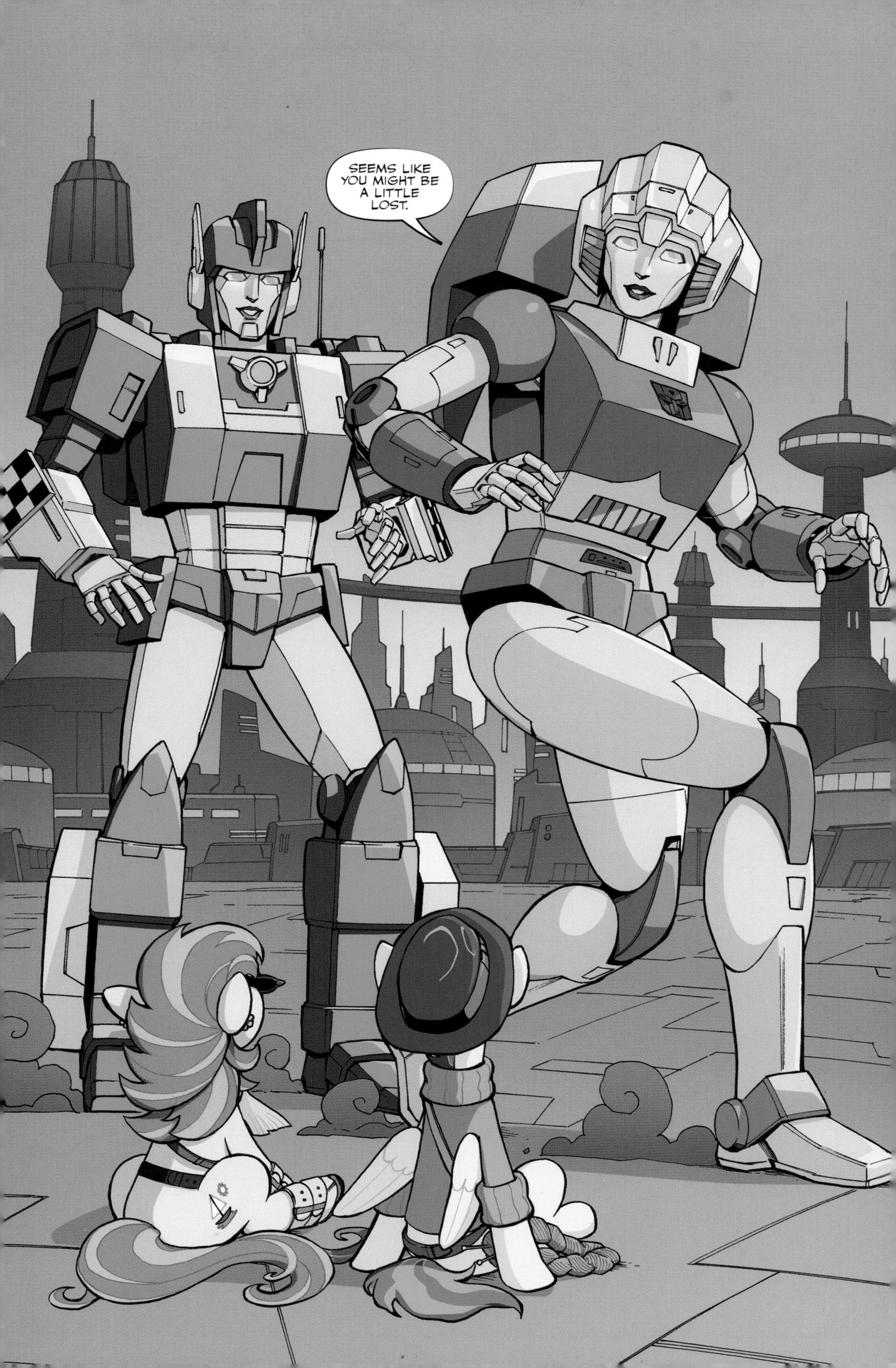
SEEMS LIKE YOU MIGHT BE A LITTLE LOST.

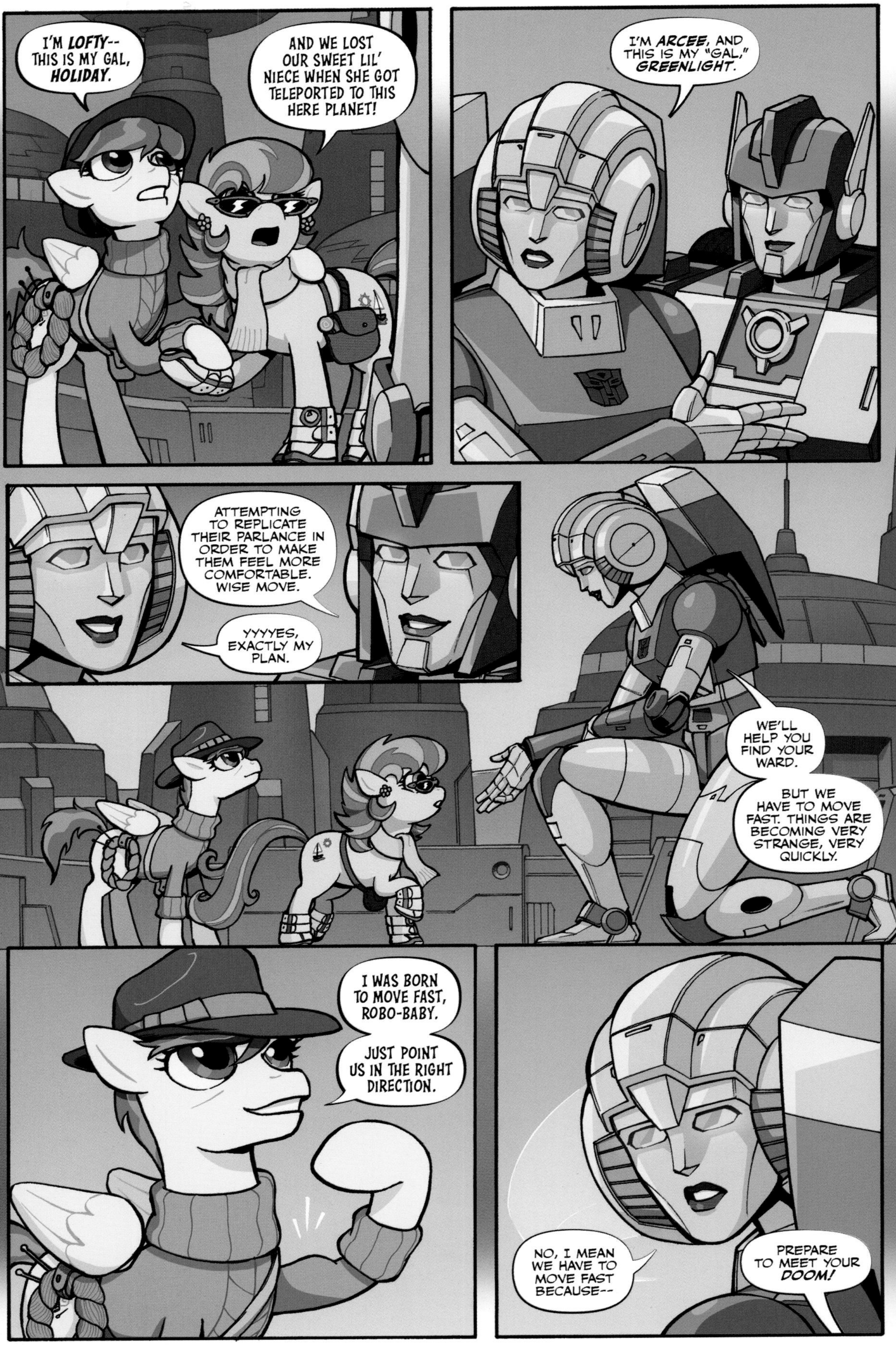
I'M LOFTY-- THIS IS MY GAL, HOLIDAY.
AND WE LOST OUR SWEET LIL' NIECE WHEN SHE GOT TELEPORTED TO THIS HERE PLANET!
I'M ARCEE, AND THIS IS MY "GAL," GREENLIGHT.
ATTEMPTING TO REPLICATE THEIR PARLANCE IN ORDER TO MAKE THEM FEEL MORE COMFORTABLE. WISE MOVE.
YYYYES, EXACTLY MY PLAN.
WE'LL HELP YOU FIND YOUR WARD.
BUT WE HAVE TO MOVE FAST. THINGS ARE BECOMING VERY STRANGE, VERY QUICKLY.
I WAS BORN TO MOVE FAST, ROBO-BABY.
JUST POINT US IN THE RIGHT DIRECTION.
NO, I MEAN WE HAVE TO MOVE FAST BECAUSE--
PREPARE TO MEET YOUR DOOM!

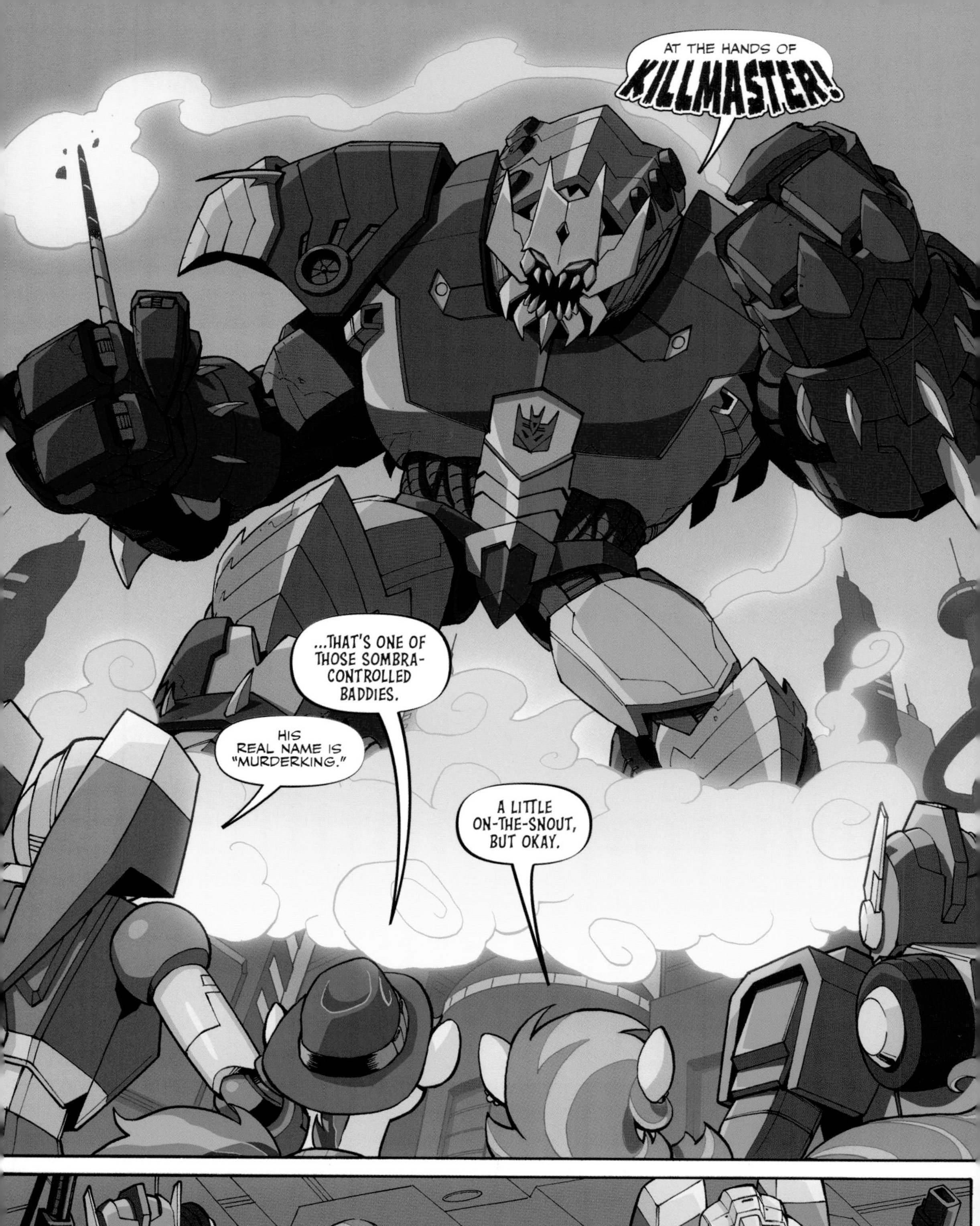
AT THE HANDS OF KILLMASTER!
...THAT'S ONE OF THOSE SOMBRA-CONTROLLED BADDIES.
HIS REAL NAME IS "MURDERKING."
A LITTLE ON-THE-SNOUT, BUT OKAY.

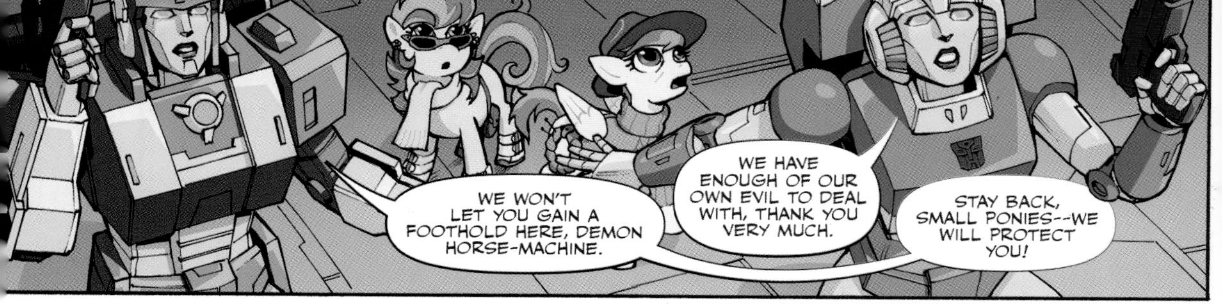
WE WON'T LET YOU GAIN A FOOTHOLD HERE, DEMON HORSE-MACHINE.
WE HAVE ENOUGH OF OUR OWN EVIL TO DEAL WITH, THANK YOU VERY MUCH.
STAY BACK, SMALL PONIES--WE WILL PROTECT YOU!

LEAVE OUR PLANET. THIS MAGIC DOESN'T BELONG HERE!

SOMBRA COULD RULE *EVERY* PLANET IF HE SO CHOSE!

AND HE DOES CHOOSE! SO THERE!

PSHEW PSHEW

PWSH PWSH

THUD

WHAT IS *THAT?!*

WHOOOOOOSSSH

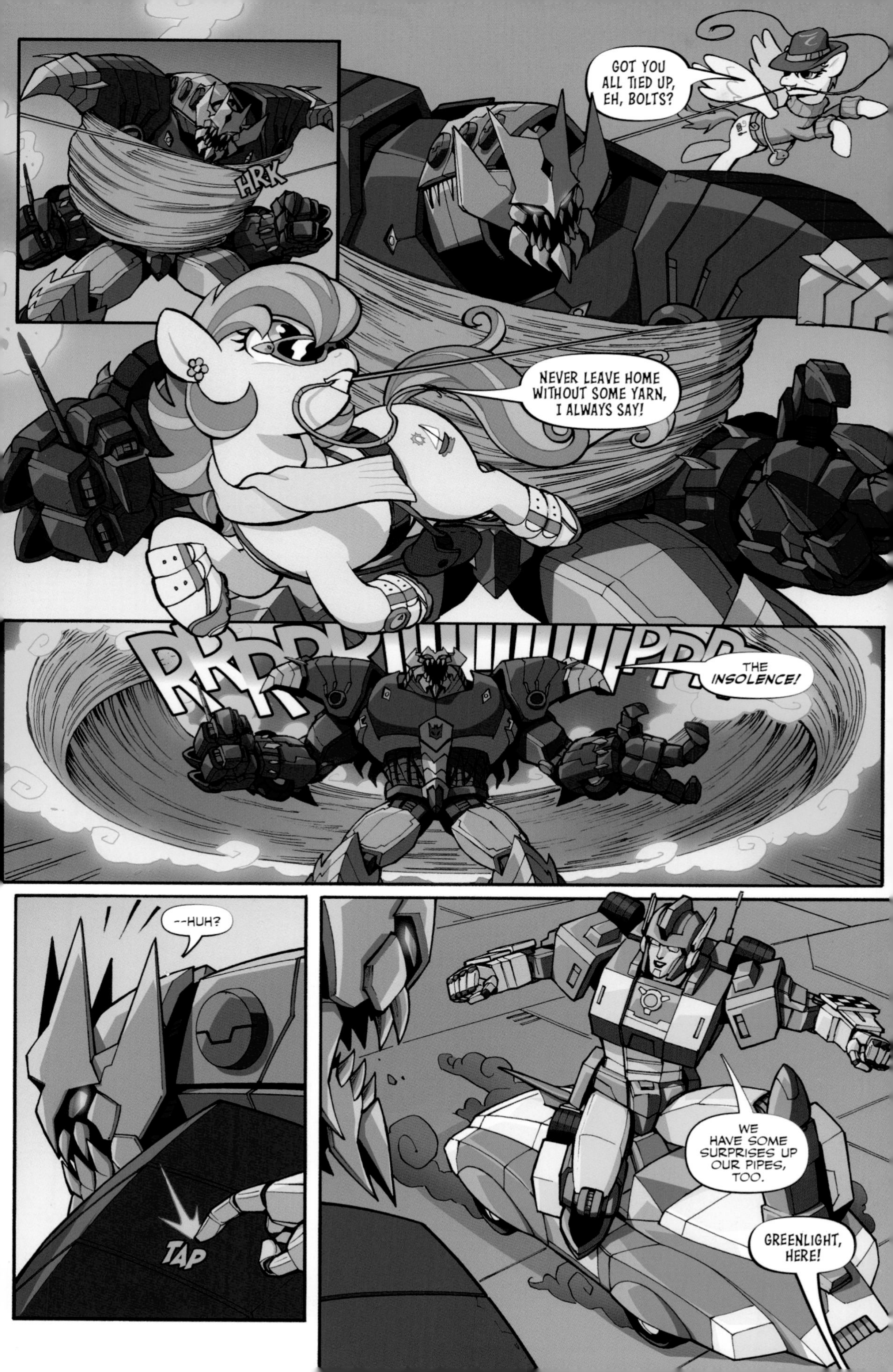
HRK
GOT YOU ALL TIED UP, EH, BOLTS?
NEVER LEAVE HOME WITHOUT SOME YARN, I ALWAYS SAY!
THE *INSOLENCE!*
--HUH?
TAP
WE HAVE SOME SURPRISES UP OUR PIPES, TOO.
GREENLIGHT, HERE!

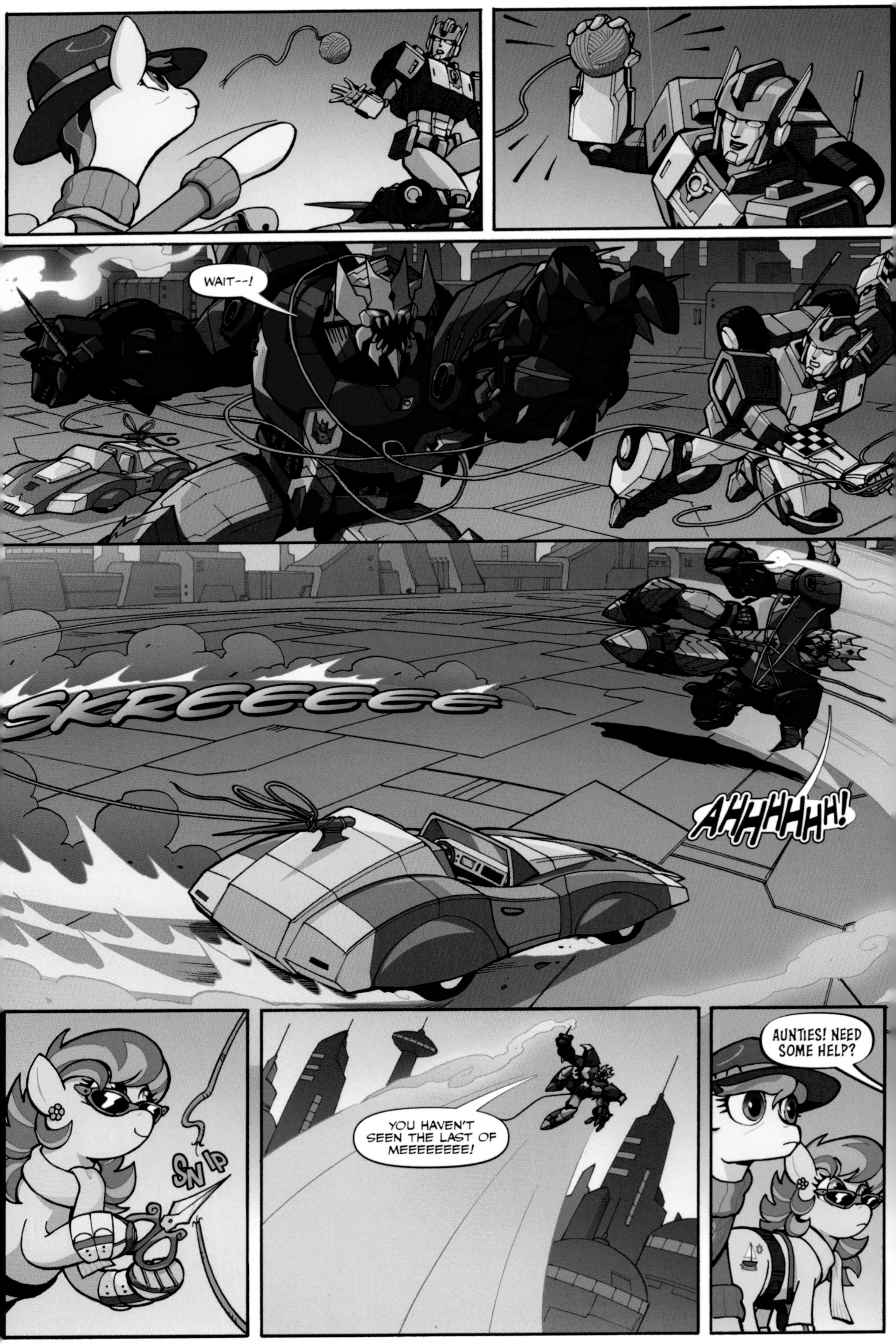
WAIT--!
SKREEEEEEE
AHHHHHH!
SNIP
YOU HAVEN'T SEEN THE LAST OF MEEEEEEEE!
AUNTIES! NEED SOME HELP?

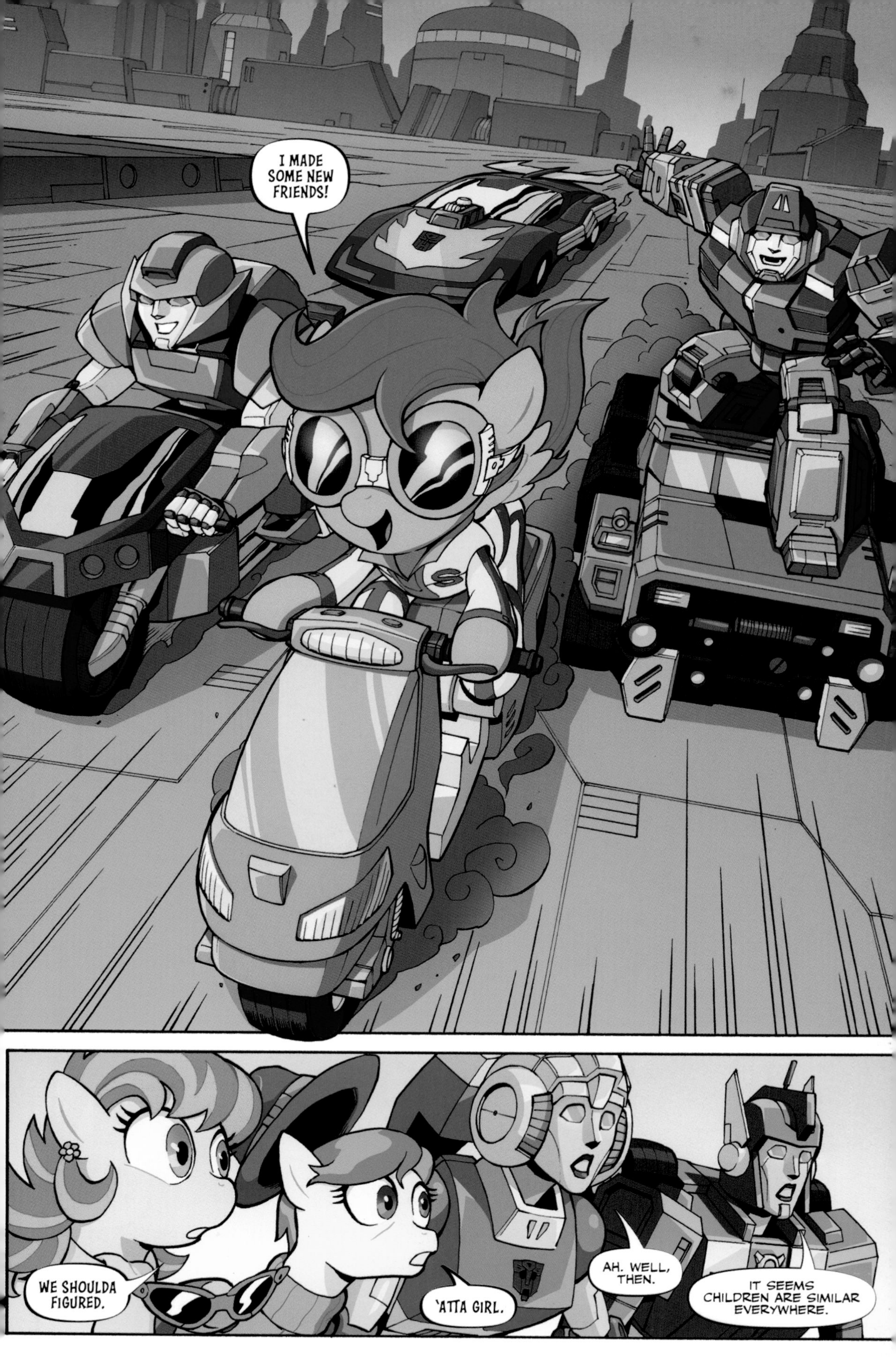
I MADE SOME NEW FRIENDS!
WE SHOULDA FIGURED.
'ATTA GIRL.
AH. WELL, THEN.
IT SEEMS CHILDREN ARE SIMILAR EVERYWHERE.

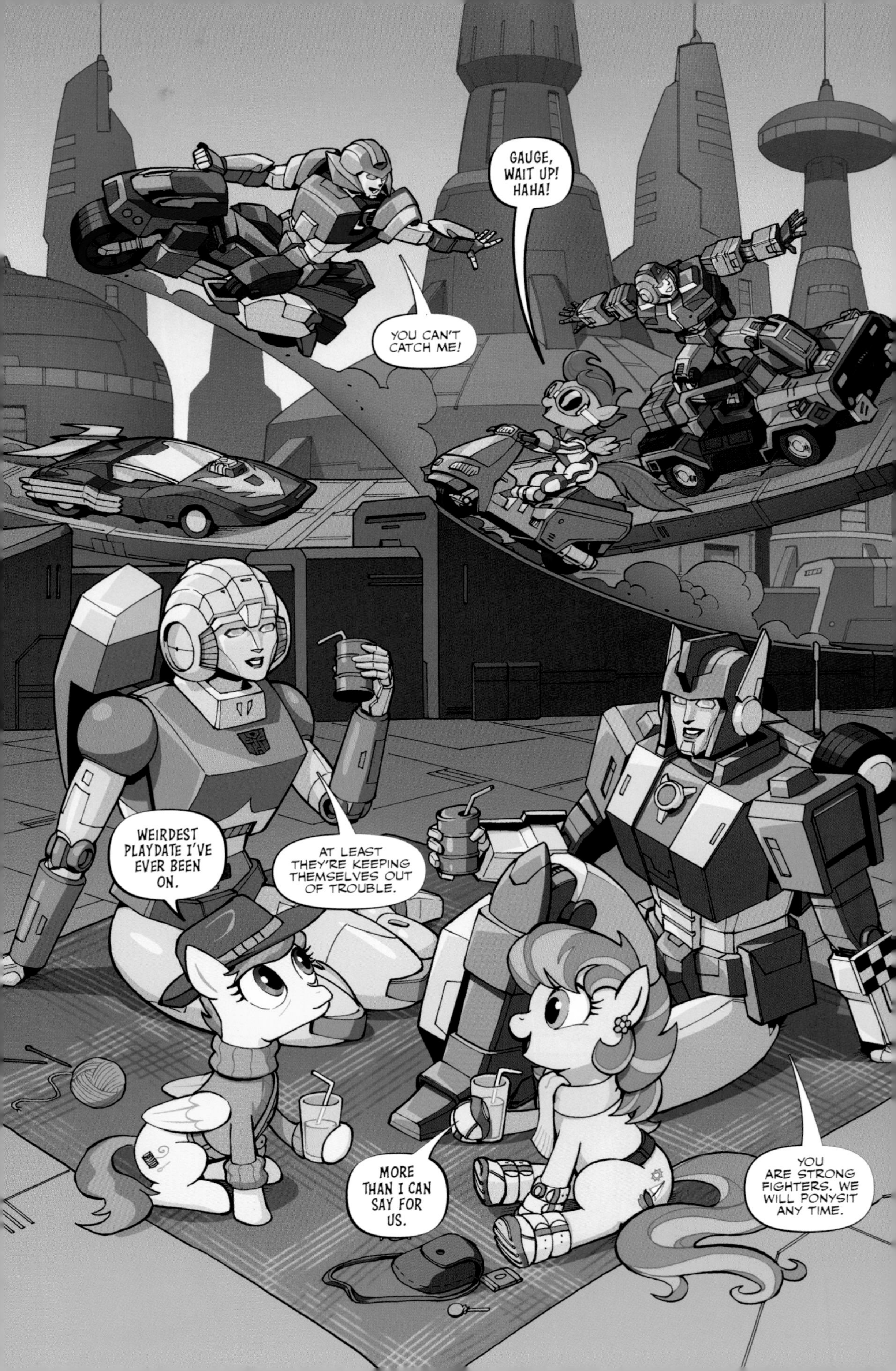
YOU CAN'T CATCH ME!
GAUGE, WAIT UP! HAHA!
WEIRDEST PLAYDATE I'VE EVER BEEN ON.
AT LEAST THEY'RE KEEPING THEMSELVES OUT OF TROUBLE.
MORE THAN I CAN SAY FOR US.
YOU ARE STRONG FIGHTERS. WE WILL PONYSIT ANY TIME.

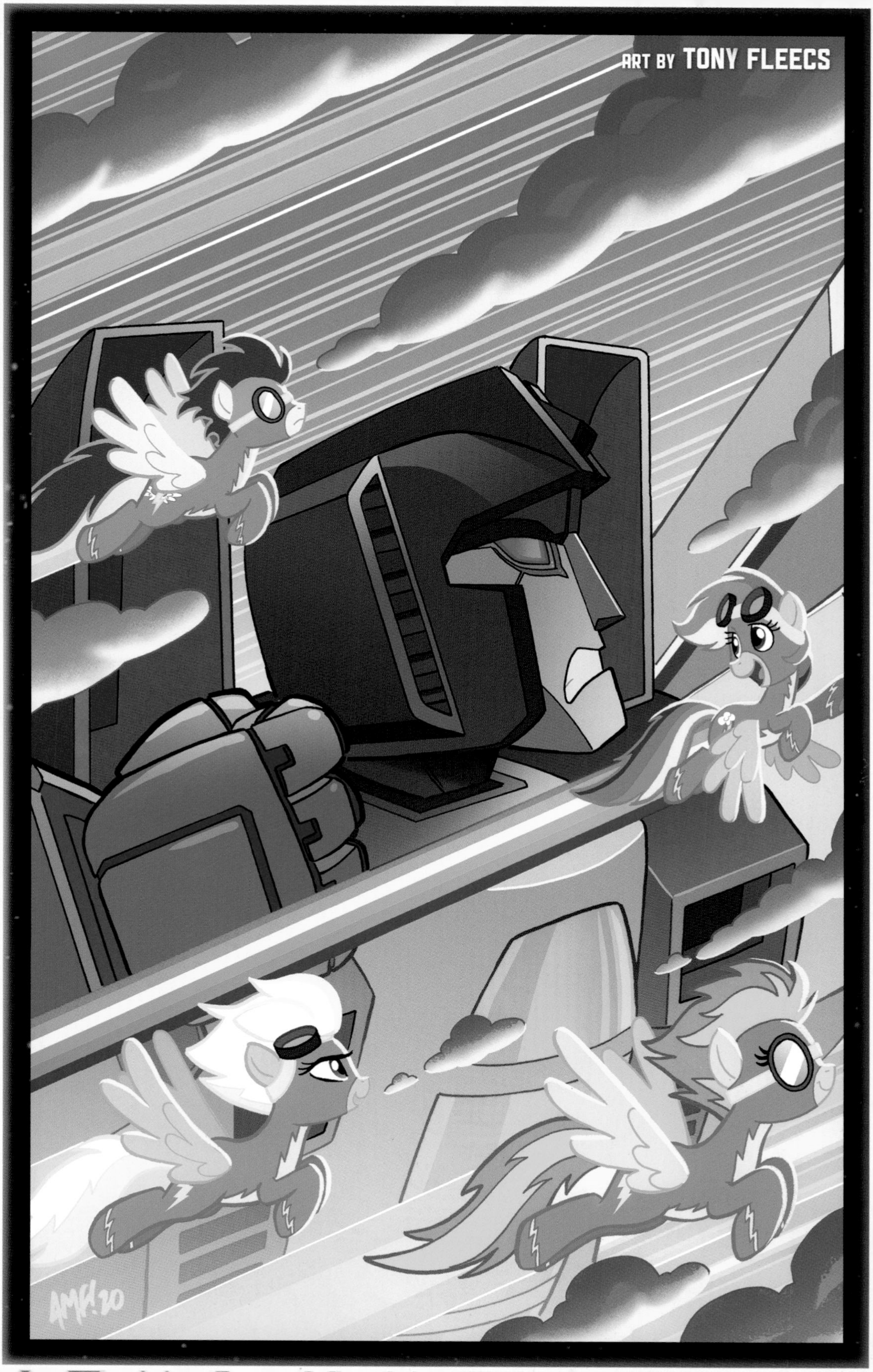
ART BY TONY FLEECS
AMF! '20

"STUNT FLYING"

WRITTEN BY **IAN FLYNN**
ART BY **PRISCILLA TRAMONTANO**
COLORS BY **JOANA LAFUENTE**
LETTERS BY **JAKE M. WOOD**

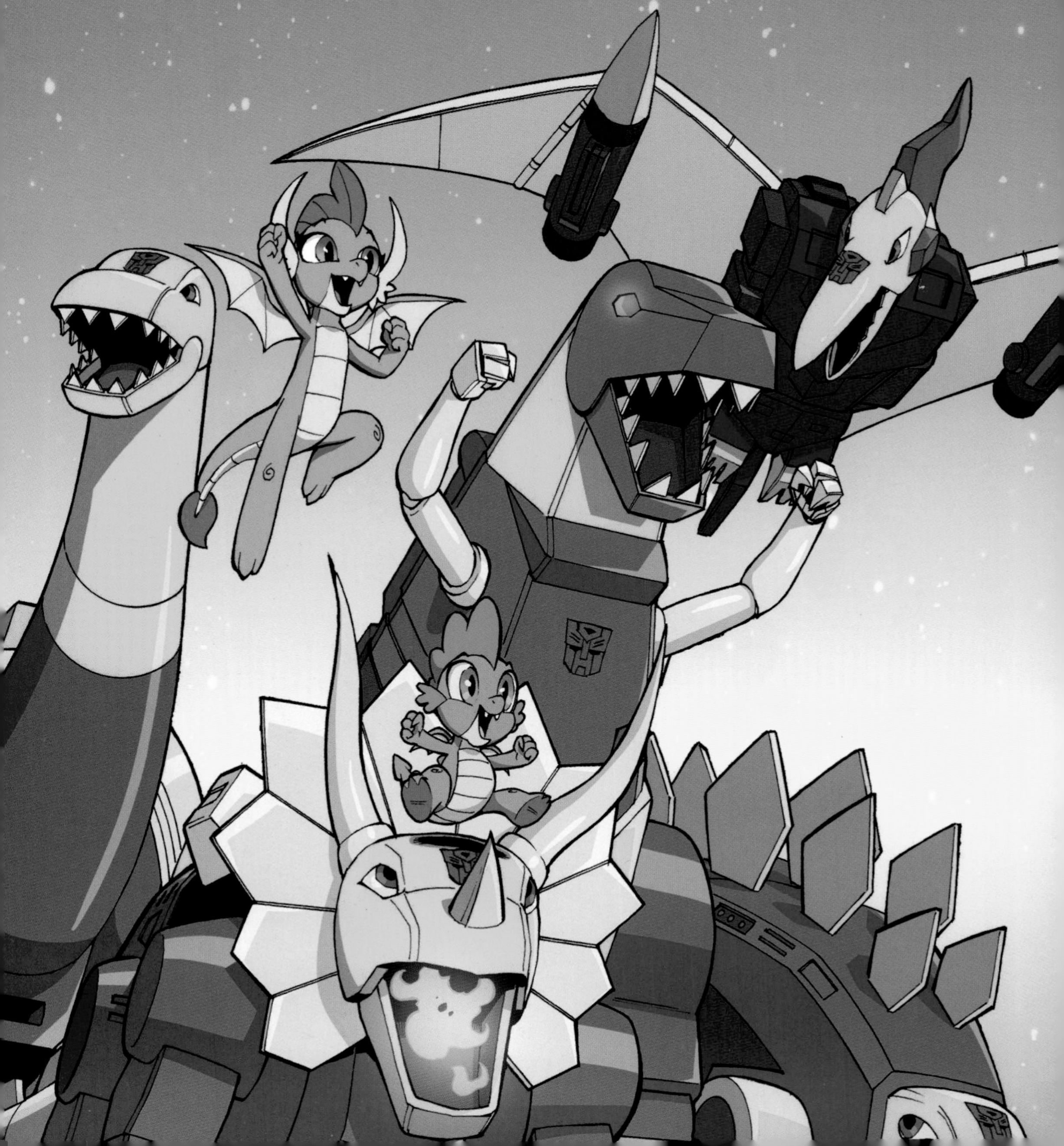

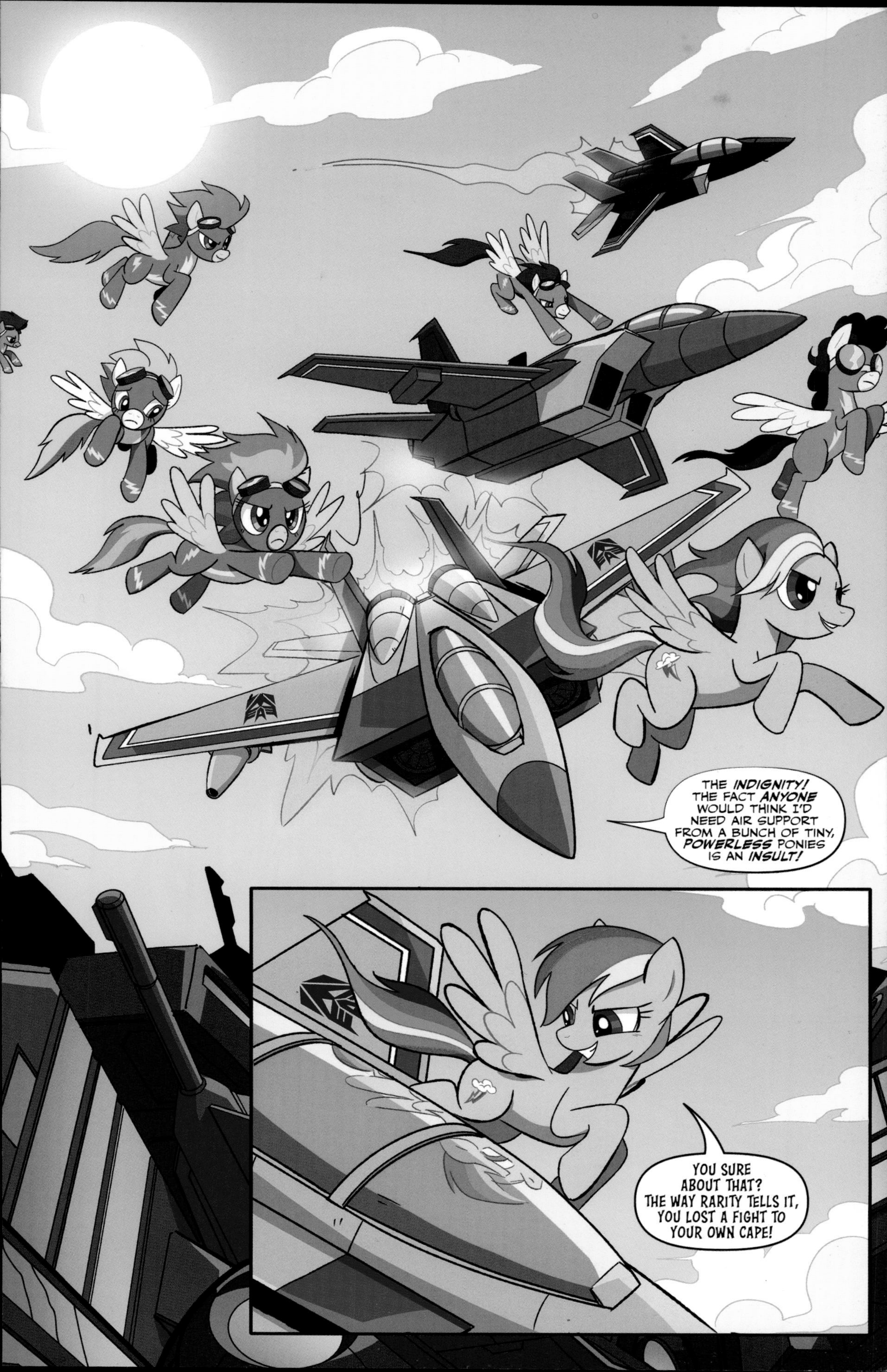
THE *INDIGNITY!* THE FACT *ANYONE* WOULD THINK I'D NEED AIR SUPPORT FROM A BUNCH OF TINY, *POWERLESS* PONIES IS AN *INSULT!*
YOU SURE ABOUT THAT? THE WAY RARITY TELLS IT, YOU LOST A FIGHT TO YOUR OWN CAPE!

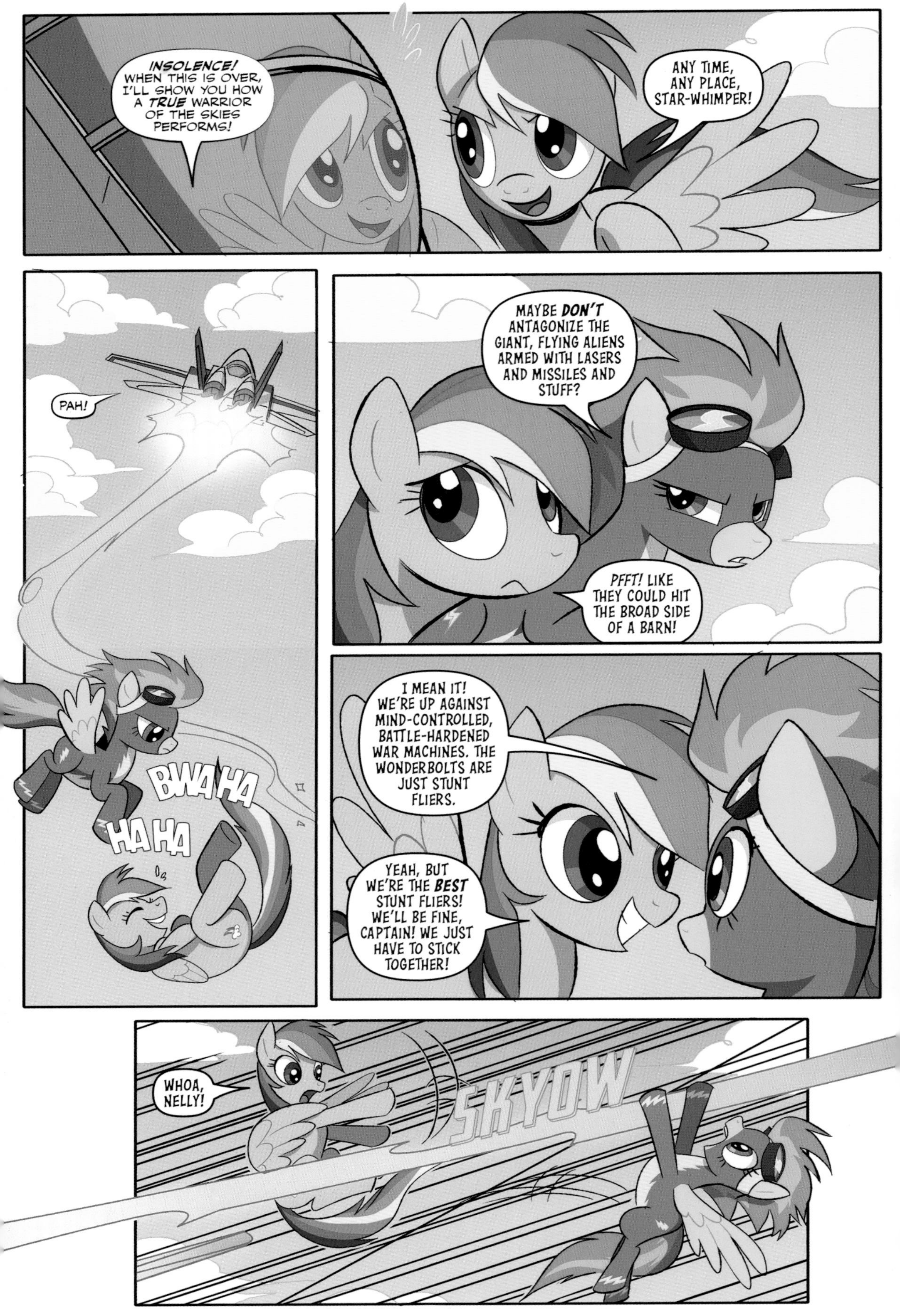
INSOLENCE! WHEN THIS IS OVER, I'LL SHOW YOU HOW A TRUE WARRIOR OF THE SKIES PERFORMS!
ANY TIME, ANY PLACE, STAR-WHIMPER!
PAH!
MAYBE DON'T ANTAGONIZE THE GIANT, FLYING ALIENS ARMED WITH LASERS AND MISSILES AND STUFF?
PFFT! LIKE THEY COULD HIT THE BROAD SIDE OF A BARN!
BWAHA
HAHA
I MEAN IT! WE'RE UP AGAINST MIND-CONTROLLED, BATTLE-HARDENED WAR MACHINES. THE WONDERBOLTS ARE JUST STUNT FLIERS.
YEAH, BUT WE'RE THE BEST STUNT FLIERS! WE'LL BE FINE, CAPTAIN! WE JUST HAVE TO STICK TOGETHER!
WHOA, NELLY!
SKYOW

SQUADRON! BOMBARD THOSE WEAK-MINDED FOOLS!

THERE'S DECEPTICONS AMONG THEM!

DID I STUTTER? *BLAST THEM!*

HOLD ON! WE'RE SUPPOSED TO DISABLE ANYPONY WE FIND SO WE CAN BREAK SOMBRA'S ENCHANTMENT!

THE FLYIN' GLUE BOTTLE'S RIGHT. WE CAN'T MAKE AN ARMY OUT OF DEAD SOLDIERS.

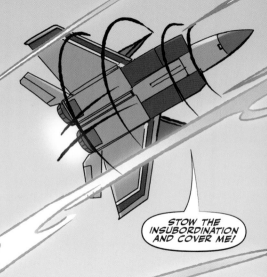

STOW THE INSUBORDINATION AND COVER ME!

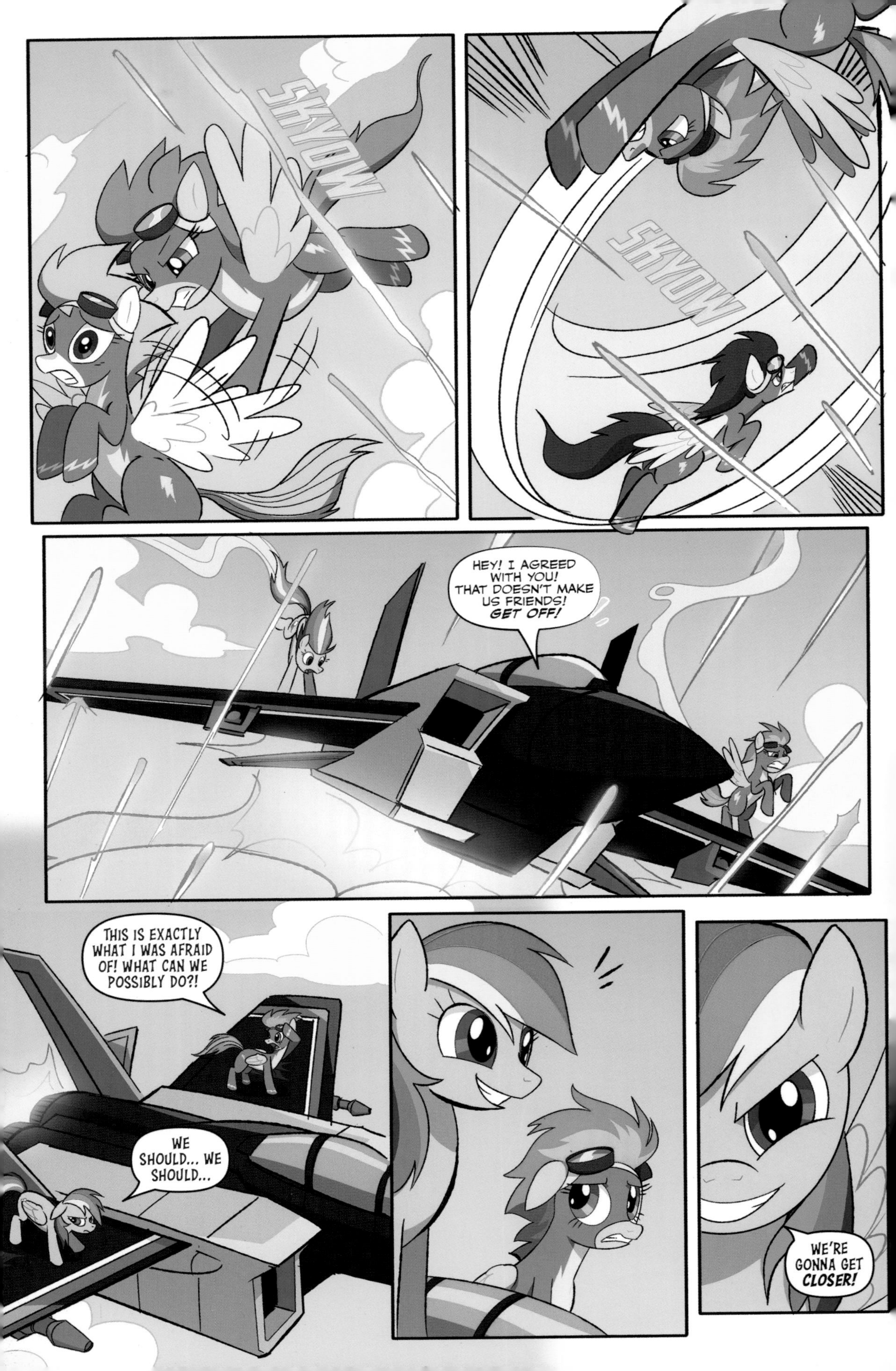
SKYOW
SKYOW
HEY! I AGREED WITH YOU! THAT DOESN'T MAKE US FRIENDS! GET OFF!
THIS IS EXACTLY WHAT I WAS AFRAID OF! WHAT CAN WE POSSIBLY DO?!
WE SHOULD... WE SHOULD...
WE'RE GONNA GET CLOSER!

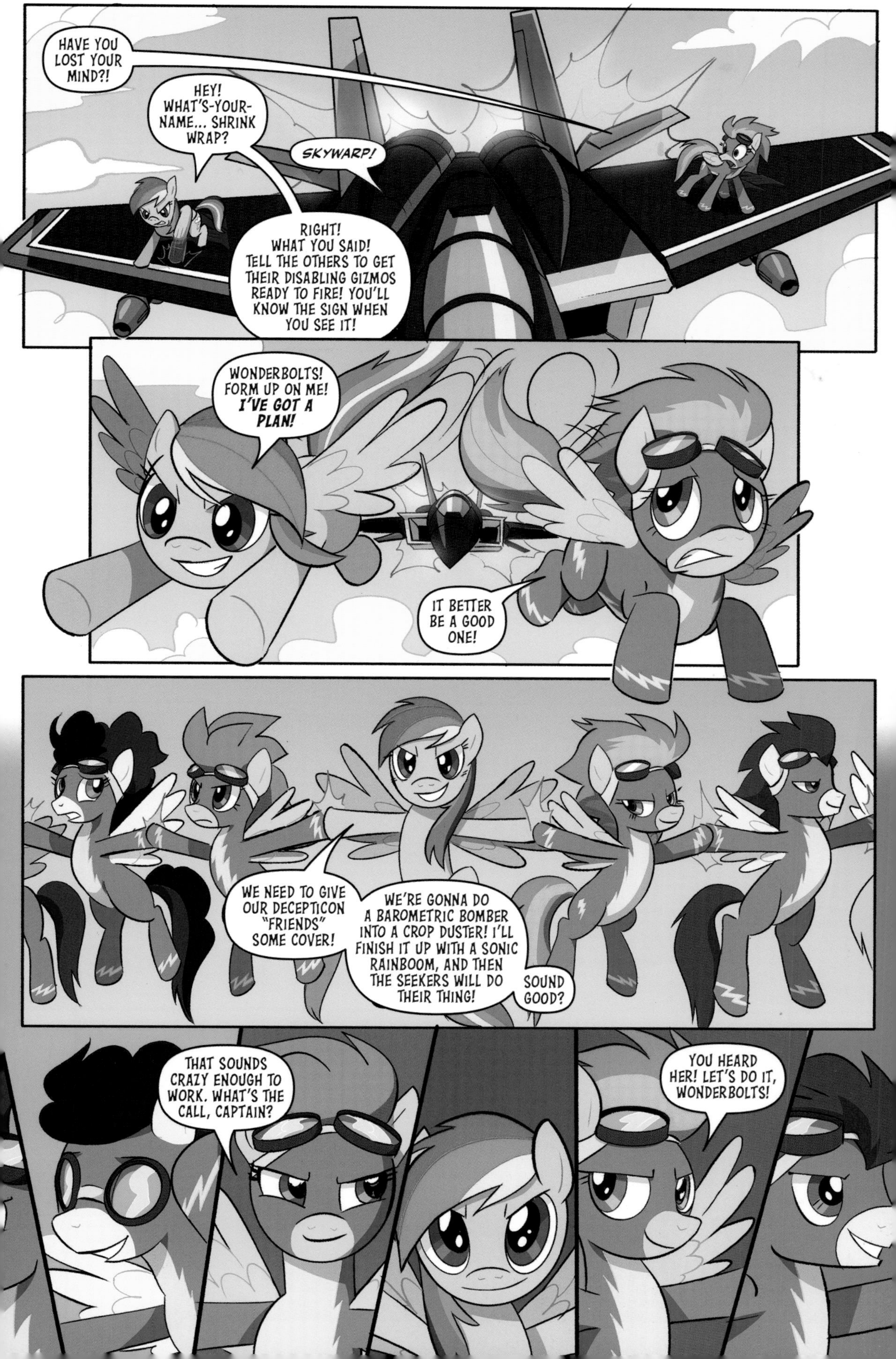
HAVE YOU LOST YOUR MIND?!
HEY! WHAT'S-YOUR-NAME... SHRINK WRAP?
SKYWARP!
RIGHT! WHAT YOU SAID! TELL THE OTHERS TO GET THEIR DISABLING GIZMOS READY TO FIRE! YOU'LL KNOW THE SIGN WHEN YOU SEE IT!
WONDERBOLTS! FORM UP ON ME! I'VE GOT A PLAN!
IT BETTER BE A GOOD ONE!
WE NEED TO GIVE OUR DECEPTICON "FRIENDS" SOME COVER!
WE'RE GONNA DO A BAROMETRIC BOMBER INTO A CROP DUSTER! I'LL FINISH IT UP WITH A SONIC RAINBOOM, AND THEN THE SEEKERS WILL DO THEIR THING!
SOUND GOOD?
THAT SOUNDS CRAZY ENOUGH TO WORK. WHAT'S THE CALL, CAPTAIN?
YOU HEARD HER! LET'S DO IT, WONDERBOLTS!

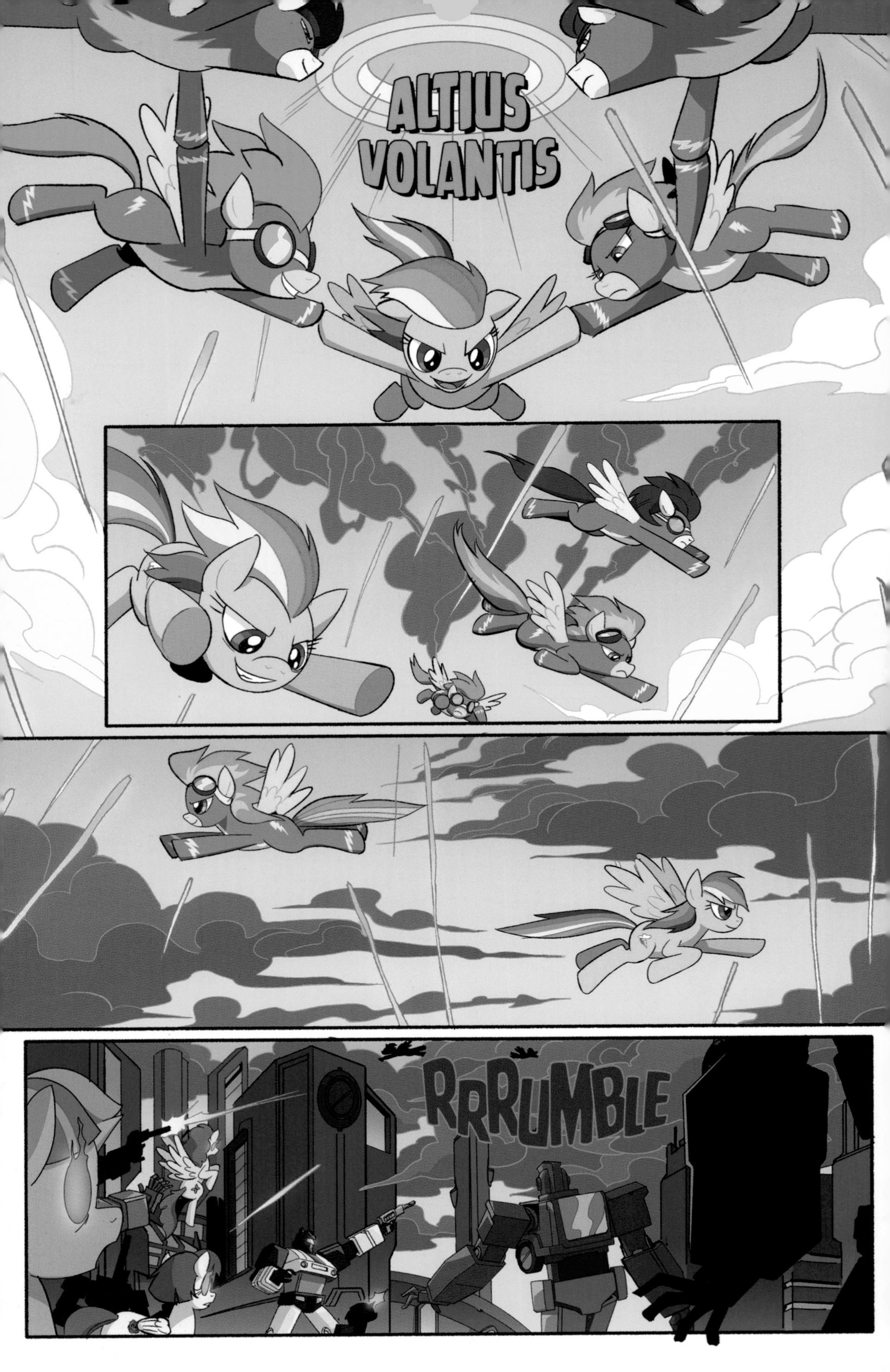
ALTIUS VOLANTIS
RRRUMBLE

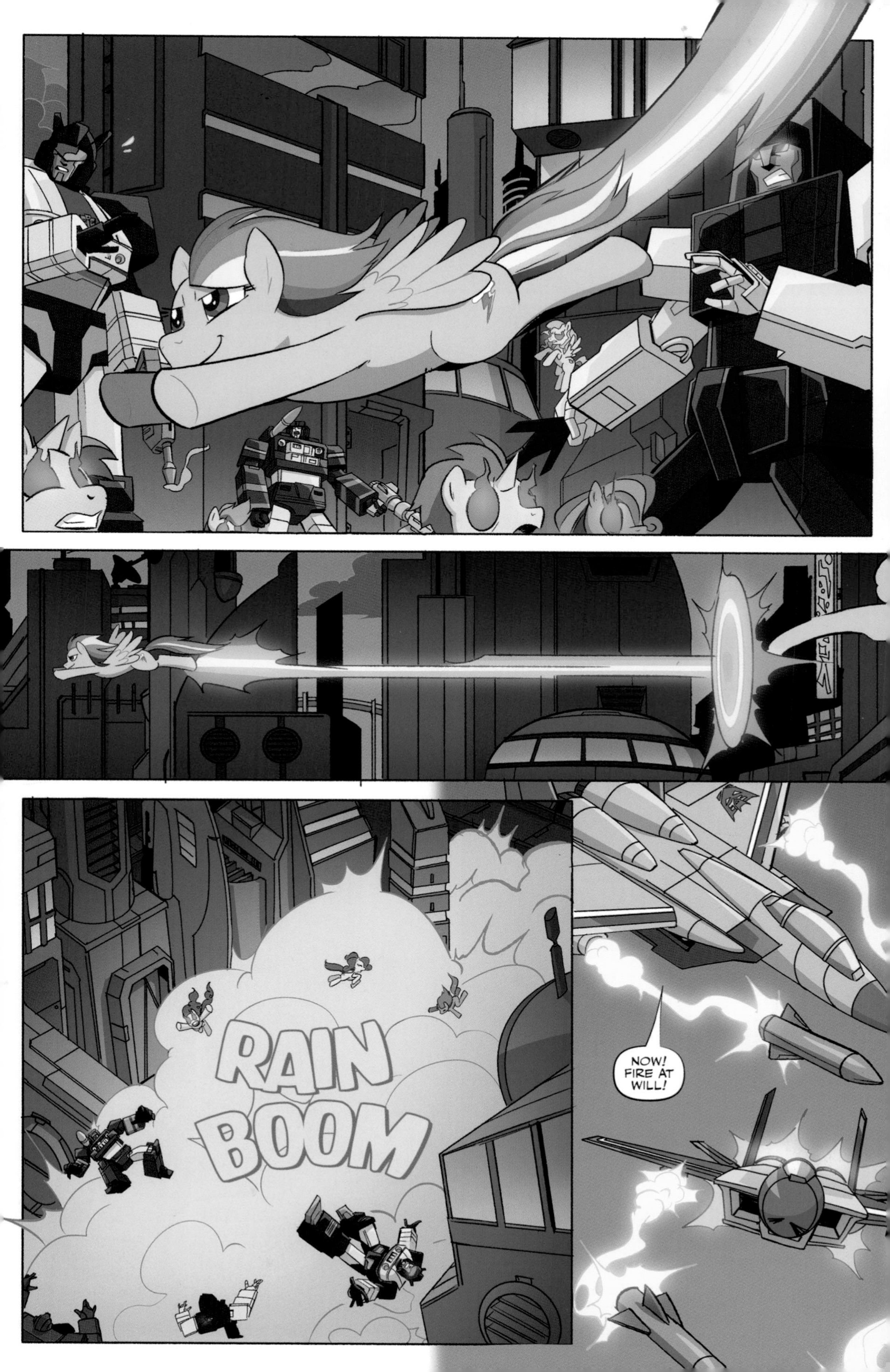
RAIN
BOOM
NOW! FIRE AT WILL!

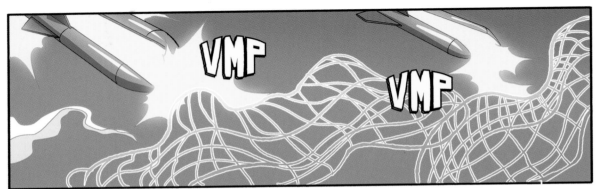

VMP

VMP

CRASH

THAT WAS *TERRIFYING!*

EH, ALL IN ALL, FLYING THROUGH THE HURRICANE THAT ONE TIME WAS WAY WORSE.

THE HURRICANE WASN'T SHOOTING AT US, CAPTAIN.

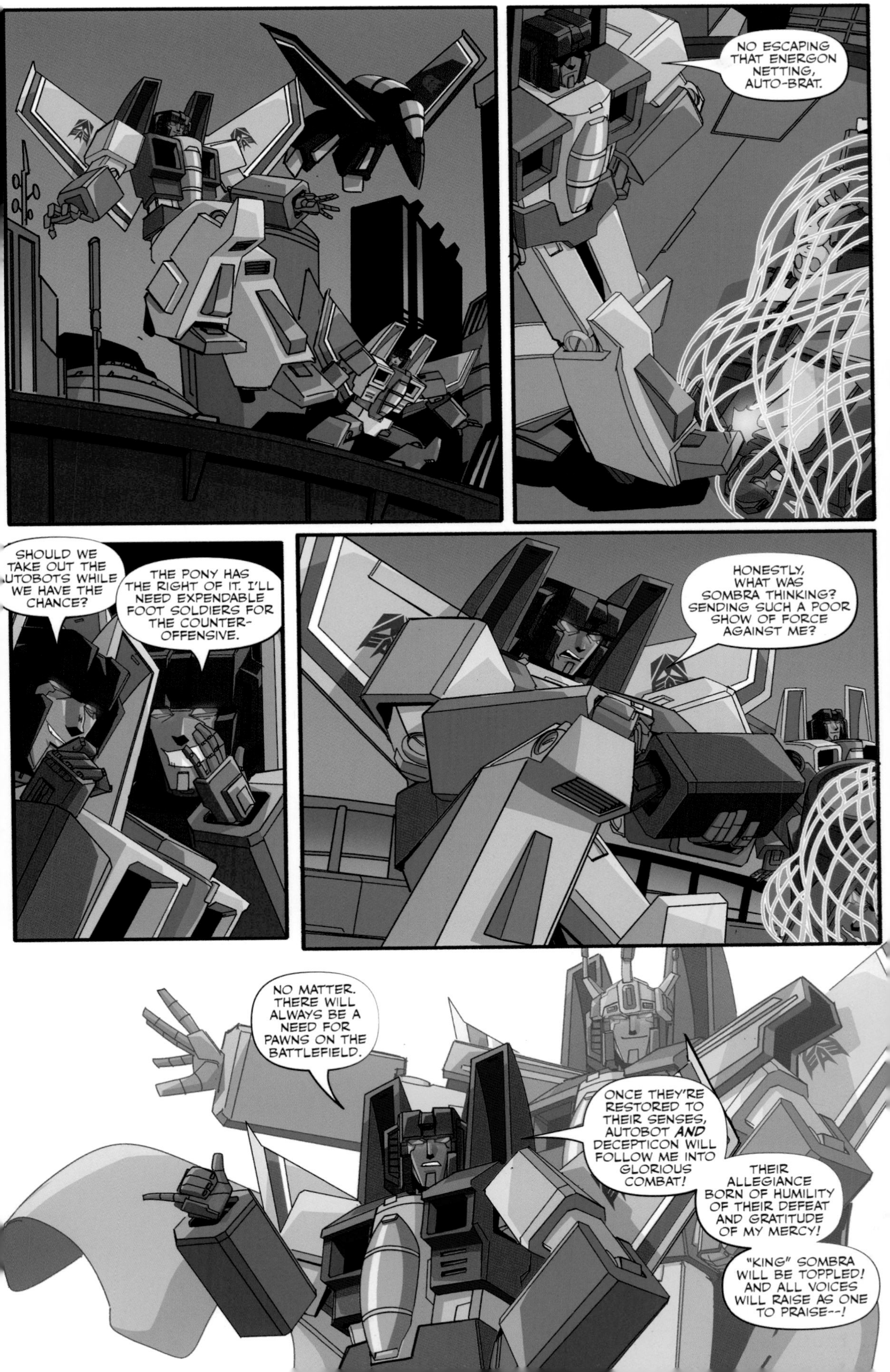
NO ESCAPING THAT ENERGON NETTING, AUTO-BRAT.
SHOULD WE TAKE OUT THE AUTOBOTS WHILE WE HAVE THE CHANCE?
THE PONY HAS THE RIGHT OF IT. I'LL NEED EXPENDABLE FOOT SOLDIERS FOR THE COUNTER-OFFENSIVE.
HONESTLY, WHAT WAS SOMBRA THINKING? SENDING SUCH A POOR SHOW OF FORCE AGAINST ME?
NO MATTER. THERE WILL ALWAYS BE A NEED FOR PAWNS ON THE BATTLEFIELD.
ONCE THEY'RE RESTORED TO THEIR SENSES, AUTOBOT *AND* DECEPTICON WILL FOLLOW ME INTO GLORIOUS COMBAT!
THEIR ALLEGIANCE BORN OF HUMILITY OF THEIR DEFEAT AND GRATITUDE OF MY MERCY!
"KING" SOMBRA WILL BE TOPPLED! AND ALL VOICES WILL RAISE AS ONE TO PRAISE--!

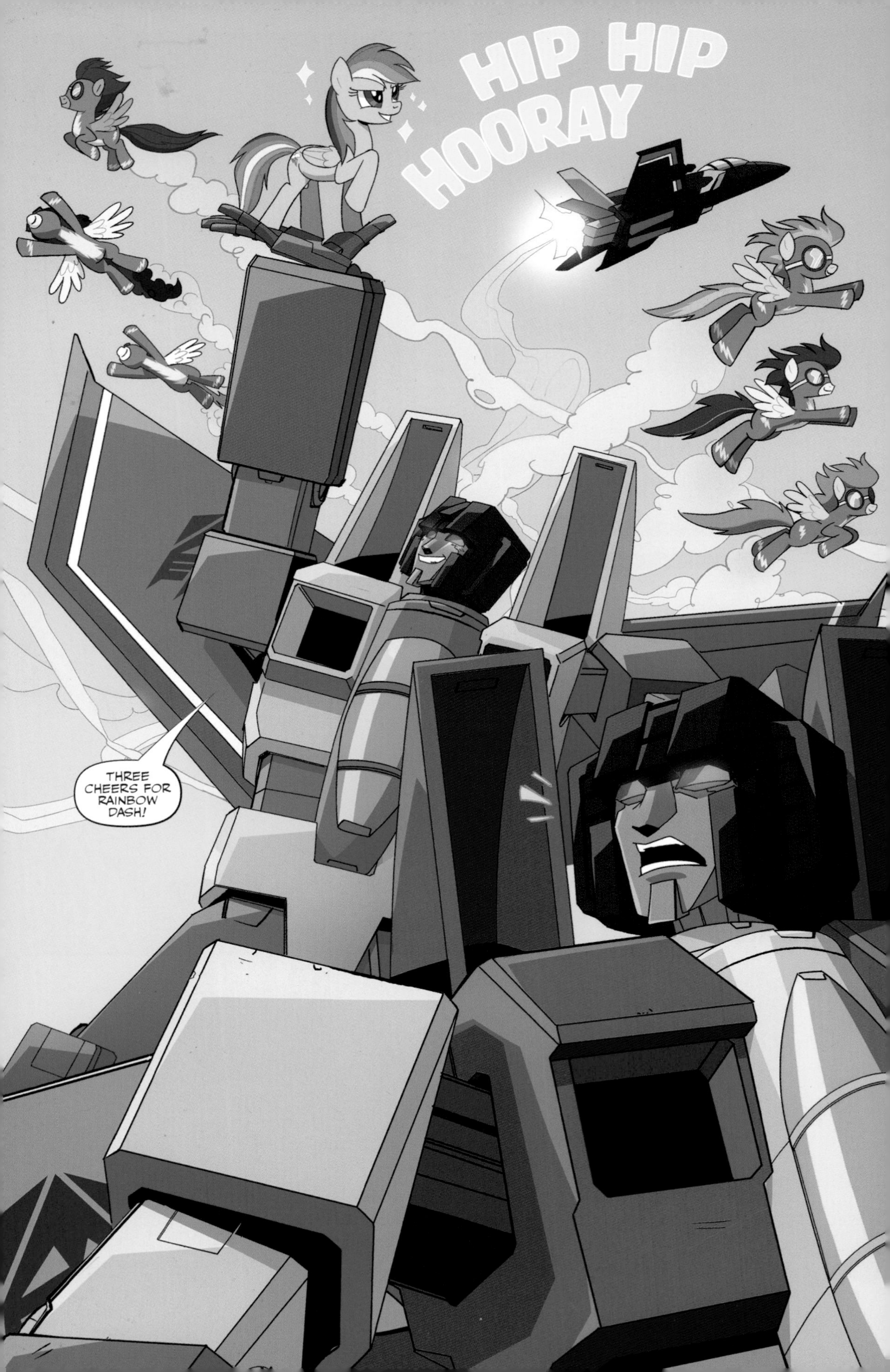
HIP HIP HOORAY
THREE CHEERS FOR RAINBOW DASH!

ART BY ADAM BRYCE THOMAS

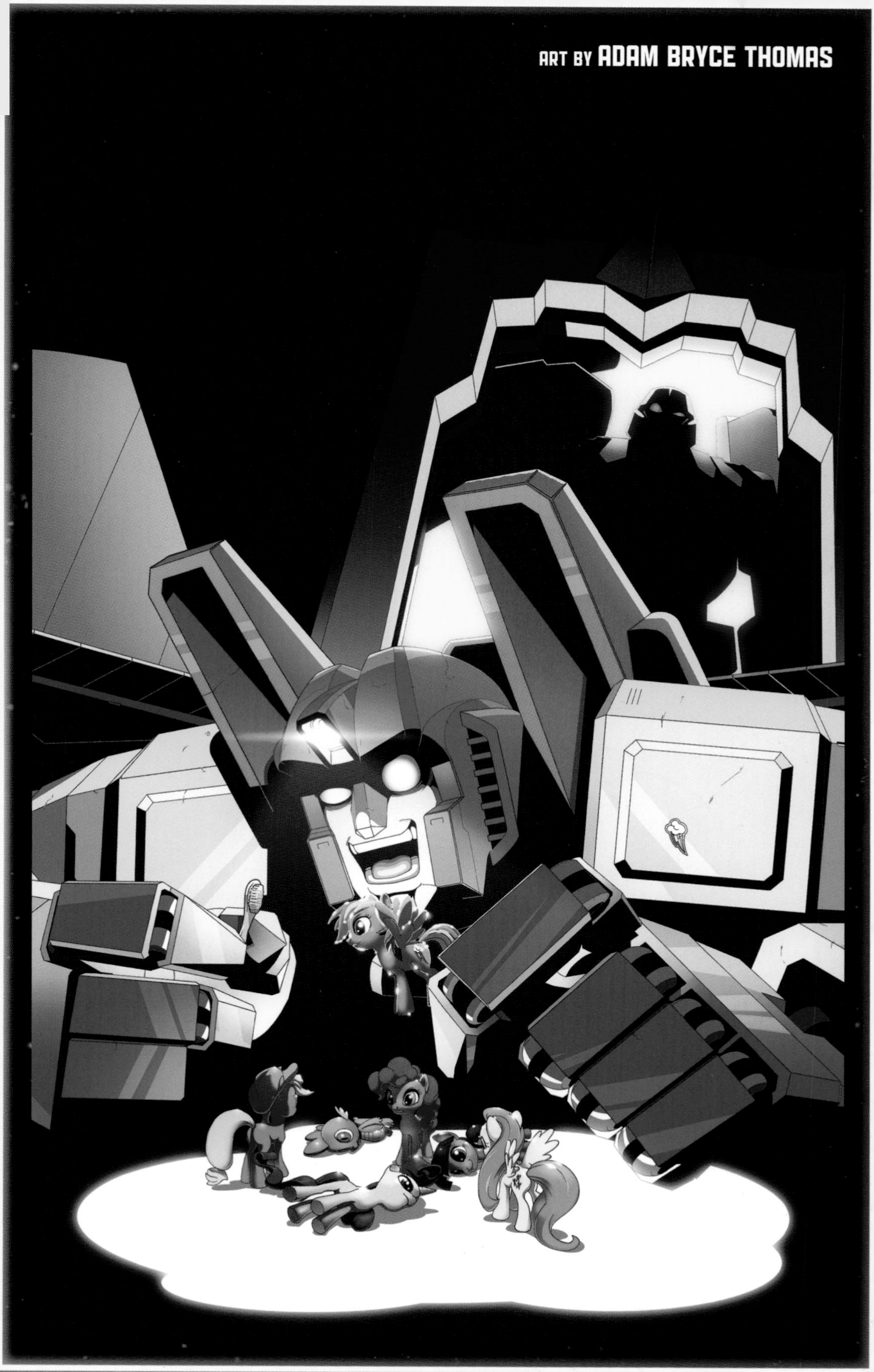

"ONE-TRICK PONY"

WRITTEN BY SAM MAGGS
ART BY TRISH FORSTNER
COLORS BY LUIS ANTONIO DELGADO
LETTERS BY NEIL UYETAKE

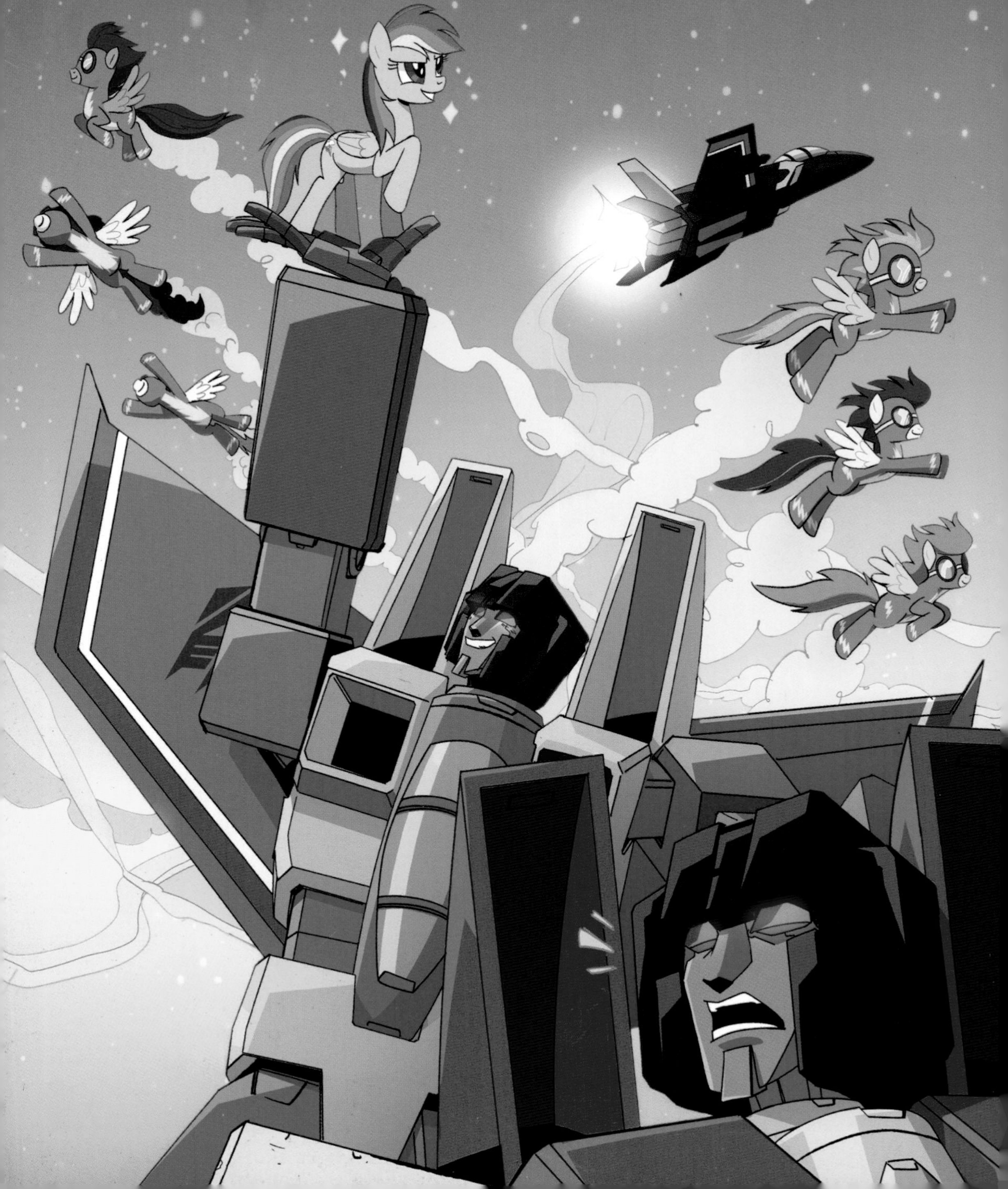

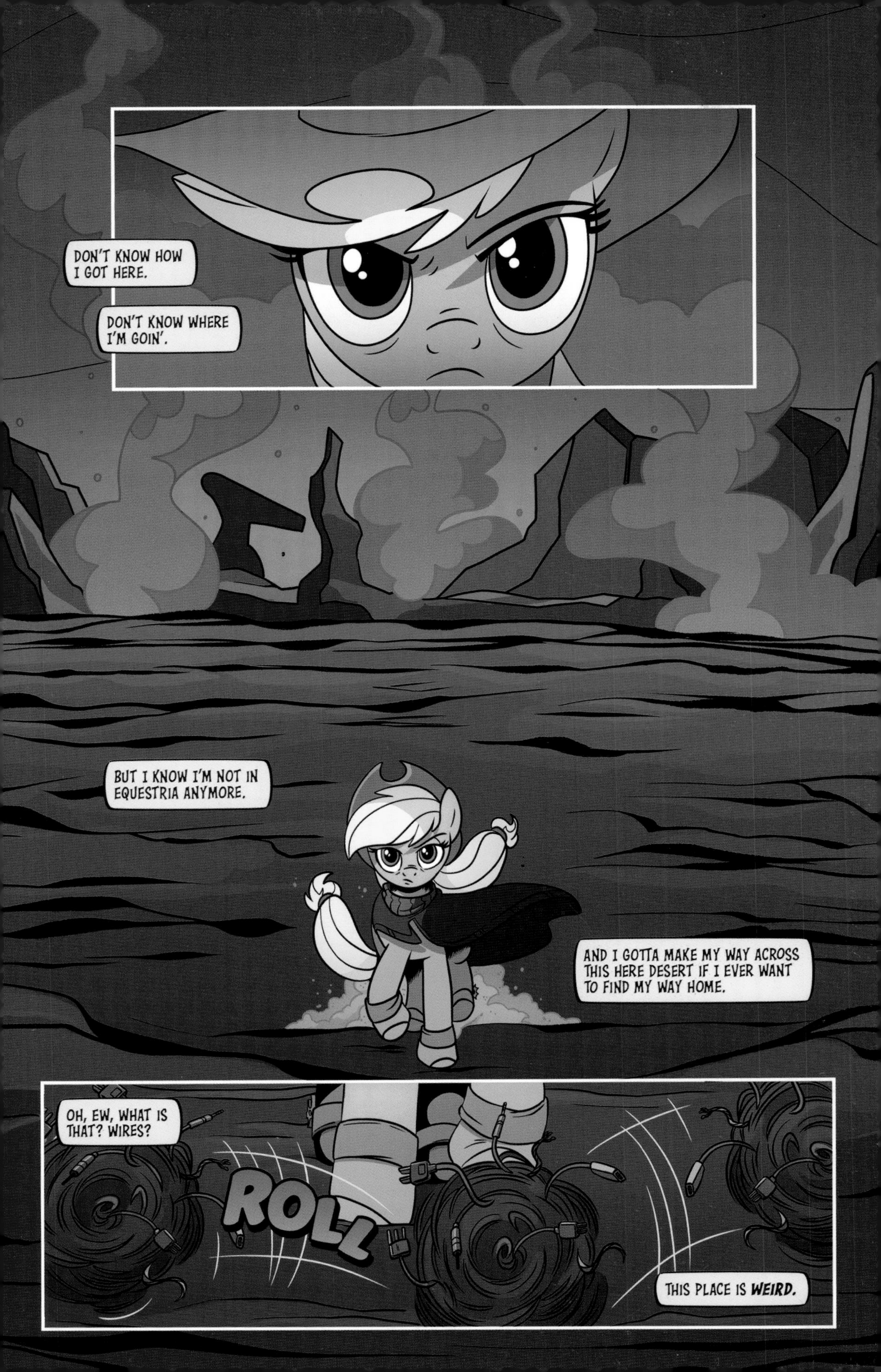
DON'T KNOW HOW I GOT HERE.
DON'T KNOW WHERE I'M GOIN'.
BUT I KNOW I'M NOT IN EQUESTRIA ANYMORE.
AND I GOTTA MAKE MY WAY ACROSS THIS HERE DESERT IF I EVER WANT TO FIND MY WAY HOME.
OH, EW, WHAT IS THAT? WIRES?
ROLL
THIS PLACE IS WEIRD.

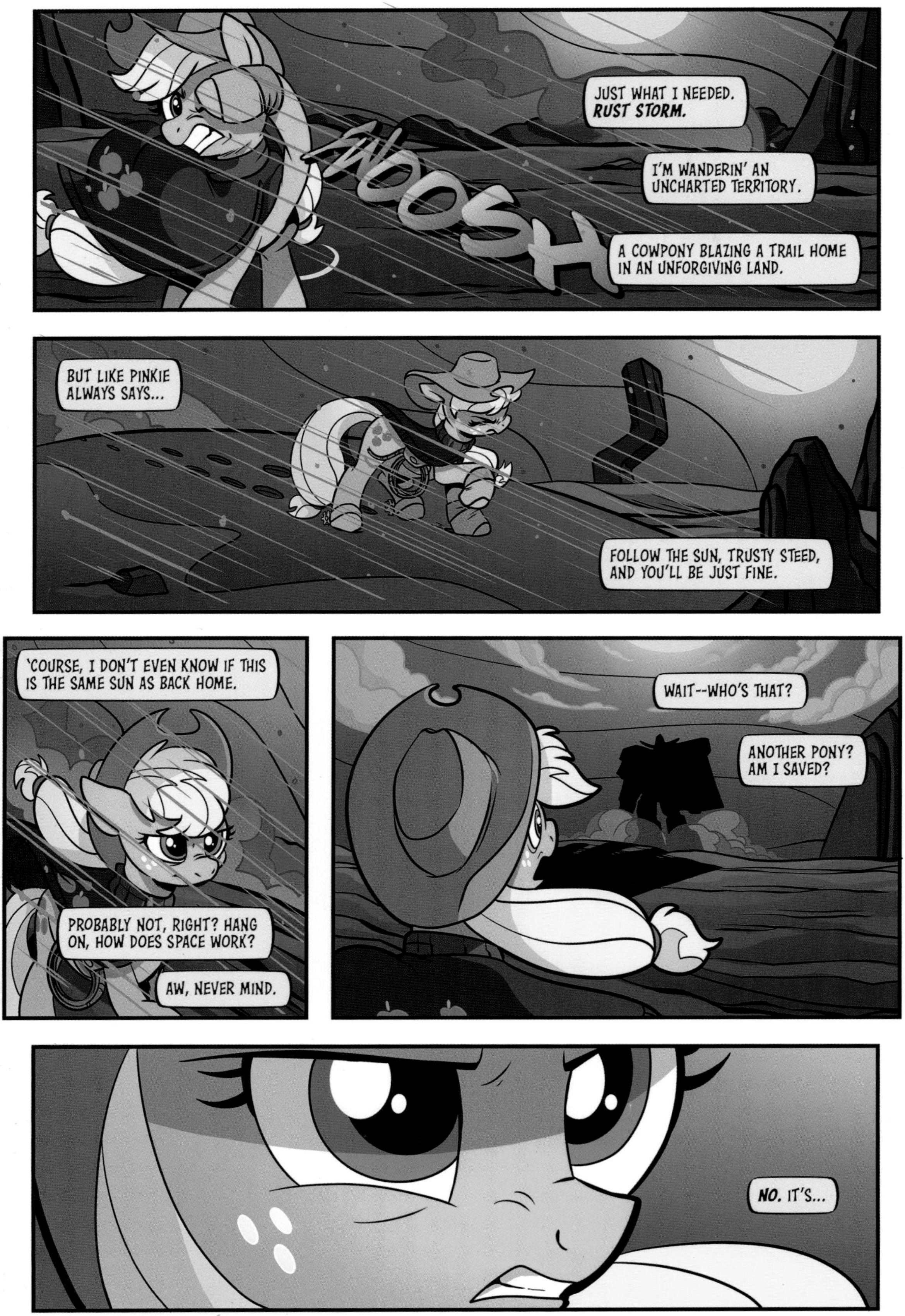
JUST WHAT I NEEDED. RUST STORM.
WOOSH
I'M WANDERIN' AN UNCHARTED TERRITORY.
A COWPONY BLAZING A TRAIL HOME IN AN UNFORGIVING LAND.
BUT LIKE PINKIE ALWAYS SAYS...
FOLLOW THE SUN, TRUSTY STEED, AND YOU'LL BE JUST FINE.
'COURSE, I DON'T EVEN KNOW IF THIS IS THE SAME SUN AS BACK HOME.
PROBABLY NOT, RIGHT? HANG ON, HOW DOES SPACE WORK?
AW, NEVER MIND.
WAIT--WHO'S THAT?
ANOTHER PONY? AM I SAVED?
NO. IT'S...

I'M WILDWHEEL.
AND THIS HERE TERRITORY IS UNDER MY PROTECTION.
NOW THAT LOOKS LIKE A 'BOT GONE BAD.
TILT
NO DISRESPECT MEANT, MISTER GIANT ROBOT PONCHO.
I'M JUST TRYNA MAKE MY WAY HOME.
TING
WELL, THEN...
YOU CAN SEE THAT WE MIGHT HAVE A LITTLE PROBLEM.
HERE WE GO.

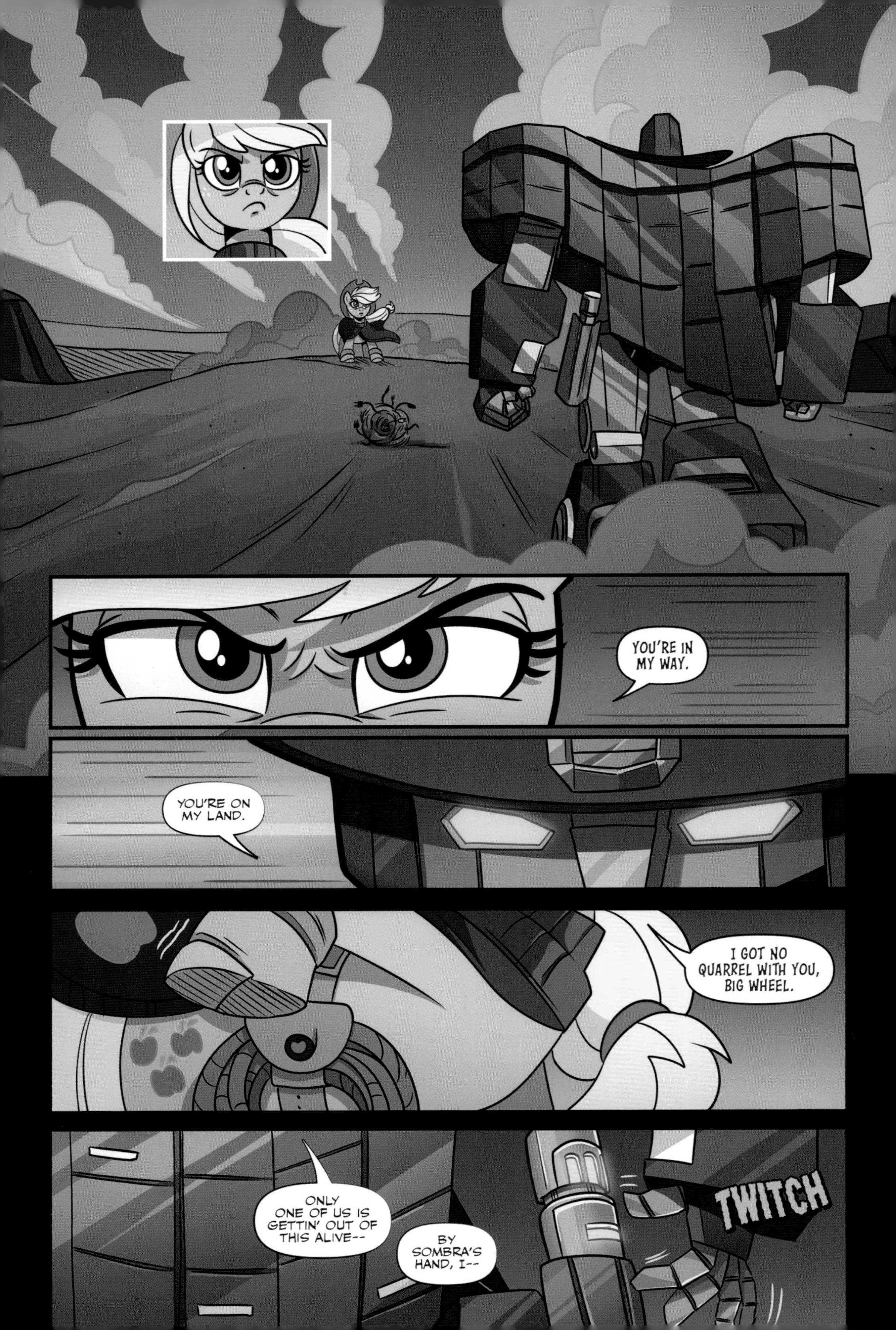
YOU'RE IN MY WAY.
YOU'RE ON MY LAND.
I GOT NO QUARREL WITH YOU, BIG WHEEL.
ONLY ONE OF US IS GETTIN' OUT OF THIS ALIVE--
BY SOMBRA'S HAND, I--
TWITCH

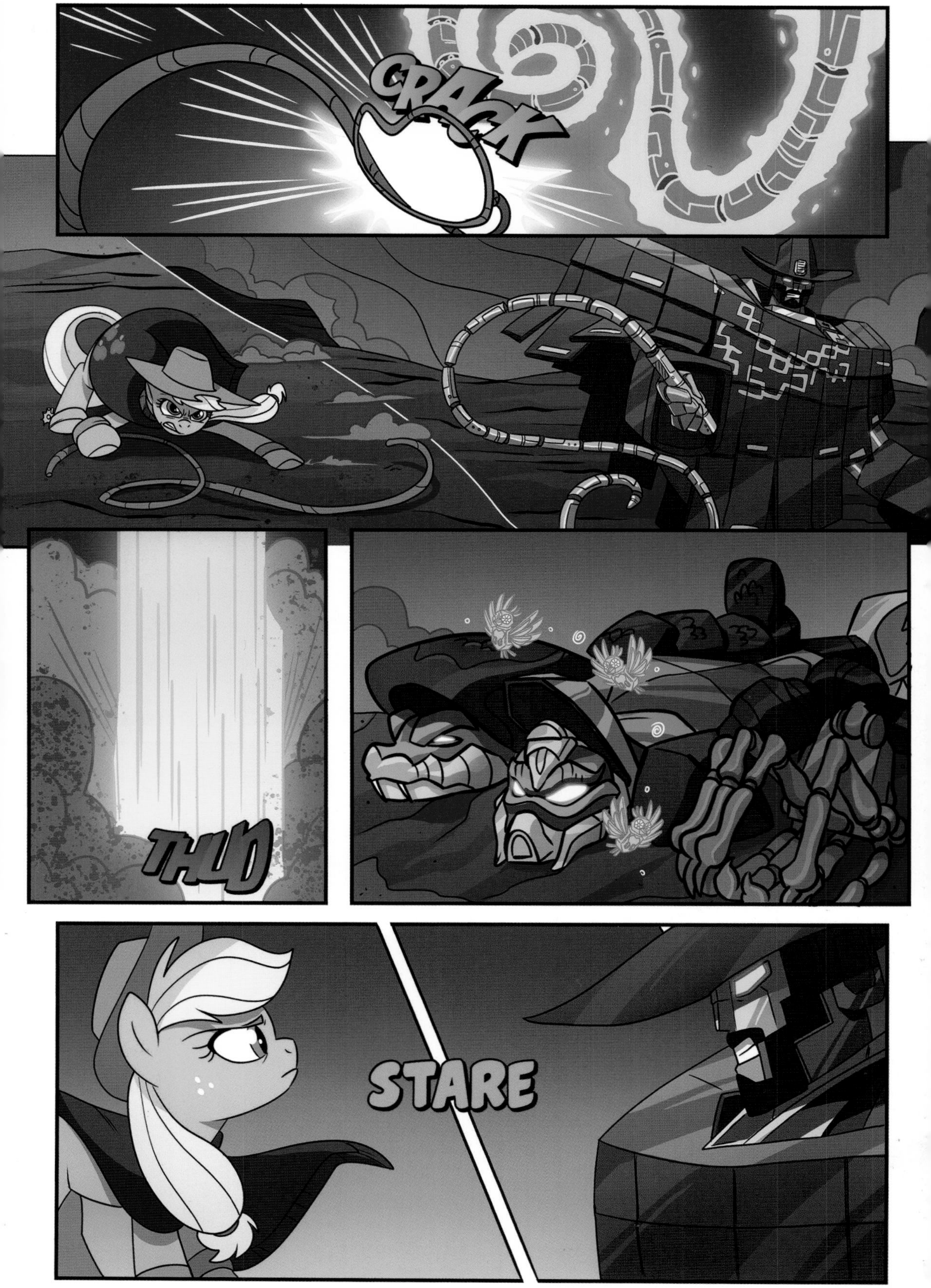
CRACK
THUD
STARE

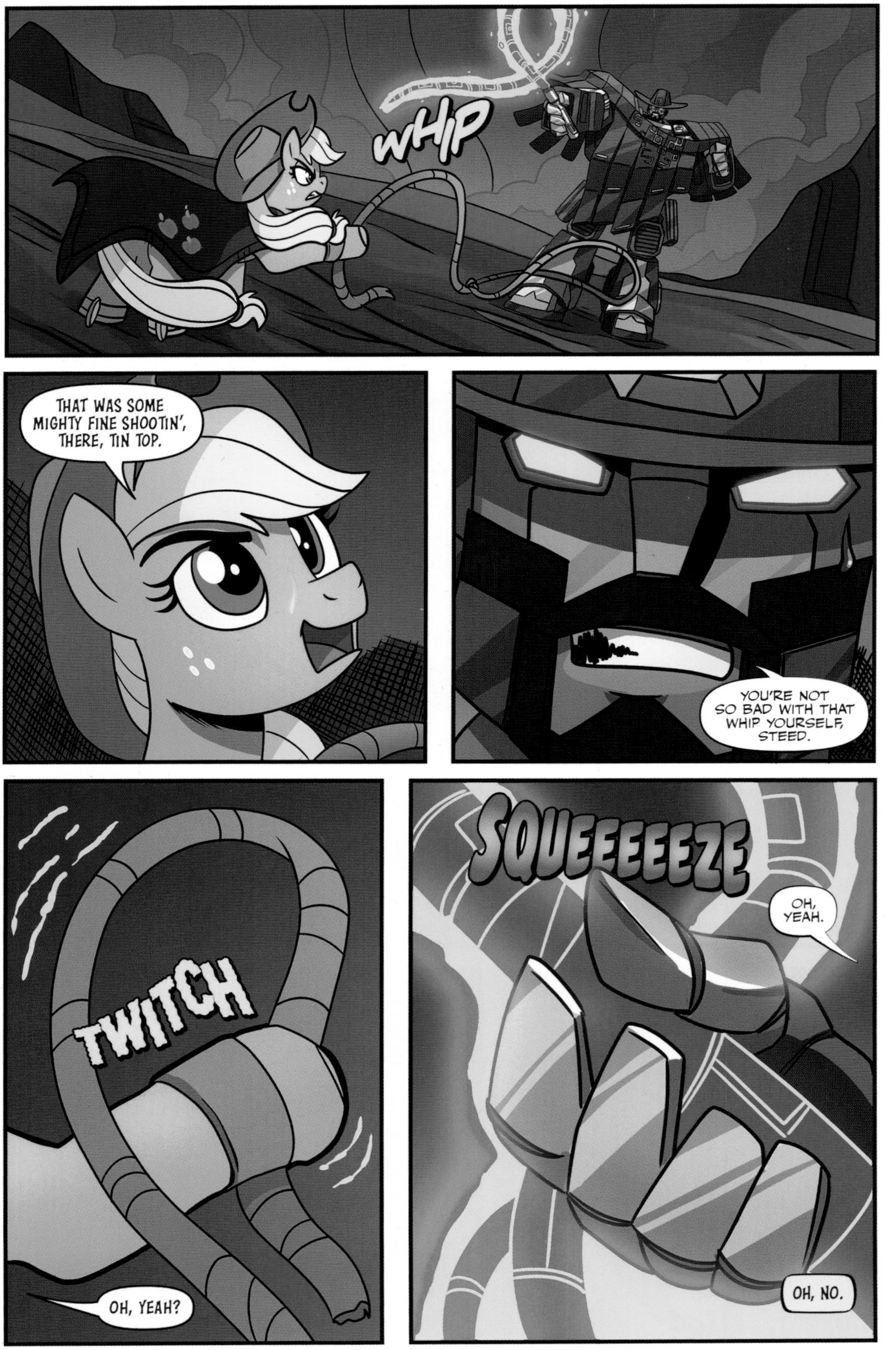
WHIP
THAT WAS SOME MIGHTY FINE SHOOTIN', THERE, TIN TOP.
YOU'RE NOT SO BAD WITH THAT WHIP YOURSELF, STEED.
TWITCH
OH, YEAH?
SQUEEEEEEZE
OH, YEAH.
OH, NO.

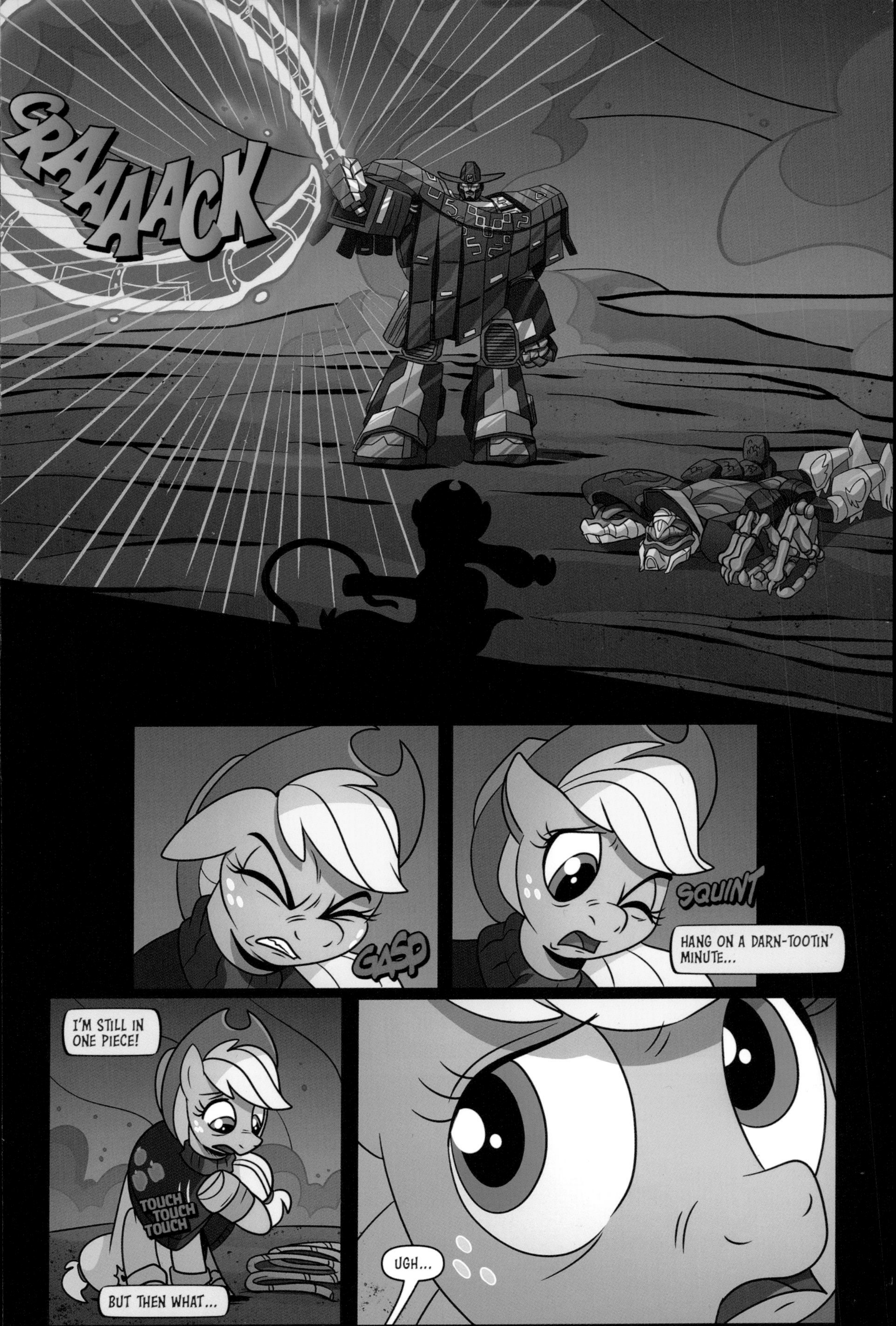
CRAAAACK
GASP
SQUINT
HANG ON A DARN-TOOTIN' MINUTE...
I'M STILL IN ONE PIECE!
TOUCH TOUCH TOUCH
BUT THEN WHAT...
UGH...

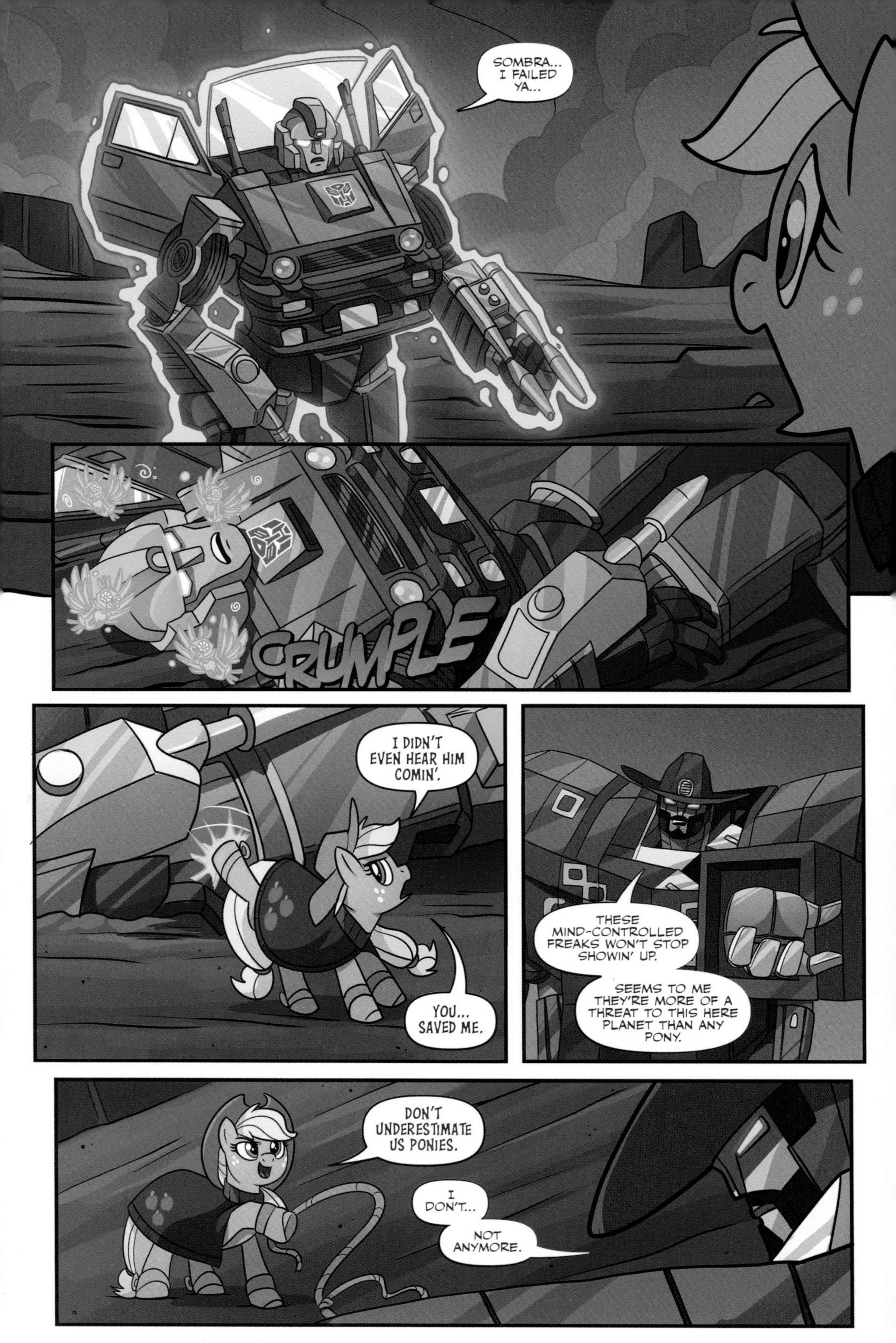
SOMBRA... I FAILED YA...
CRUMPLE
I DIDN'T EVEN HEAR HIM COMIN'.
YOU... SAVED ME.
THESE MIND-CONTROLLED FREAKS WON'T STOP SHOWIN' UP.
SEEMS TO ME THEY'RE MORE OF A THREAT TO THIS HERE PLANET THAN ANY PONY.
DON'T UNDERESTIMATE US PONIES.
I DON'T...
NOT ANYMORE.

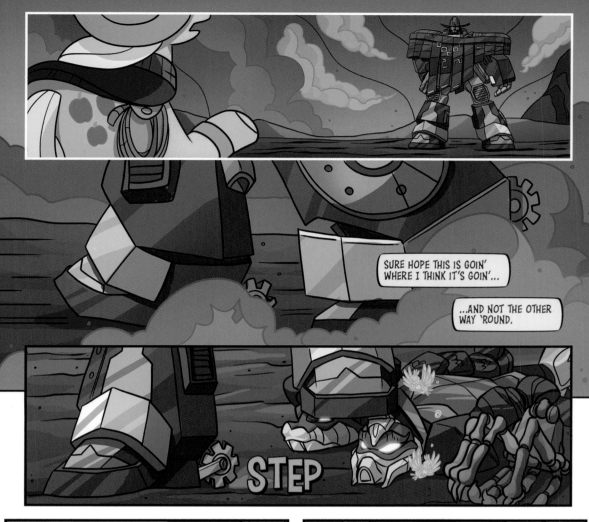

SURE HOPE THIS IS GOIN' WHERE I THINK IT'S GOIN'...

...AND NOT THE OTHER WAY 'ROUND.

STEP

I'LL HELP YOU FIND YOUR WAY HOME.

YOU'VE EARNED MY RESPECT, HORSE.

WELL, I RECKON YOU WEREN'T TOO BAD YERSELF!

OH, YOU WON'T REGRET THIS, WILD PONCHO, I PROMISE YOU THAT.

SHAKE SHAKE SHAKE

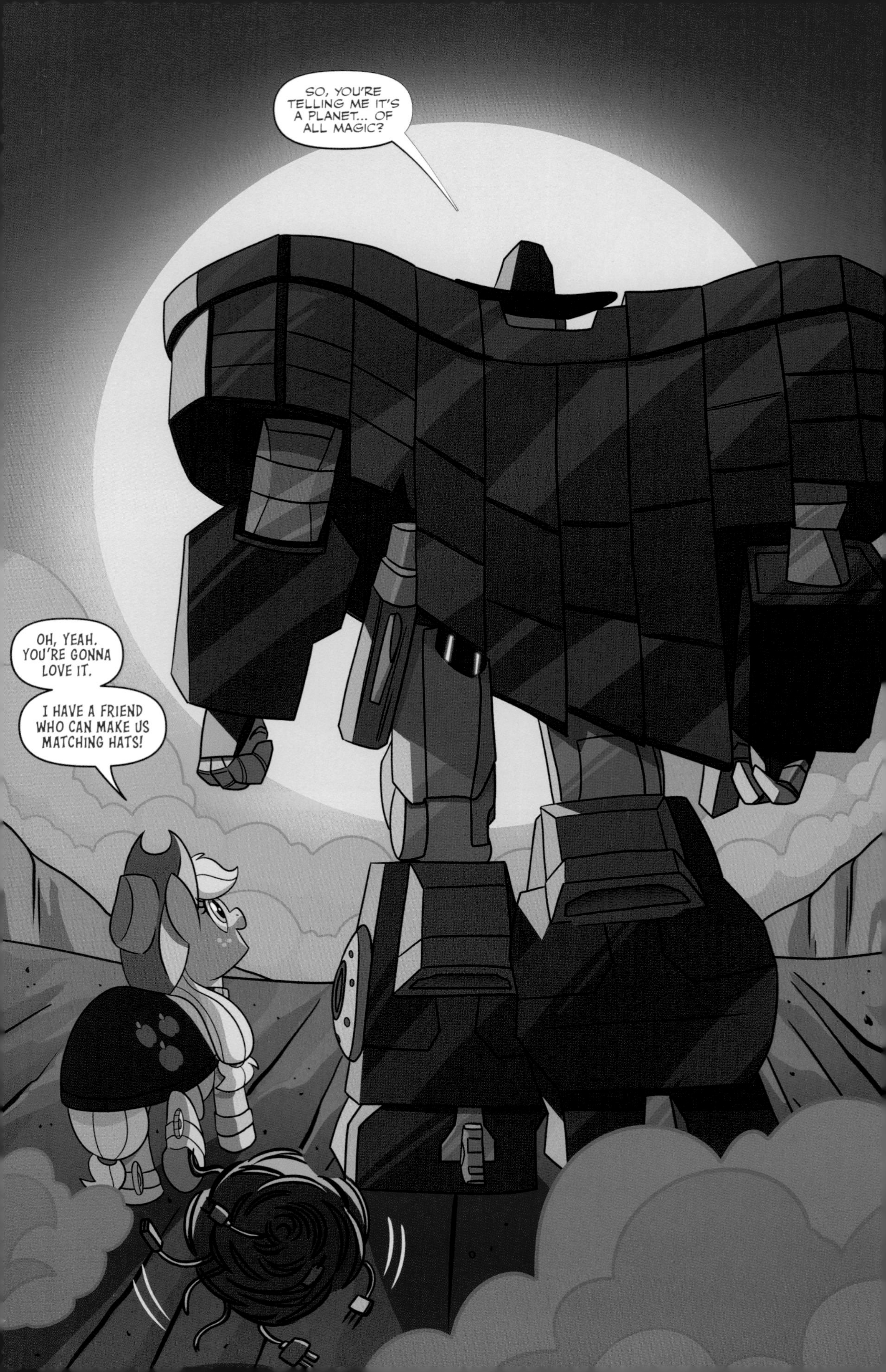
SO, YOU'RE TELLING ME IT'S A PLANET... OF ALL MAGIC?
OH, YEAH. YOU'RE GONNA LOVE IT.
I HAVE A FRIEND WHO CAN MAKE US MATCHING HATS!

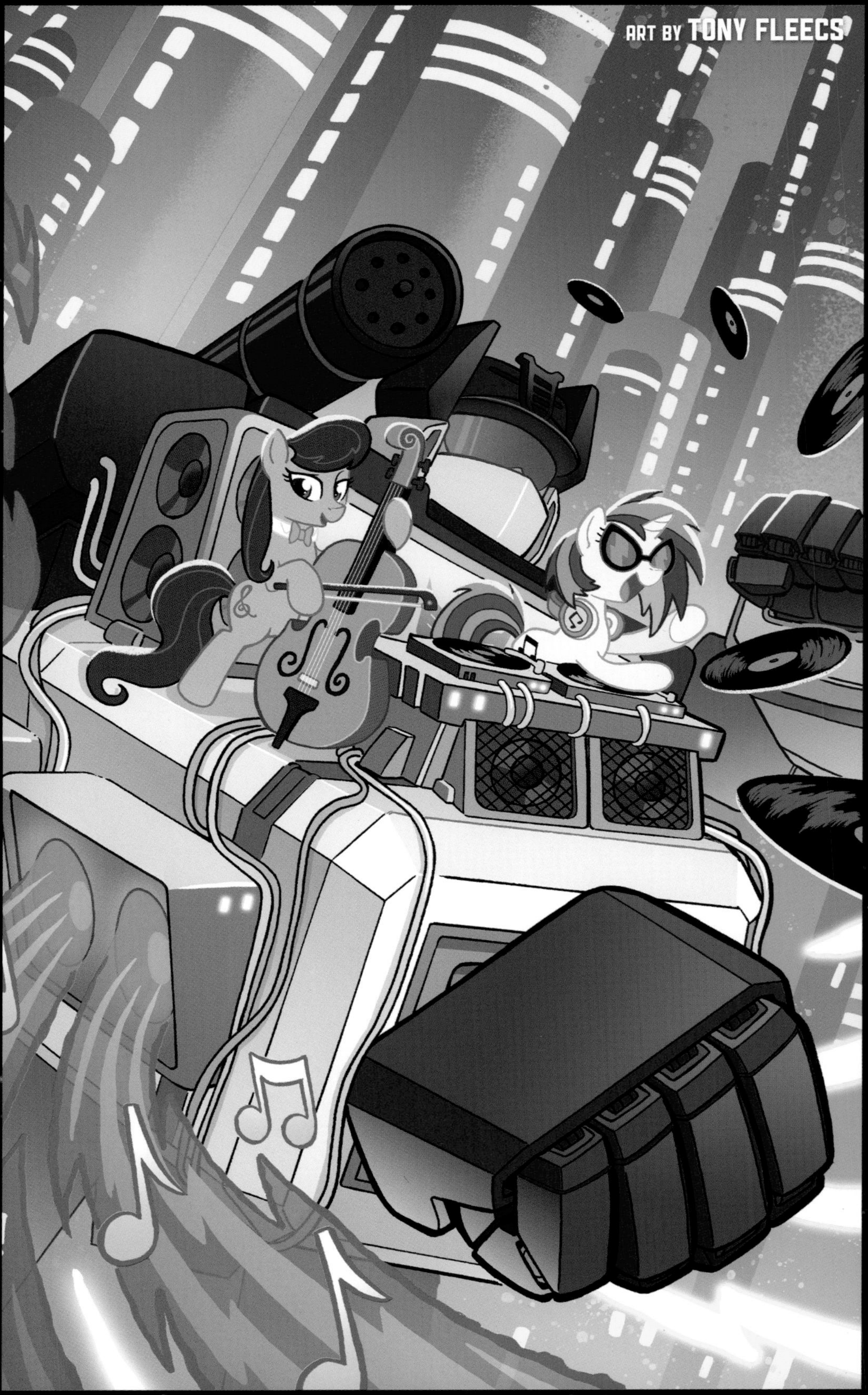
ART BY TONY FLEECS

"SICK BEATS"

WRITTEN AND DRAWN BY **TONY FLEECS**
COLOR FLATS BY **LAUREN PERRY**
COLORS BY **TONY FLEECS**
LETTERS BY **JAKE M. WOOD**

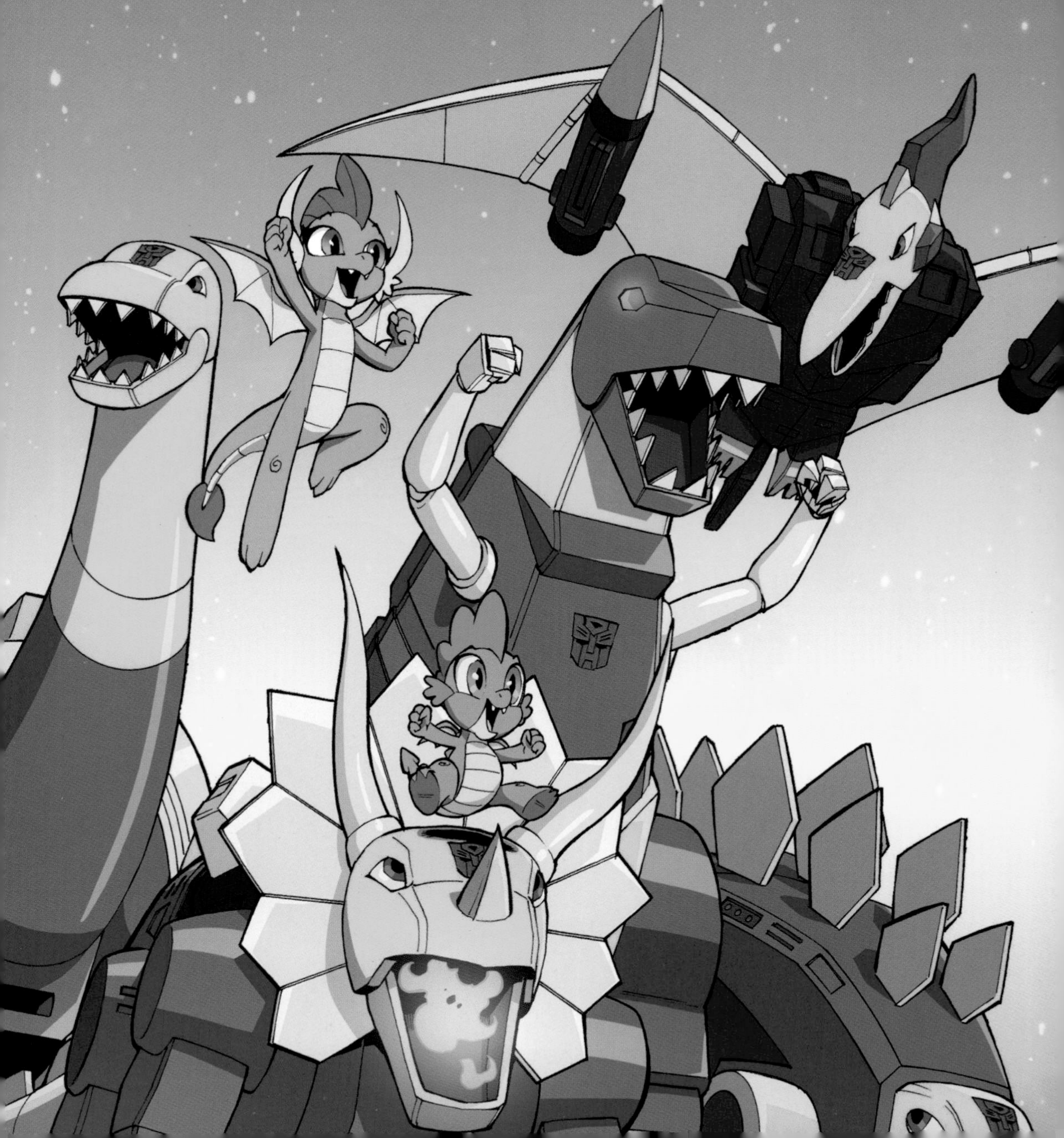

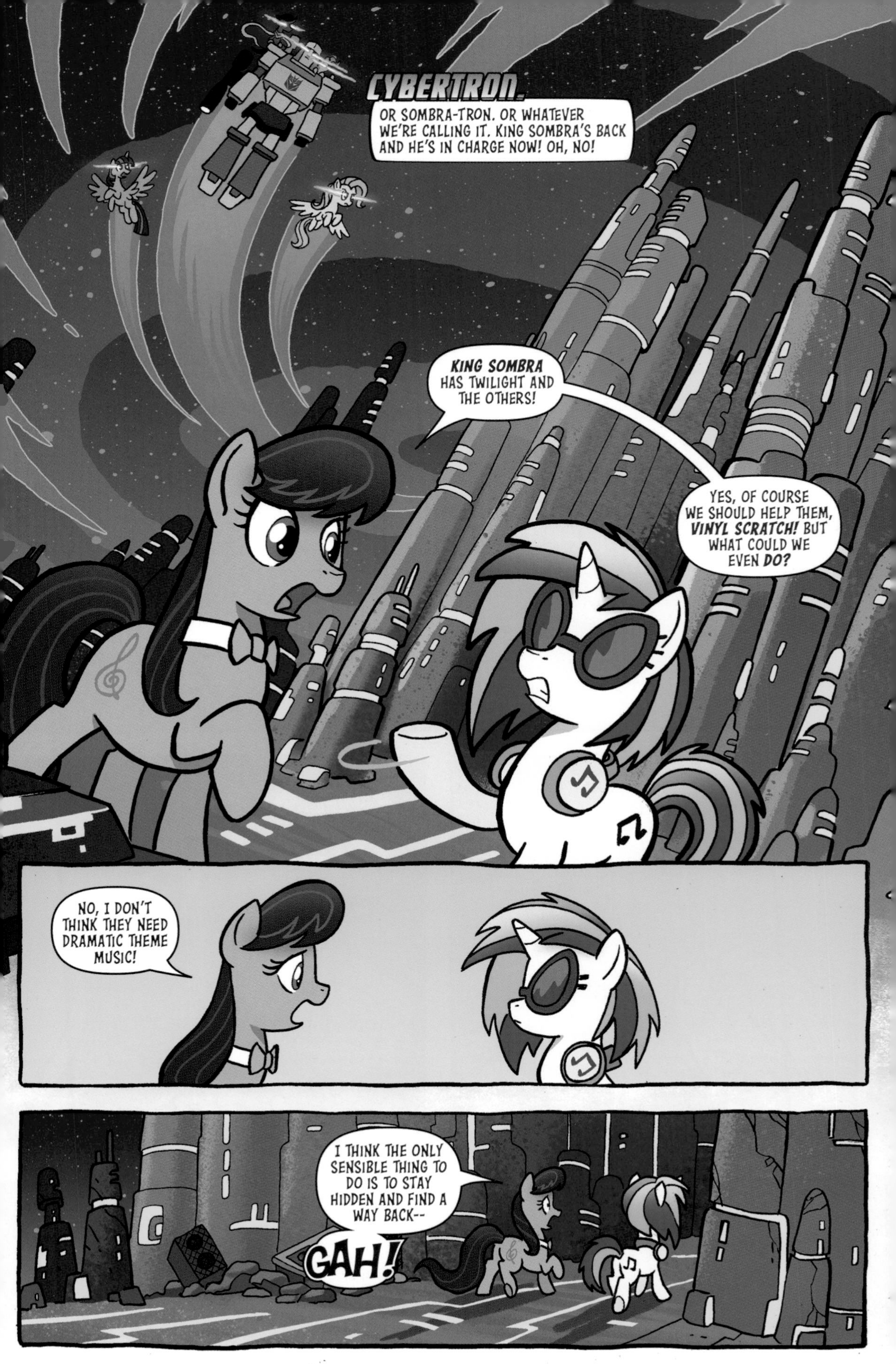

CYBERTRON.
OR SOMBRA-TRON. OR WHATEVER WE'RE CALLING IT. KING SOMBRA'S BACK AND HE'S IN CHARGE NOW! OH, NO!
KING SOMBRA HAS TWILIGHT AND THE OTHERS!
YES, OF COURSE WE SHOULD HELP THEM, VINYL SCRATCH! BUT WHAT COULD WE EVEN DO?
NO, I DON'T THINK THEY NEED DRAMATIC THEME MUSIC!
I THINK THE ONLY SENSIBLE THING TO DO IS TO STAY HIDDEN AND FIND A WAY BACK--
GAH!

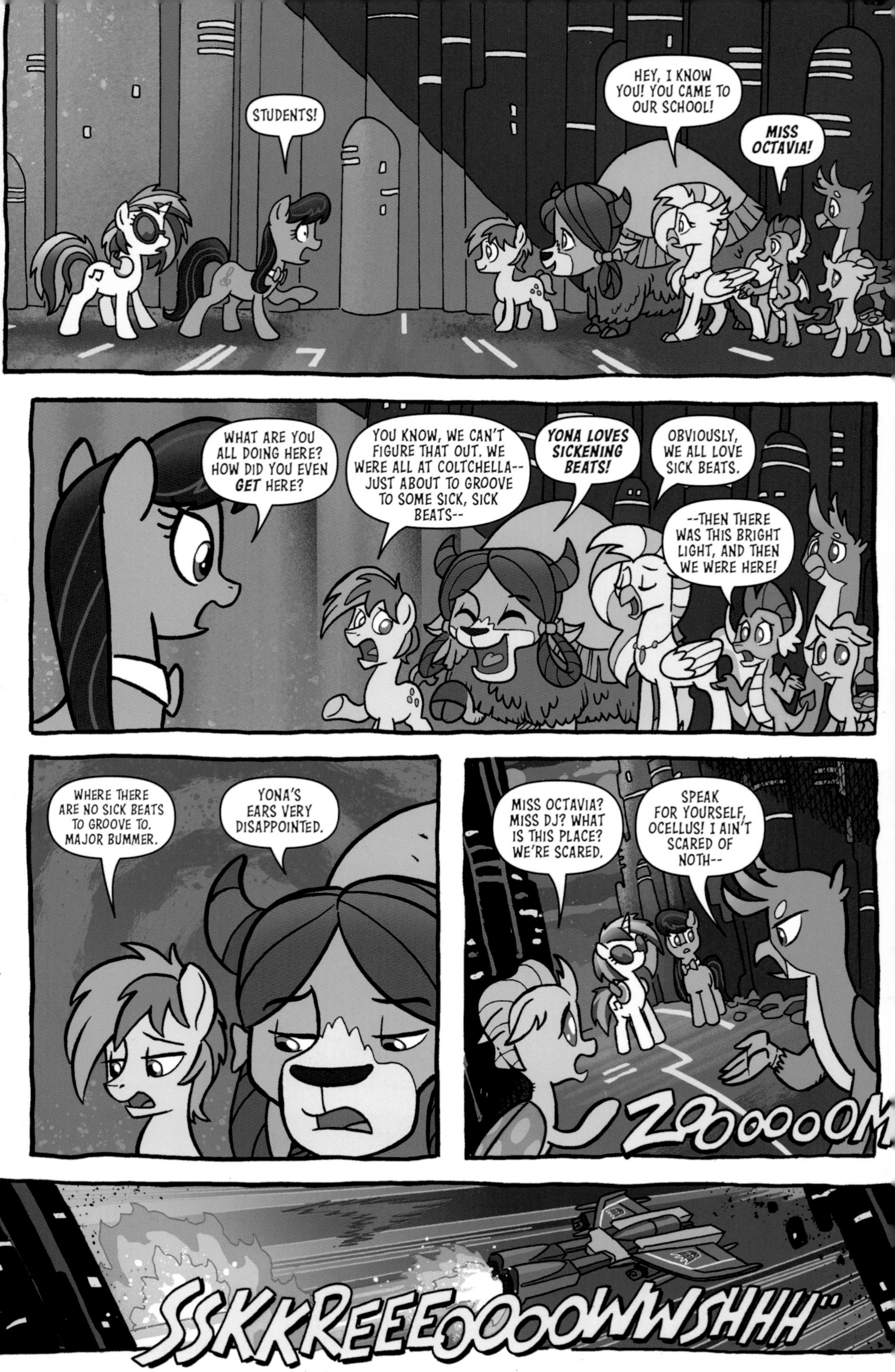

STUDENTS!
HEY, I KNOW YOU! YOU CAME TO OUR SCHOOL!
MISS OCTAVIA!
WHAT ARE YOU ALL DOING HERE? HOW DID YOU EVEN GET HERE?
YOU KNOW, WE CAN'T FIGURE THAT OUT. WE WERE ALL AT COLTCHELLA-- JUST ABOUT TO GROOVE TO SOME SICK, SICK BEATS--
YONA LOVES SICKENING BEATS!
OBVIOUSLY, WE ALL LOVE SICK BEATS.
--THEN THERE WAS THIS BRIGHT LIGHT, AND THEN WE WERE HERE!
WHERE THERE ARE NO SICK BEATS TO GROOVE TO. MAJOR BUMMER.
YONA'S EARS VERY DISAPPOINTED.
MISS OCTAVIA? MISS DJ? WHAT IS THIS PLACE? WE'RE SCARED.
SPEAK FOR YOURSELF, OCELLUS! I AIN'T SCARED OF NOTH--
ZOOOOOOM
SSKKREEEOOOOOWWSHHH

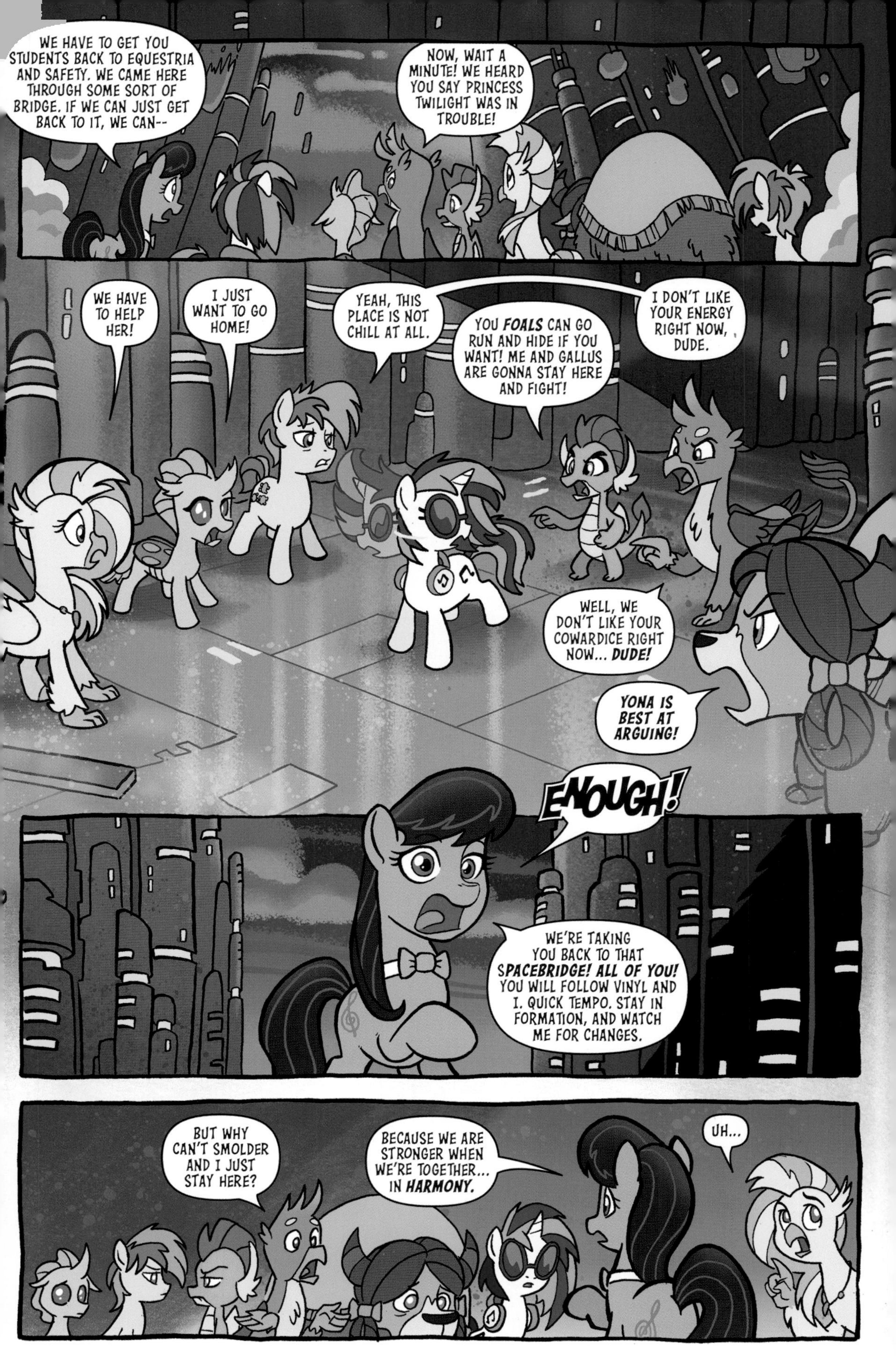
WE HAVE TO GET YOU STUDENTS BACK TO EQUESTRIA AND SAFETY. WE CAME HERE THROUGH SOME SORT OF BRIDGE. IF WE CAN JUST GET BACK TO IT, WE CAN--
NOW, WAIT A MINUTE! WE HEARD YOU SAY PRINCESS TWILIGHT WAS IN TROUBLE!
WE HAVE TO HELP HER!
I JUST WANT TO GO HOME!
YEAH, THIS PLACE IS NOT CHILL AT ALL.
I DON'T LIKE YOUR ENERGY RIGHT NOW, DUDE.
YOU FOALS CAN GO RUN AND HIDE IF YOU WANT! ME AND GALLUS ARE GONNA STAY HERE AND FIGHT!
WELL, WE DON'T LIKE YOUR COWARDICE RIGHT NOW... DUDE!
YONA IS BEST AT ARGUING!
ENOUGH!
WE'RE TAKING YOU BACK TO THAT SPACEBRIDGE! ALL OF YOU! YOU WILL FOLLOW VINYL AND I. QUICK TEMPO. STAY IN FORMATION, AND WATCH ME FOR CHANGES.
BUT WHY CAN'T SMOLDER AND I JUST STAY HERE?
BECAUSE WE ARE STRONGER WHEN WE'RE TOGETHER... IN HARMONY.
UH...

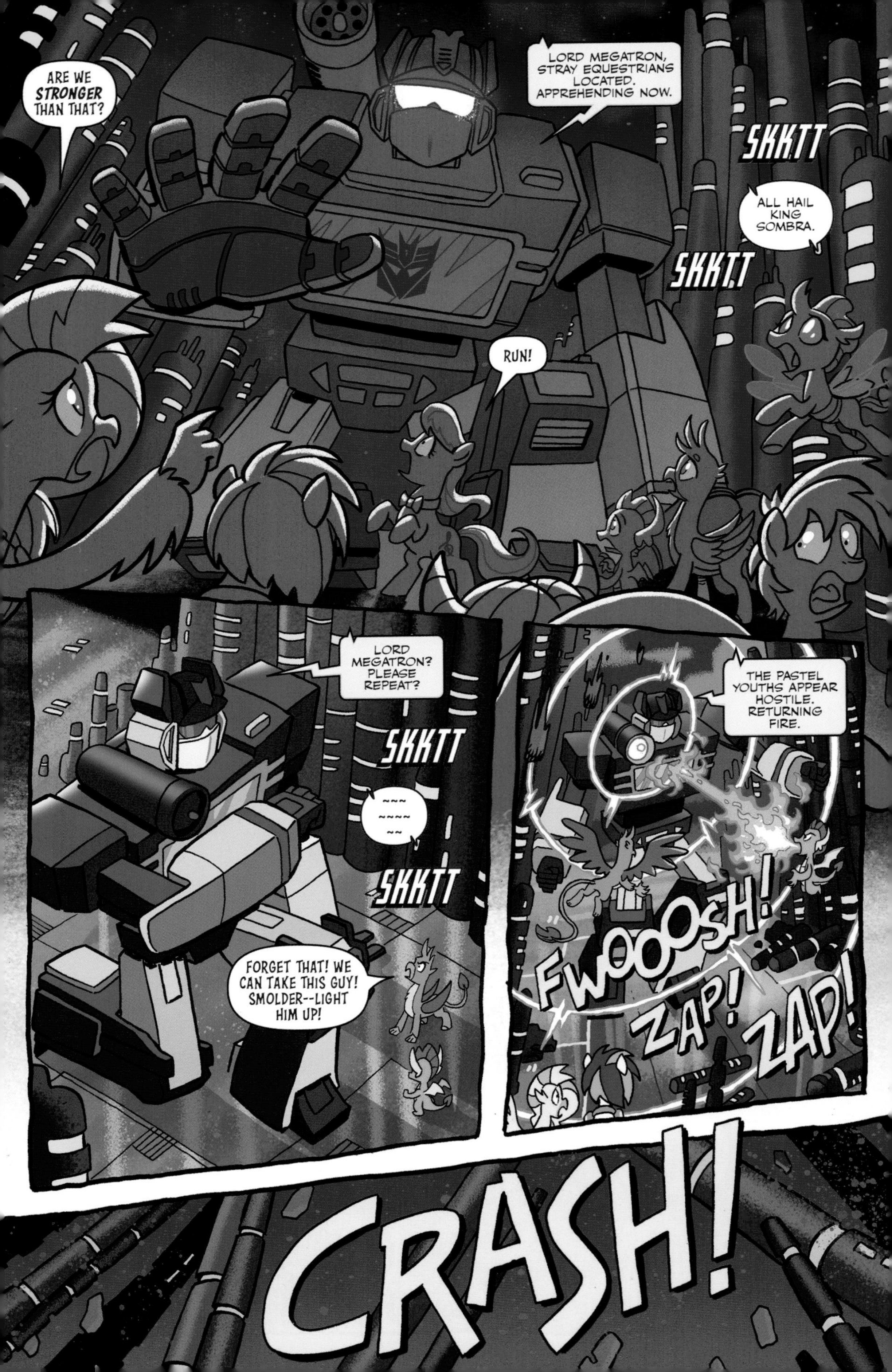
ARE WE STRONGER THAN THAT?
LORD MEGATRON, STRAY EQUESTRIANS LOCATED. APPREHENDING NOW.
SKKTT
ALL HAIL KING SOMBRA.
SKKTT
RUN!
LORD MEGATRON? PLEASE REPEAT?
SKKTT
~~~ ~~~~ ~~
SKKTT
FORGET THAT! WE CAN TAKE THIS GUY! SMOLDER--LIGHT HIM UP!
THE PASTEL YOUTHS APPEAR HOSTILE. RETURNING FIRE.
FWOOOSH!
ZAP!
ZAP!
CRASH!
~~~

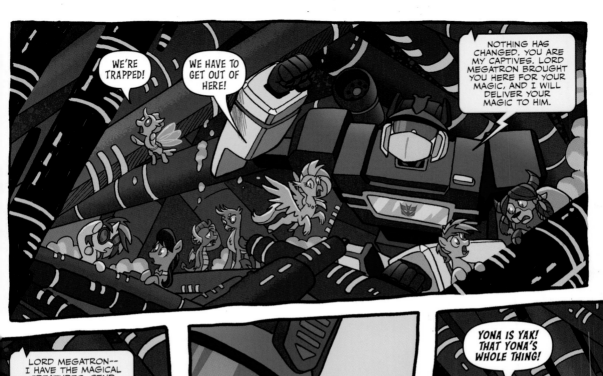

We're trapped!

We have to get out of here!

Nothing has changed. You are my captives. Lord Megatron brought you here for your magic, and I will deliver your magic to him.

Lord Megatron-- I have the magical creatures. Send Contructicons to my coordinates for excavation and extraction.

Lord Megatron?

SKKTT

It doesn't sound like he's in right now, guy.

Do not mock me, Buffalo!

Hey, I'M A GRIFFON! YONA'S the Buffalo!

Yona is Yak! That Yona's whole thing!

Students, don't taunt the giant robot!

Silence!

Witness the strength...

...OF SOUNDWAVE!

BZZ

AAAAWWWWWWW!

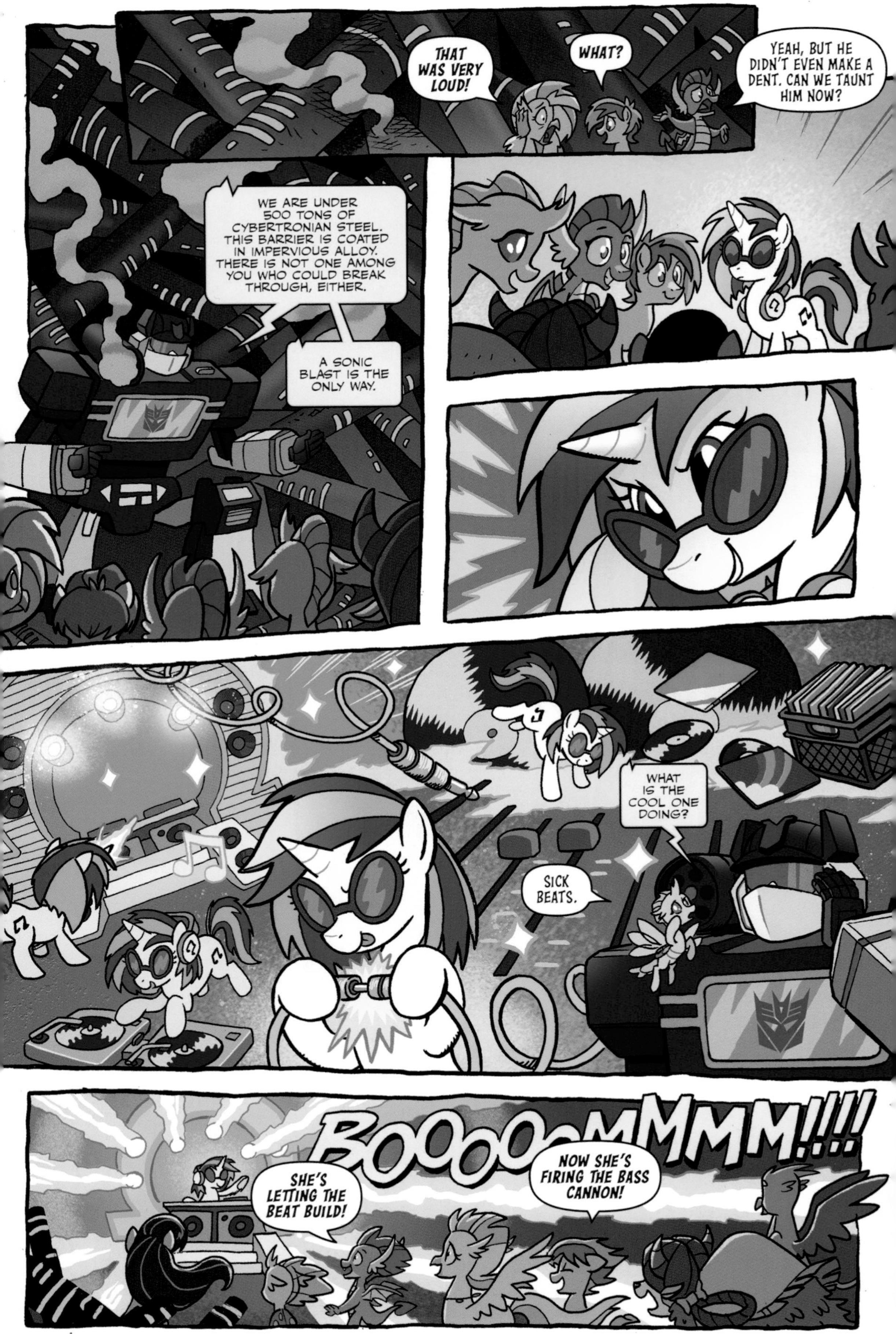
THAT WAS VERY LOUD!
WHAT?
YEAH, BUT HE DIDN'T EVEN MAKE A DENT. CAN WE TAUNT HIM NOW?
WE ARE UNDER 500 TONS OF CYBERTRONIAN STEEL. THIS BARRIER IS COATED IN IMPERVIOUS ALLOY. THERE IS NOT ONE AMONG YOU WHO COULD BREAK THROUGH, EITHER.
A SONIC BLAST IS THE ONLY WAY.
WHAT IS THE COOL ONE DOING?
SICK BEATS.
BOOOOOMMMMM!!!!
SHE'S LETTING THE BEAT BUILD!
NOW SHE'S FIRING THE BASS CANNON!

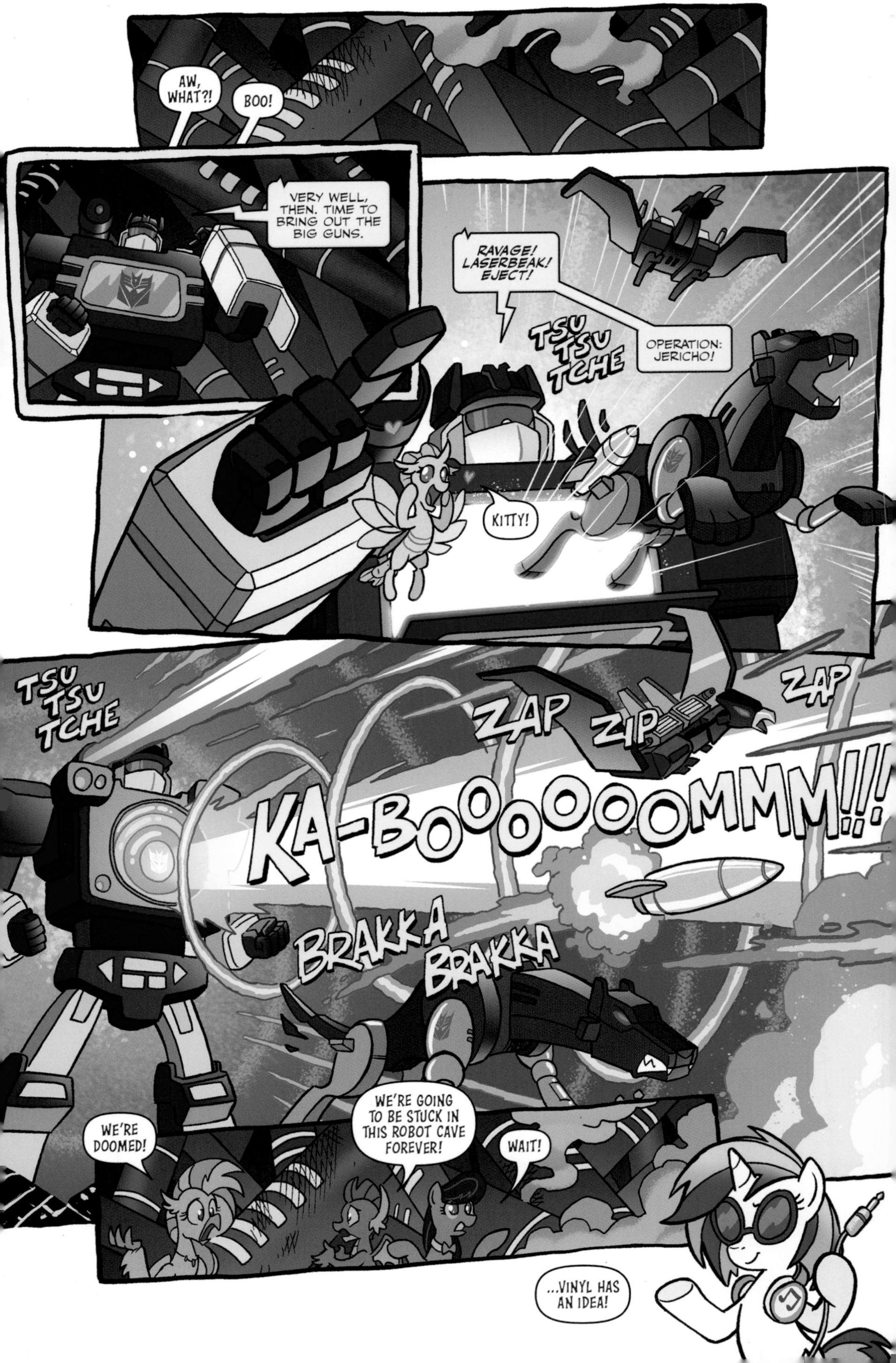
AW, WHAT?!
BOO!
VERY WELL, THEN. TIME TO BRING OUT THE BIG GUNS.
RAVAGE! LASERBEAK! EJECT!
TSU TSU TCHE
OPERATION: JERICHO!
KITTY!
TSU TSU TCHE
ZAP
ZIP
ZAP
KA-BOOOOOOOMMMM!!!
BRAKKA
BRAKKA
WE'RE DOOMED!
WE'RE GOING TO BE STUCK IN THIS ROBOT CAVE FOREVER!
WAIT!
...VINYL HAS AN IDEA!

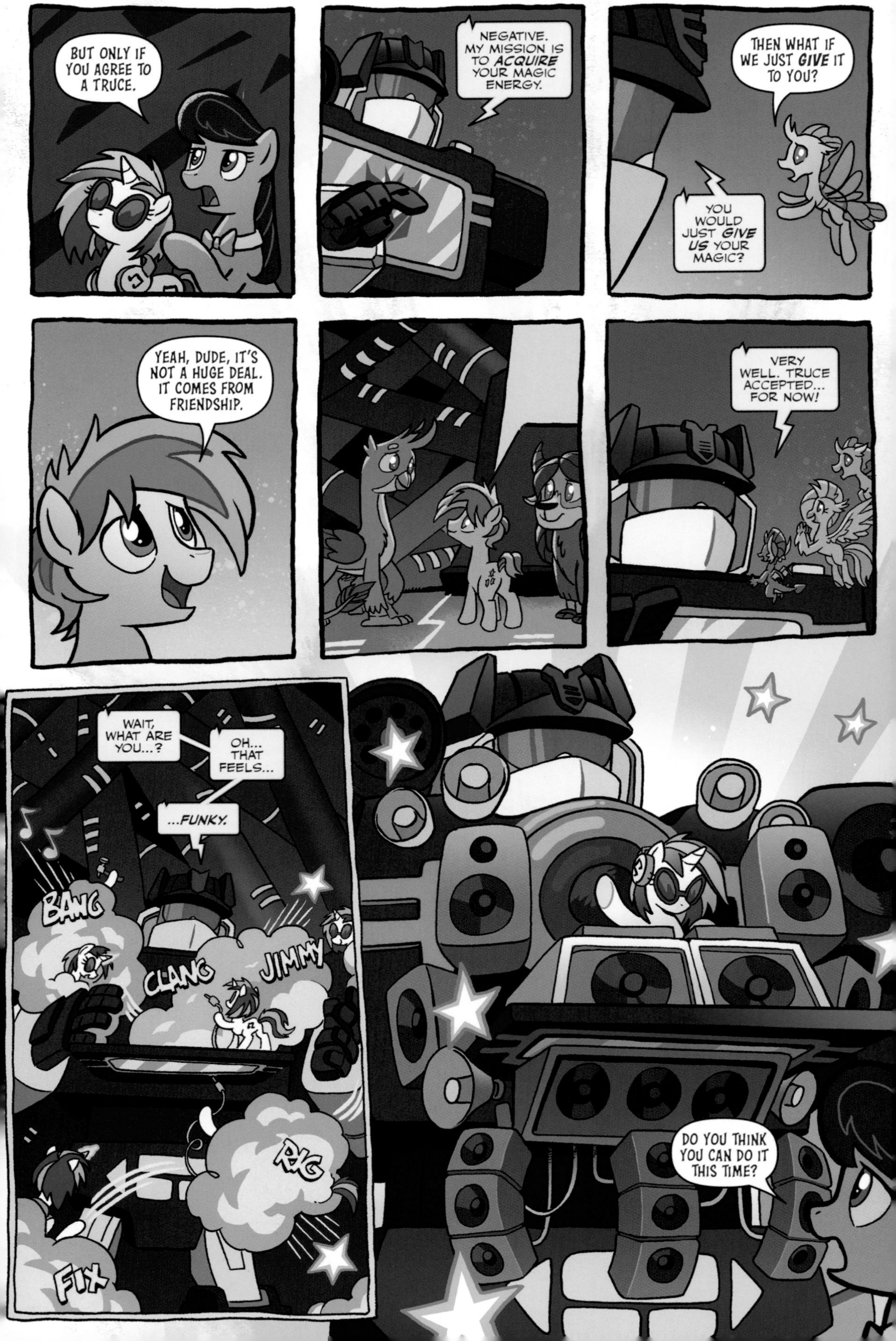
BUT ONLY IF YOU AGREE TO A TRUCE.
NEGATIVE. MY MISSION IS TO ACQUIRE YOUR MAGIC ENERGY.
THEN WHAT IF WE JUST GIVE IT TO YOU?
YOU WOULD JUST GIVE US YOUR MAGIC?
YEAH, DUDE, IT'S NOT A HUGE DEAL. IT COMES FROM FRIENDSHIP.
VERY WELL. TRUCE ACCEPTED... FOR NOW!
WAIT, WHAT ARE YOU...?
OH... THAT FEELS...
...FUNKY.
BANG
CLANG
JIMMY
RIG
FIX
DO YOU THINK YOU CAN DO IT THIS TIME?

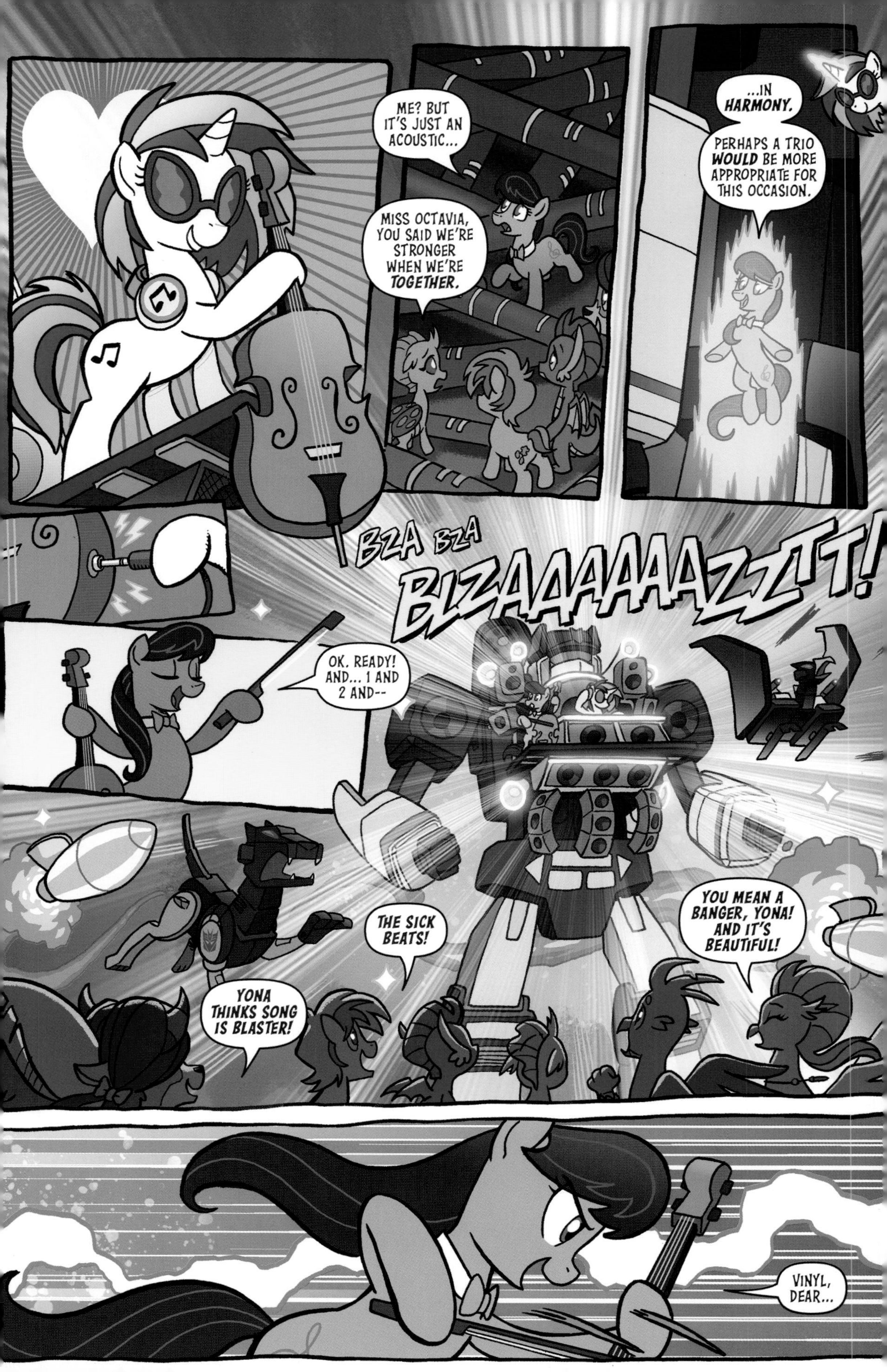
ME? BUT IT'S JUST AN ACOUSTIC...
MISS OCTAVIA, YOU SAID WE'RE STRONGER WHEN WE'RE TOGETHER.
...IN HARMONY.
PERHAPS A TRIO WOULD BE MORE APPROPRIATE FOR THIS OCCASION.
BZA BZA
BLZAAAAAAZZTT!
OK. READY! AND... 1 AND 2 AND--
THE SICK BEATS!
YOU MEAN A BANGER, YONA! AND IT'S BEAUTIFUL!
YONA THINKS SONG IS BLASTER!
VINYL, DEAR...

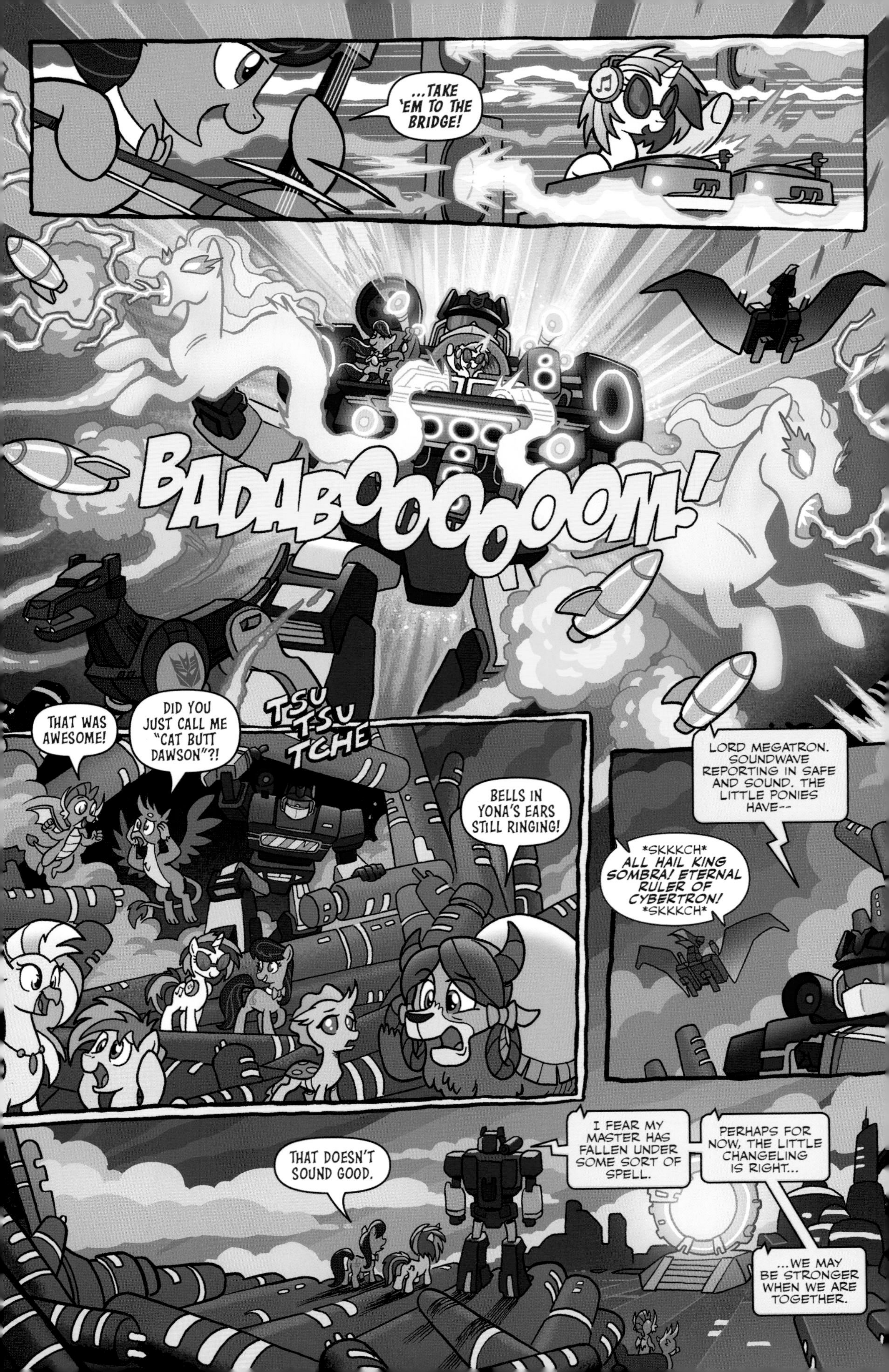

...TAKE 'EM TO THE BRIDGE!
BADABOOOOOOOM!
TSU TSU TSU TCHE
THAT WAS AWESOME!
DID YOU JUST CALL ME "CAT BUTT DAWSON"?!
BELLS IN YONA'S EARS STILL RINGING!
LORD MEGATRON. SOUNDWAVE REPORTING IN SAFE AND SOUND. THE LITTLE PONIES HAVE--
SKKKCH ALL HAIL KING SOMBRA! ETERNAL RULER OF CYBERTRON! *SKKKCH*
THAT DOESN'T SOUND GOOD.
I FEAR MY MASTER HAS FALLEN UNDER SOME SORT OF SPELL.
PERHAPS FOR NOW, THE LITTLE CHANGELING IS RIGHT...
...WE MAY BE STRONGER WHEN WE ARE TOGETHER.

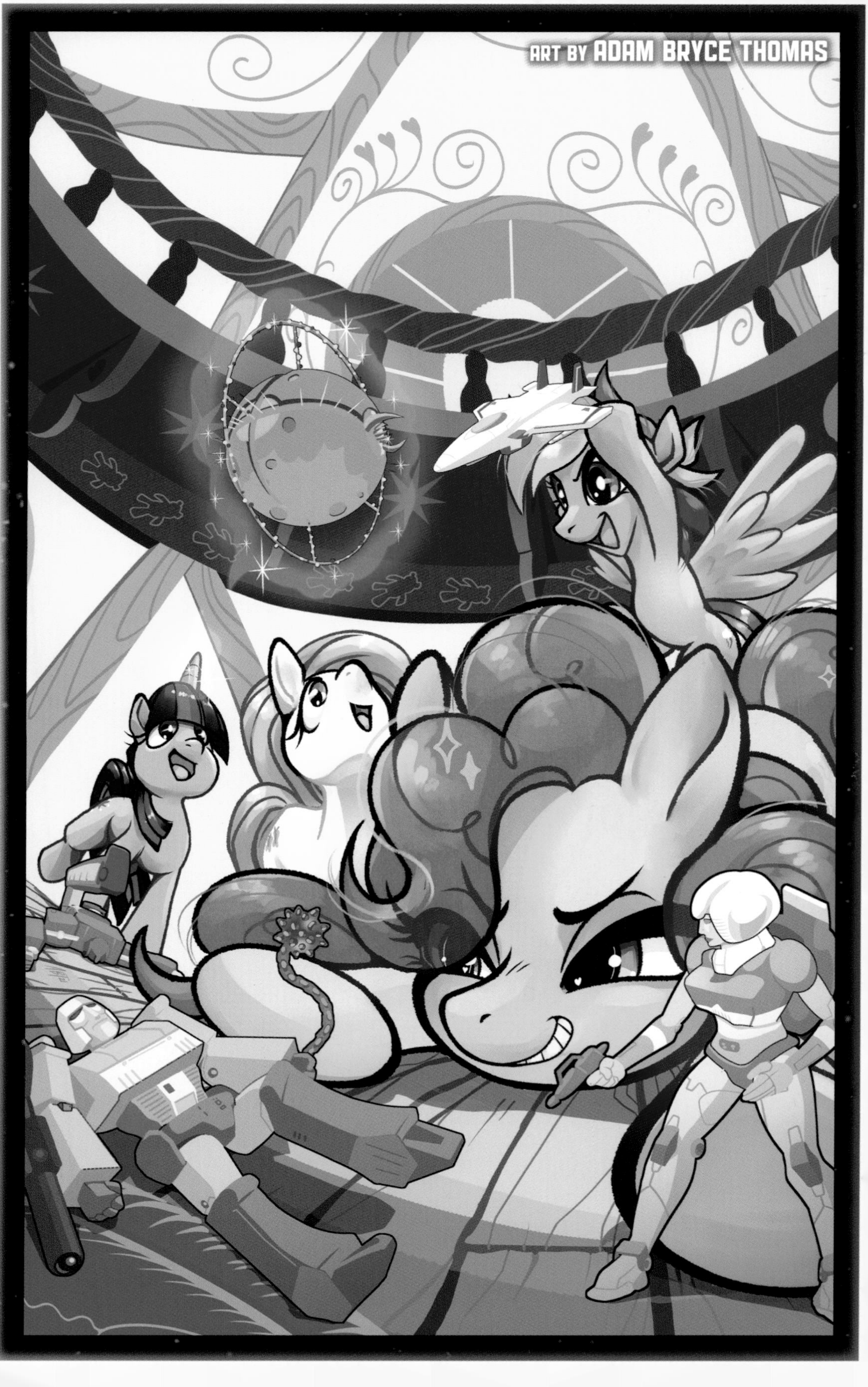
ART BY ADAM BRYCE THOMAS

"THE BEAUTY OF CYBERTRON"

WRITTEN BY JAMES ASMUS
ART BY PRISCILLA TRAMONTANO
COLORS BY LUIS ANTONIO DELGADO
LETTERS BY NEIL UYETAKE

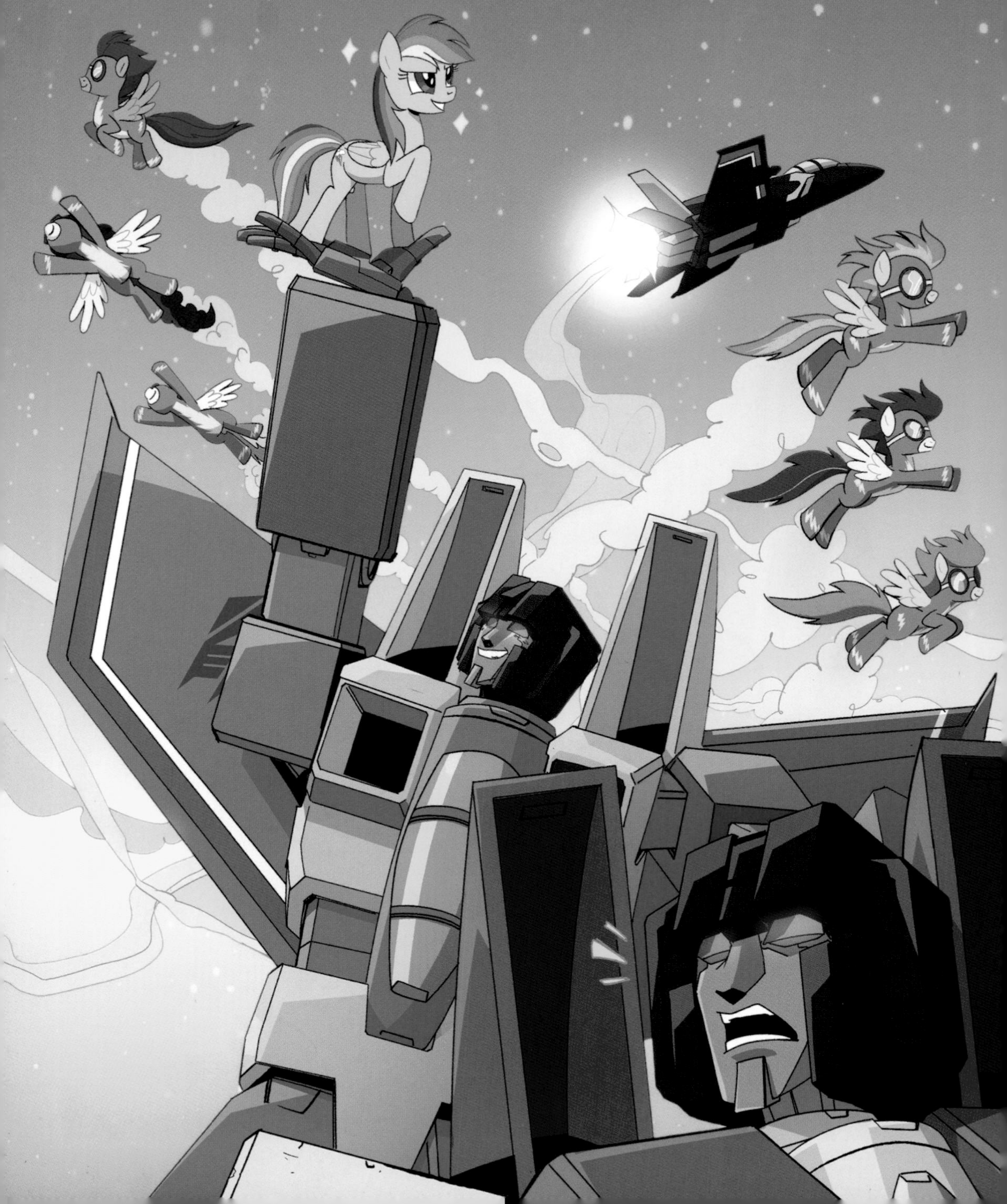

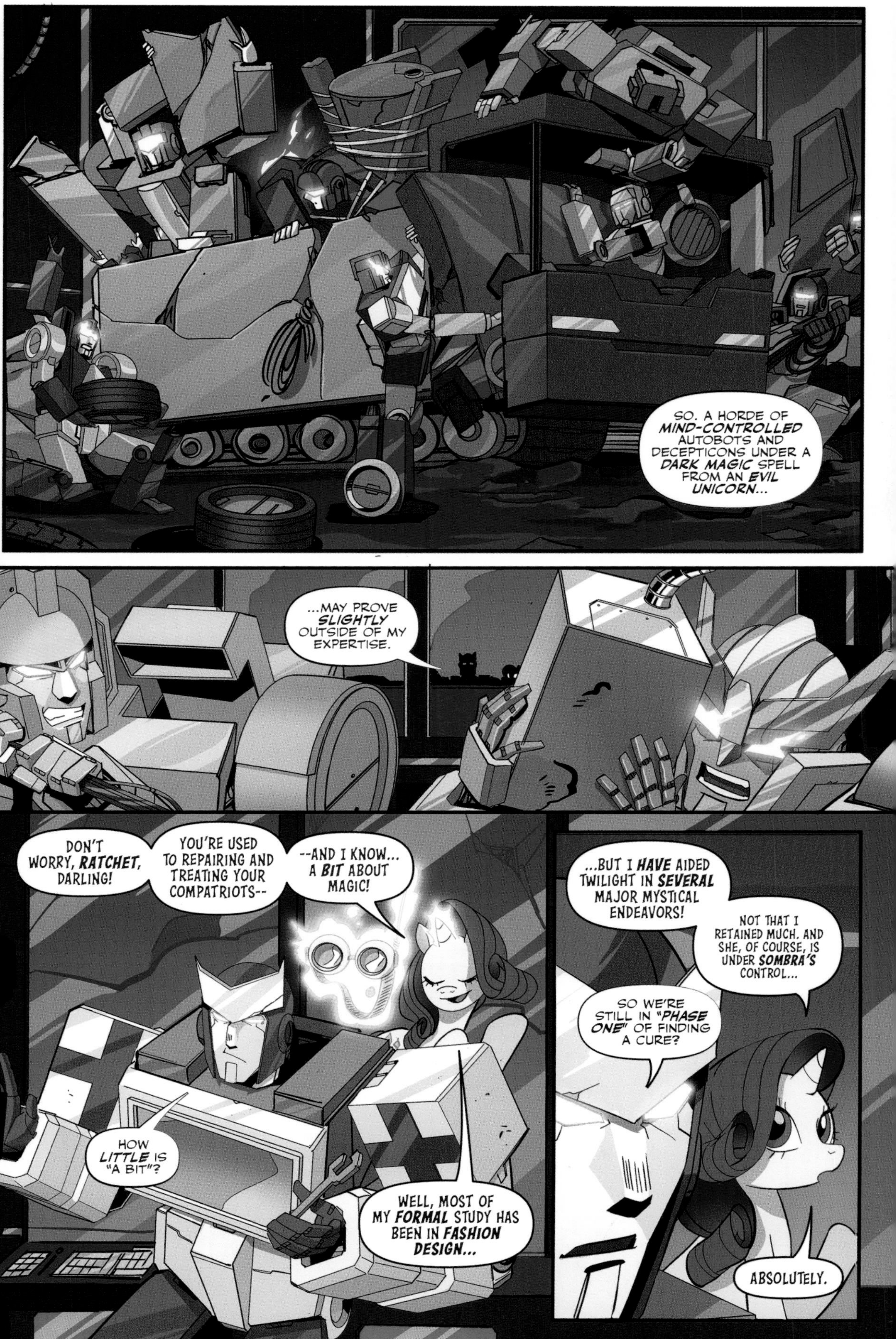
SO. A HORDE OF MIND-CONTROLLED AUTOBOTS AND DECEPTICONS UNDER A DARK MAGIC SPELL FROM AN EVIL UNICORN...
...MAY PROVE SLIGHTLY OUTSIDE OF MY EXPERTISE.
DON'T WORRY, RATCHET, DARLING!
YOU'RE USED TO REPAIRING AND TREATING YOUR COMPATRIOTS--
--AND I KNOW... A BIT ABOUT MAGIC!
HOW LITTLE IS "A BIT"?
WELL, MOST OF MY FORMAL STUDY HAS BEEN IN FASHION DESIGN...
...BUT I HAVE AIDED TWILIGHT IN SEVERAL MAJOR MYSTICAL ENDEAVORS!
NOT THAT I RETAINED MUCH. AND SHE, OF COURSE, IS UNDER SOMBRA'S CONTROL...
SO WE'RE STILL IN "PHASE ONE" OF FINDING A CURE?
ABSOLUTELY.

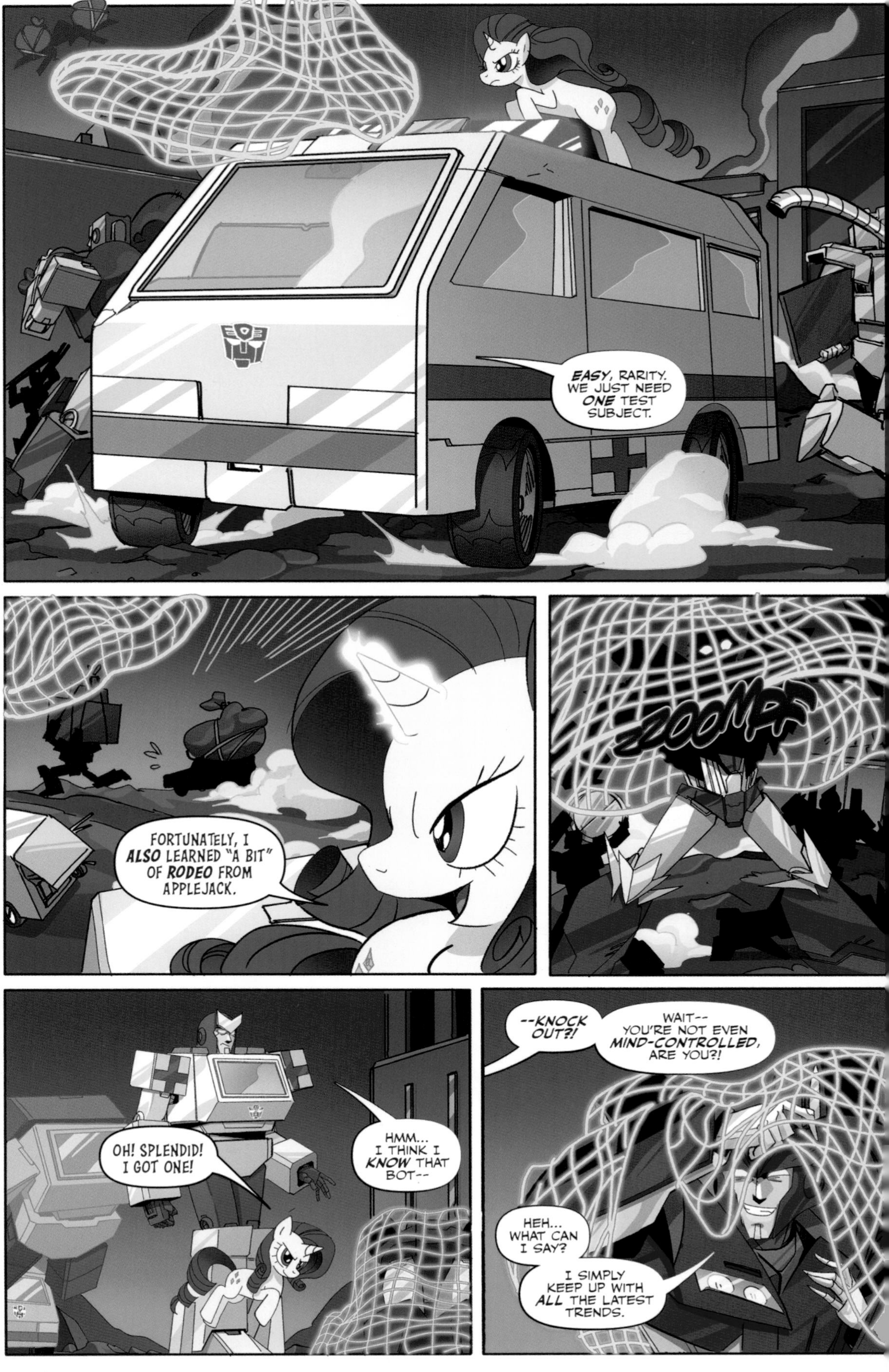
EASY, RARITY. WE JUST NEED ONE TEST SUBJECT.
FORTUNATELY, I ALSO LEARNED "A BIT" OF RODEO FROM APPLEJACK.
ZOOMPF
OH! SPLENDID! I GOT ONE!
HMM... I THINK I KNOW THAT BOT--
--KNOCK OUT?!
WAIT-- YOU'RE NOT EVEN MIND-CONTROLLED, ARE YOU?!
HEH... WHAT CAN I SAY?
I SIMPLY KEEP UP WITH ALL THE LATEST TRENDS.

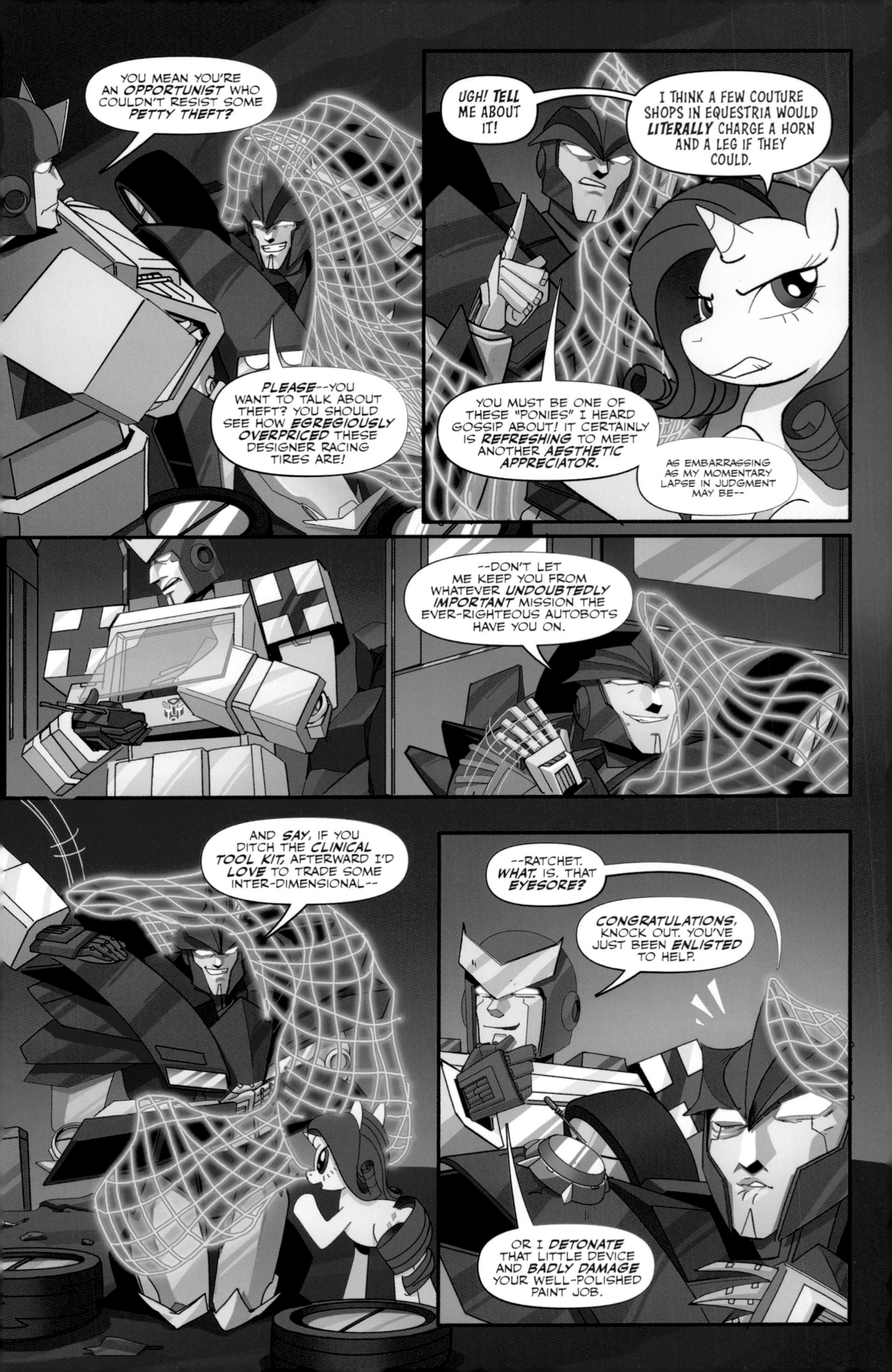
YOU MEAN YOU'RE AN OPPORTUNIST WHO COULDN'T RESIST SOME PETTY THEFT?
PLEASE--YOU WANT TO TALK ABOUT THEFT? YOU SHOULD SEE HOW EGREGIOUSLY OVERPRICED THESE DESIGNER RACING TIRES ARE!
UGH! TELL ME ABOUT IT!
I THINK A FEW COUTURE SHOPS IN EQUESTRIA WOULD LITERALLY CHARGE A HORN AND A LEG IF THEY COULD.
YOU MUST BE ONE OF THESE "PONIES" I HEARD GOSSIP ABOUT! IT CERTAINLY IS REFRESHING TO MEET ANOTHER AESTHETIC APPRECIATOR.
AS EMBARRASSING AS MY MOMENTARY LAPSE IN JUDGMENT MAY BE--
--DON'T LET ME KEEP YOU FROM WHATEVER UNDOUBTEDLY IMPORTANT MISSION THE EVER-RIGHTEOUS AUTOBOTS HAVE YOU ON.
AND SAY, IF YOU DITCH THE CLINICAL TOOL KIT, AFTERWARD I'D LOVE TO TRADE SOME INTER-DIMENSIONAL--
--RATCHET. WHAT. IS. THAT EYESORE?
CONGRATULATIONS, KNOCK OUT. YOU'VE JUST BEEN ENLISTED TO HELP.
OR I DETONATE THAT LITTLE DEVICE AND BADLY DAMAGE YOUR WELL-POLISHED PAINT JOB.

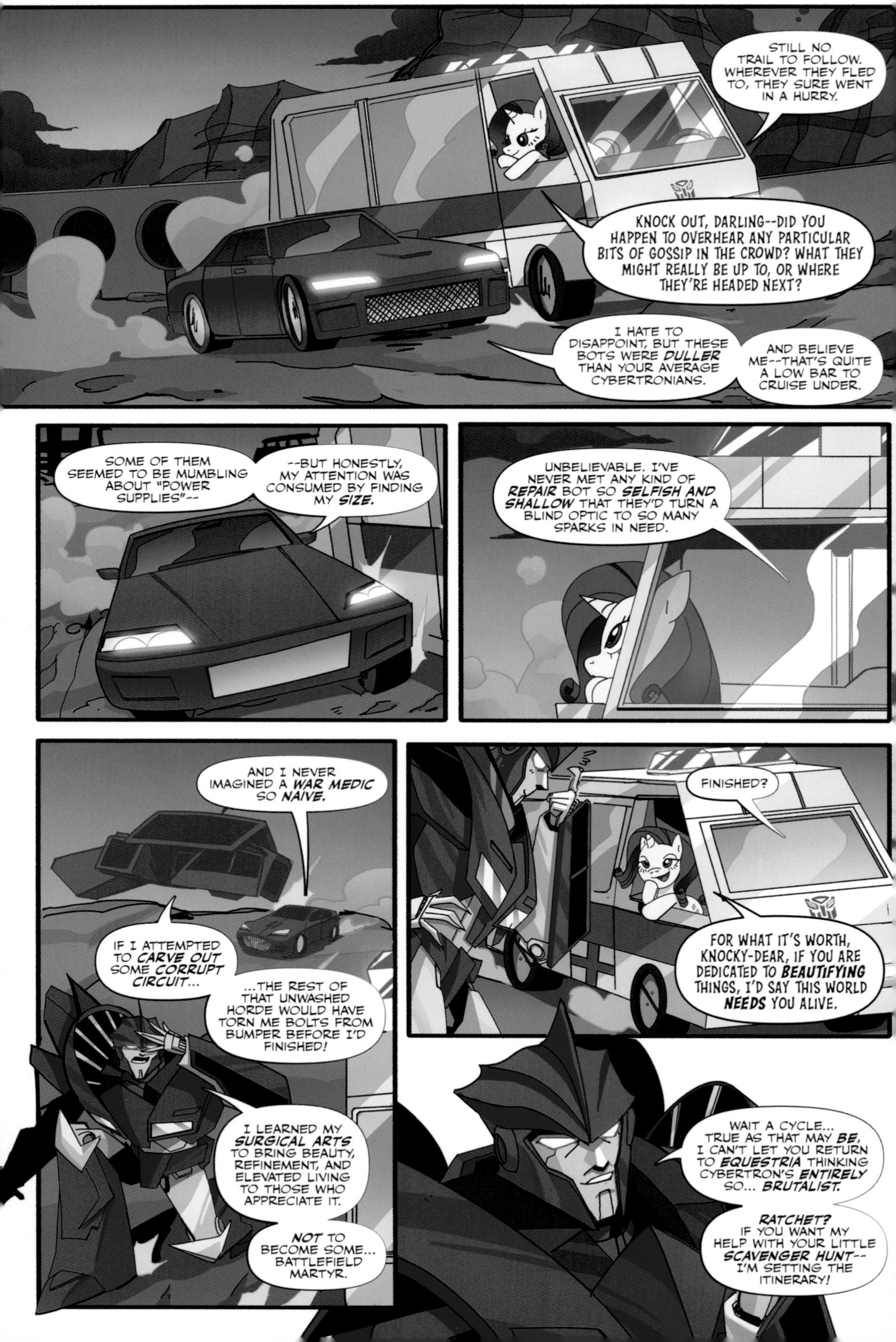
STILL NO TRAIL TO FOLLOW. WHEREVER THEY FLED TO, THEY SURE WENT IN A HURRY.
KNOCK OUT, DARLING--DID YOU HAPPEN TO OVERHEAR ANY PARTICULAR BITS OF GOSSIP IN THE CROWD? WHAT THEY MIGHT REALLY BE UP TO, OR WHERE THEY'RE HEADED NEXT?
I HATE TO DISAPPOINT, BUT THESE BOTS WERE DULLER THAN YOUR AVERAGE CYBERTRONIANS.
AND BELIEVE ME--THAT'S QUITE A LOW BAR TO CRUISE UNDER.
SOME OF THEM SEEMED TO BE MUMBLING ABOUT "POWER SUPPLIES"--
--BUT HONESTLY, MY ATTENTION WAS CONSUMED BY FINDING MY SIZE.
UNBELIEVABLE. I'VE NEVER MET ANY KIND OF REPAIR BOT SO SELFISH AND SHALLOW THAT THEY'D TURN A BLIND OPTIC TO SO MANY SPARKS IN NEED.
AND I NEVER IMAGINED A WAR MEDIC SO NAIVE.
IF I ATTEMPTED TO CARVE OUT SOME CORRUPT CIRCUIT...
...THE REST OF THAT UNWASHED HORDE WOULD HAVE TORN ME BOLTS FROM BUMPER BEFORE I'D FINISHED!
I LEARNED MY SURGICAL ARTS TO BRING BEAUTY, REFINEMENT, AND ELEVATED LIVING TO THOSE WHO APPRECIATE IT.
NOT TO BECOME SOME... BATTLEFIELD MARTYR.
FINISHED?
FOR WHAT IT'S WORTH, KNOCKY-DEAR, IF YOU ARE DEDICATED TO BEAUTIFYING THINGS, I'D SAY THIS WORLD NEEDS YOU ALIVE.
WAIT A CYCLE... TRUE AS THAT MAY BE, I CAN'T LET YOU RETURN TO EQUESTRIA THINKING CYBERTRON'S ENTIRELY SO... BRUTALIST.
RATCHET? IF YOU WANT MY HELP WITH YOUR LITTLE SCAVENGER HUNT-- I'M SETTING THE ITINERARY!

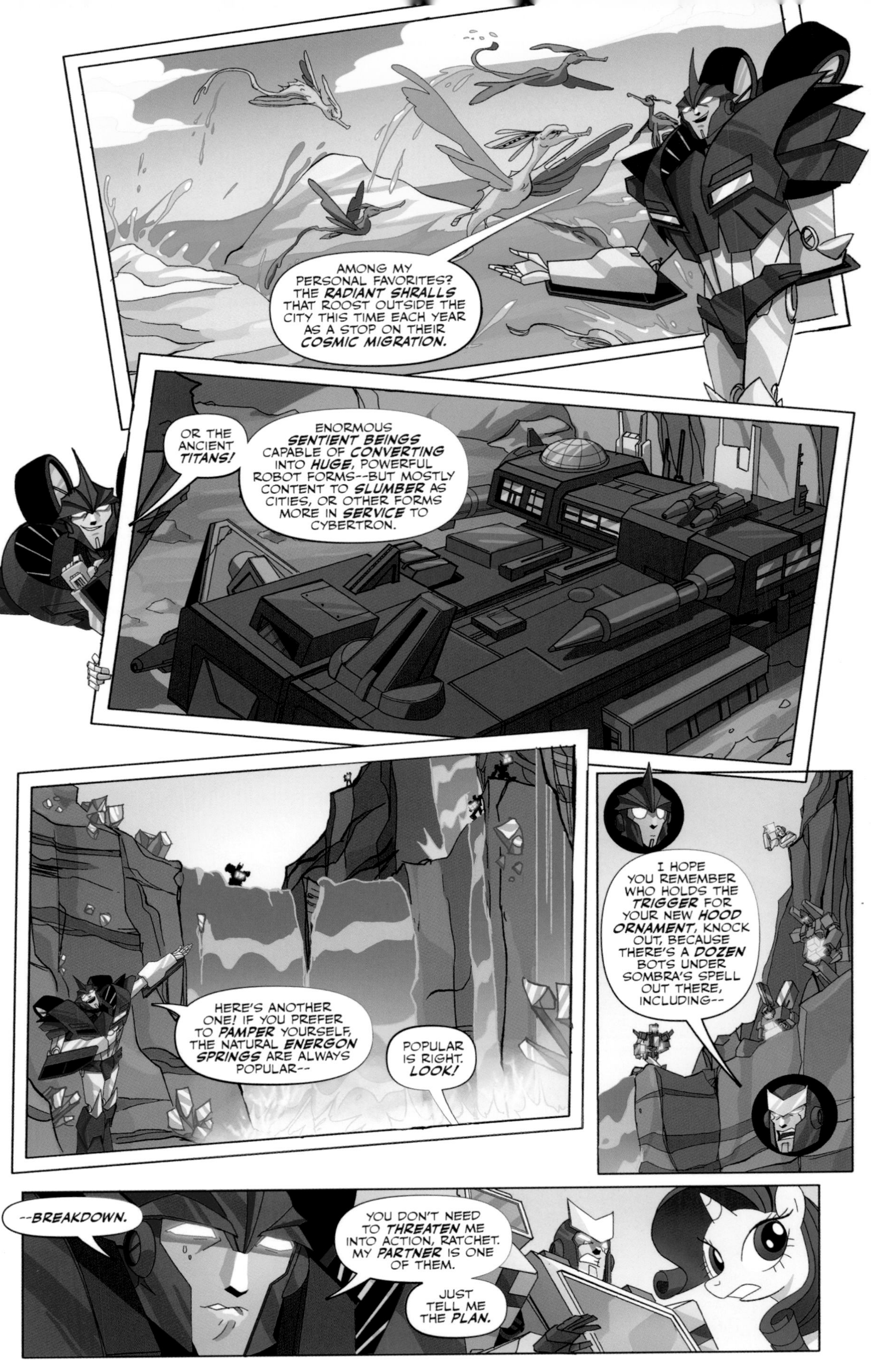
AMONG MY PERSONAL FAVORITES? THE RADIANT SHRALLS THAT ROOST OUTSIDE THE CITY THIS TIME EACH YEAR AS A STOP ON THEIR COSMIC MIGRATION.
OR THE ANCIENT TITANS!
ENORMOUS SENTIENT BEINGS CAPABLE OF CONVERTING INTO HUGE, POWERFUL ROBOT FORMS--BUT MOSTLY CONTENT TO SLUMBER AS CITIES, OR OTHER FORMS MORE IN SERVICE TO CYBERTRON.
HERE'S ANOTHER ONE! IF YOU PREFER TO PAMPER YOURSELF, THE NATURAL ENERGON SPRINGS ARE ALWAYS POPULAR--
POPULAR IS RIGHT. LOOK!
I HOPE YOU REMEMBER WHO HOLDS THE TRIGGER FOR YOUR NEW HOOD ORNAMENT, KNOCK OUT, BECAUSE THERE'S A DOZEN BOTS UNDER SOMBRA'S SPELL OUT THERE, INCLUDING--
--BREAKDOWN.
YOU DON'T NEED TO THREATEN ME INTO ACTION, RATCHET. MY PARTNER IS ONE OF THEM.
JUST TELL ME THE PLAN.

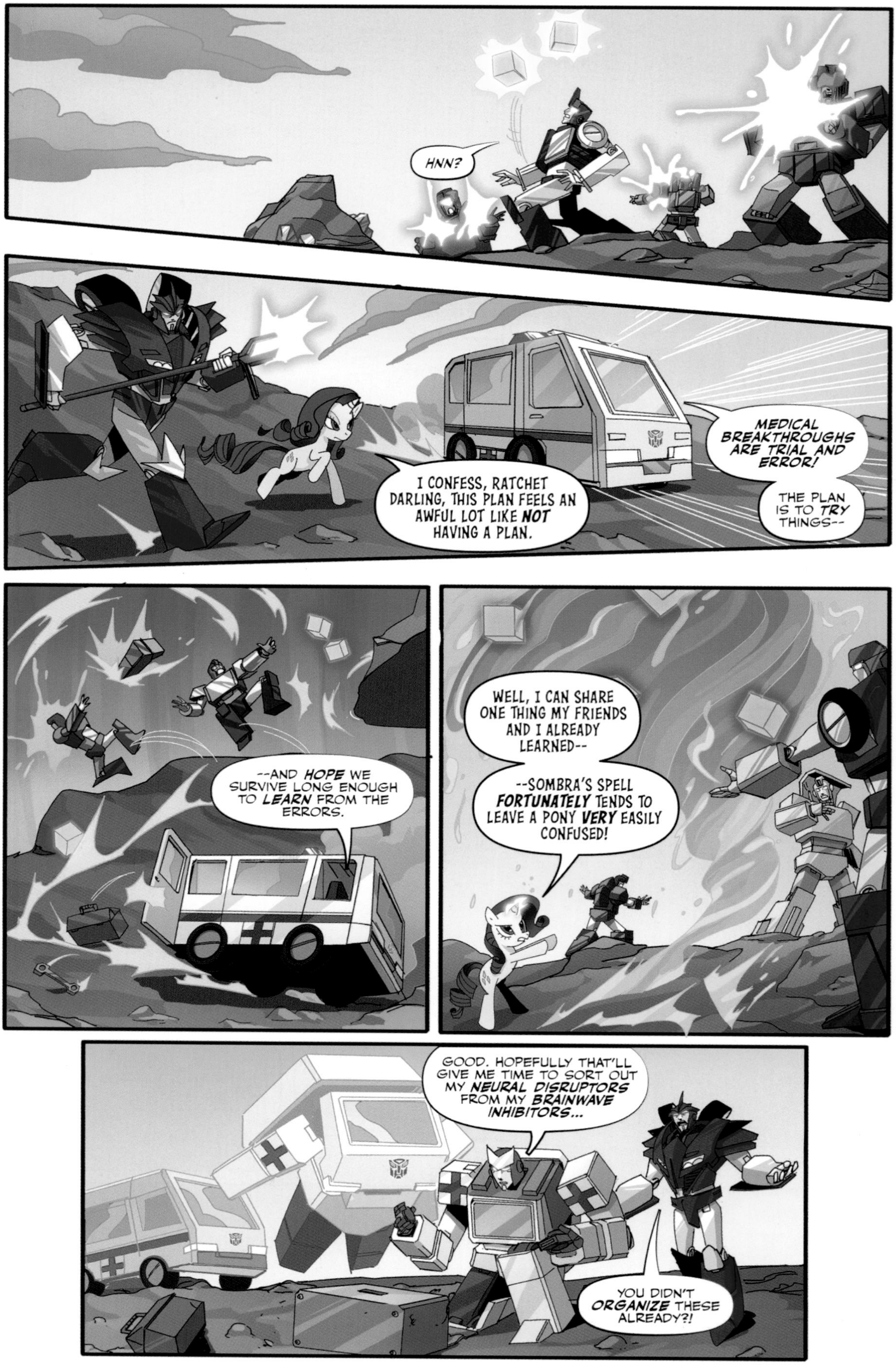
HNN?
I CONFESS, RATCHET DARLING, THIS PLAN FEELS AN AWFUL LOT LIKE NOT HAVING A PLAN.
MEDICAL BREAKTHROUGHS ARE TRIAL AND ERROR!
THE PLAN IS TO TRY THINGS--
--AND HOPE WE SURVIVE LONG ENOUGH TO LEARN FROM THE ERRORS.
WELL, I CAN SHARE ONE THING MY FRIENDS AND I ALREADY LEARNED--
--SOMBRA'S SPELL FORTUNATELY TENDS TO LEAVE A PONY VERY EASILY CONFUSED!
GOOD. HOPEFULLY THAT'LL GIVE ME TIME TO SORT OUT MY NEURAL DISRUPTORS FROM MY BRAINWAVE INHIBITORS...
YOU DIDN'T ORGANIZE THESE ALREADY?!

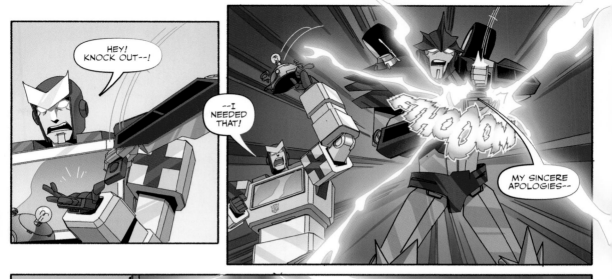

HEY! KNOCK OUT--!

--I NEEDED THAT!

MY SINCERE APOLOGIES--

G'HAA!

--BUT THEY NEED IT *MORE*.

WE MUST *RETURN*... TO LORD SOMBRA...

BREAKDOWN! DID IT WORK?

IT *BETTER* HAVE! BECAUSE YOU'RE LETTING HALF OUR OTHER TEST SUBJECTS SLIP AWAY!

RETURN... TO LORD SOMBRA...

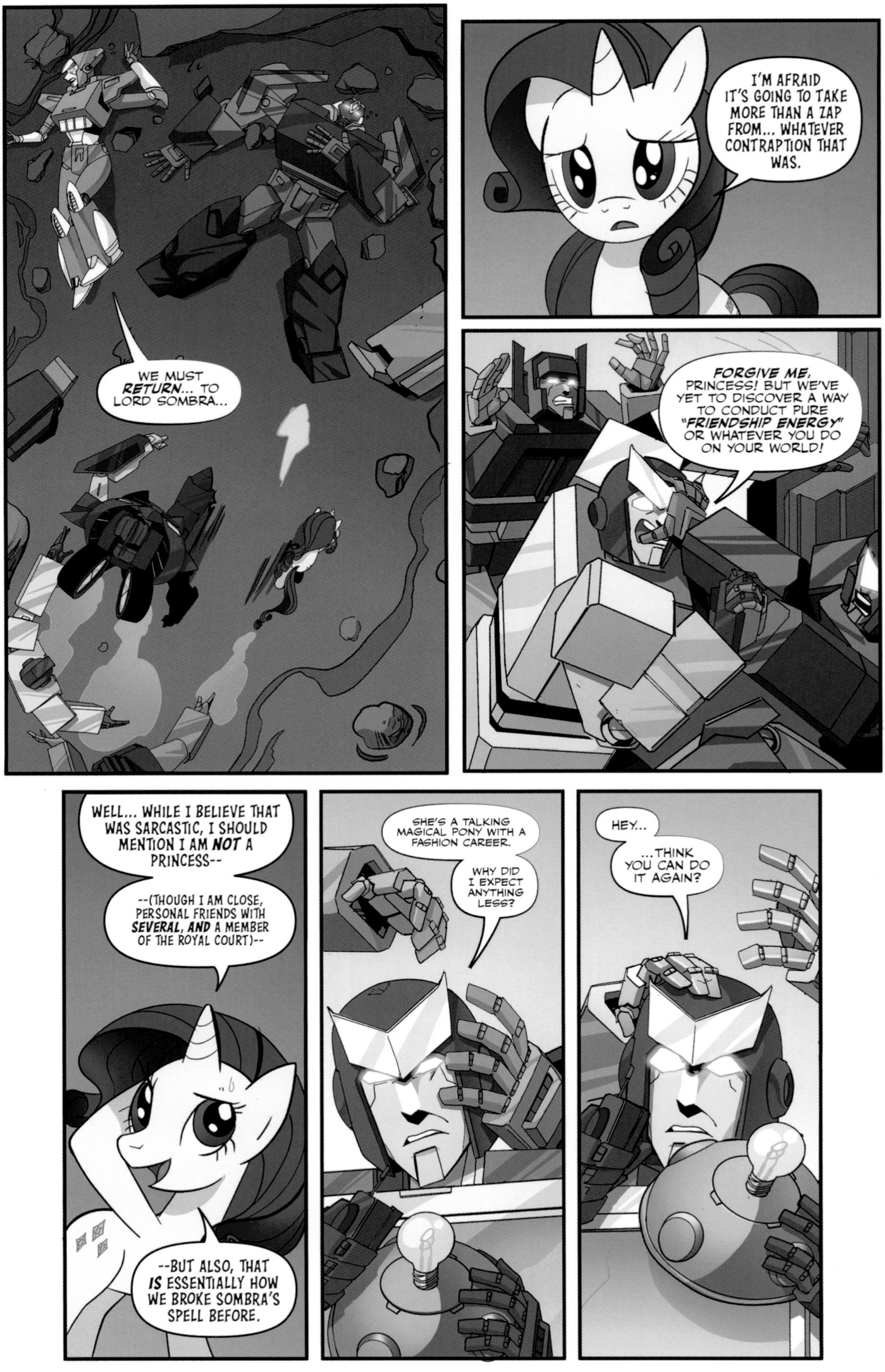
WE MUST RETURN... TO LORD SOMBRA...
I'M AFRAID IT'S GOING TO TAKE MORE THAN A ZAP FROM... WHATEVER CONTRAPTION THAT WAS.
FORGIVE ME, PRINCESS! BUT WE'VE YET TO DISCOVER A WAY TO CONDUCT PURE "FRIENDSHIP ENERGY" OR WHATEVER YOU DO ON YOUR WORLD!
WELL... WHILE I BELIEVE THAT WAS SARCASTIC, I SHOULD MENTION I AM NOT A PRINCESS--
--(THOUGH I AM CLOSE, PERSONAL FRIENDS WITH SEVERAL, AND A MEMBER OF THE ROYAL COURT)--
--BUT ALSO, THAT IS ESSENTIALLY HOW WE BROKE SOMBRA'S SPELL BEFORE.
SHE'S A TALKING MAGICAL PONY WITH A FASHION CAREER.
WHY DID I EXPECT ANYTHING LESS?
HEY...
...THINK YOU CAN DO IT AGAIN?

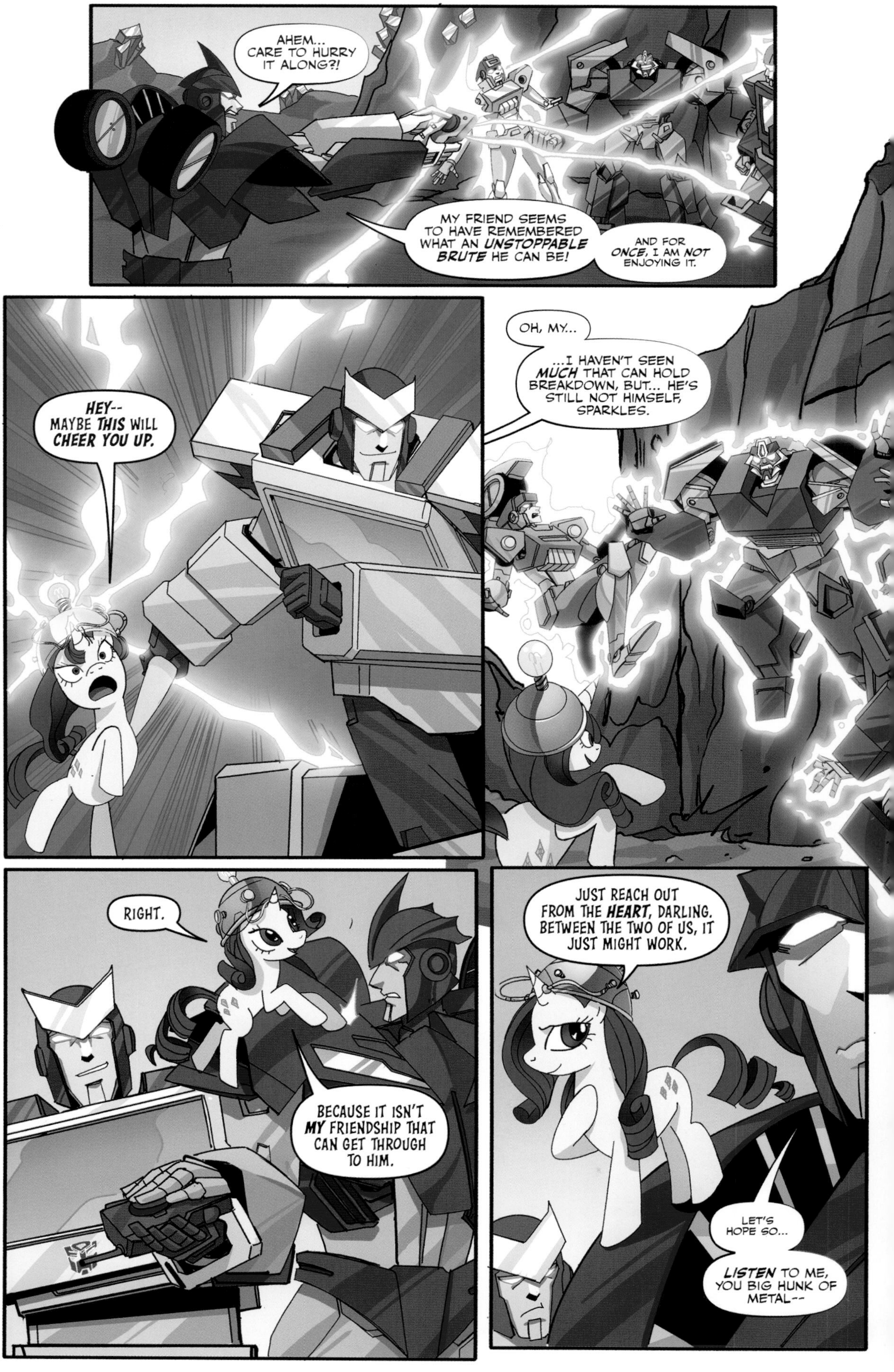
AHEM... CARE TO HURRY IT ALONG?!
MY FRIEND SEEMS TO HAVE REMEMBERED WHAT AN *UNSTOPPABLE BRUTE* HE CAN BE!
AND FOR *ONCE*, I AM *NOT* ENJOYING IT.
HEY-- MAYBE **THIS** WILL **CHEER YOU UP.**
OH, MY...
...I HAVEN'T SEEN *MUCH* THAT CAN HOLD BREAKDOWN, BUT... HE'S STILL NOT HIMSELF, SPARKLES.
RIGHT.
BECAUSE IT ISN'T *MY* FRIENDSHIP THAT CAN GET THROUGH TO HIM.
JUST REACH OUT FROM THE *HEART*, DARLING. BETWEEN THE TWO OF US, IT JUST MIGHT WORK.
LET'S HOPE SO...
LISTEN TO ME, YOU BIG HUNK OF METAL--

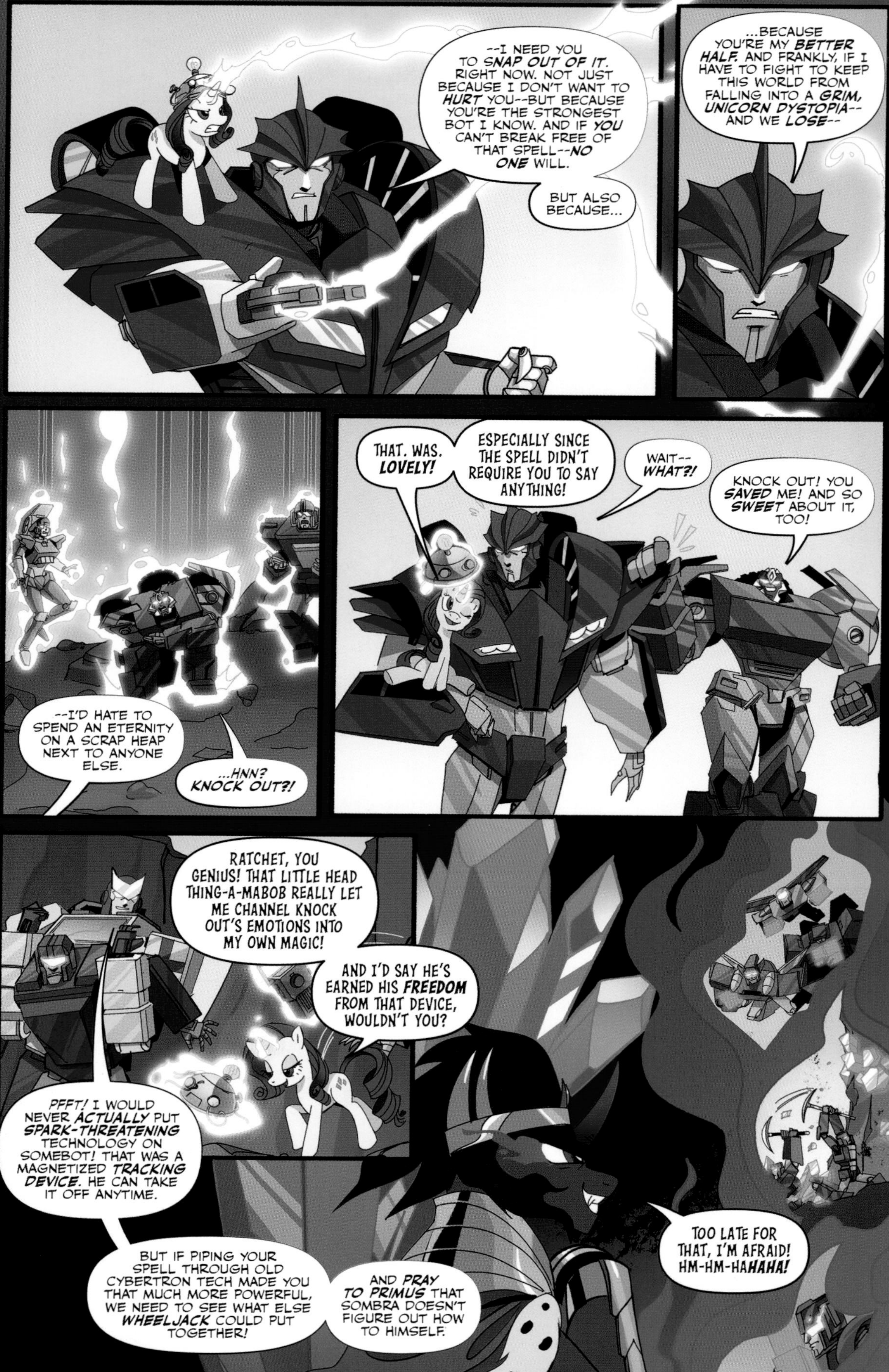
--I NEED YOU TO SNAP OUT OF IT. RIGHT NOW. NOT JUST BECAUSE I DON'T WANT TO HURT YOU--BUT BECAUSE YOU'RE THE STRONGEST BOT I KNOW. AND IF YOU CAN'T BREAK FREE OF THAT SPELL--NO ONE WILL.
BUT ALSO BECAUSE...
...BECAUSE YOU'RE MY BETTER HALF. AND FRANKLY, IF I HAVE TO FIGHT TO KEEP THIS WORLD FROM FALLING INTO A GRIM, UNICORN DYSTOPIA--AND WE LOSE--
--I'D HATE TO SPEND AN ETERNITY ON A SCRAP HEAP NEXT TO ANYONE ELSE.
...HNN? KNOCK OUT?!
THAT. WAS. LOVELY!
ESPECIALLY SINCE THE SPELL DIDN'T REQUIRE YOU TO SAY ANYTHING!
WAIT--WHAT?!
KNOCK OUT! YOU SAVED ME! AND SO SWEET ABOUT IT, TOO!
RATCHET, YOU GENIUS! THAT LITTLE HEAD THING-A-MABOB REALLY LET ME CHANNEL KNOCK OUT'S EMOTIONS INTO MY OWN MAGIC!
AND I'D SAY HE'S EARNED HIS FREEDOM FROM THAT DEVICE, WOULDN'T YOU?
PFFT! I WOULD NEVER ACTUALLY PUT SPARK-THREATENING TECHNOLOGY ON SOMEBOT! THAT WAS A MAGNETIZED TRACKING DEVICE. HE CAN TAKE IT OFF ANYTIME.
BUT IF PIPING YOUR SPELL THROUGH OLD CYBERTRON TECH MADE YOU THAT MUCH MORE POWERFUL, WE NEED TO SEE WHAT ELSE WHEELJACK COULD PUT TOGETHER!
AND PRAY TO PRIMUS THAT SOMBRA DOESN'T FIGURE OUT HOW TO HIMSELF.
TOO LATE FOR THAT, I'M AFRAID! HM-HM-HAHAHA!

ART BY TONY FLEECS

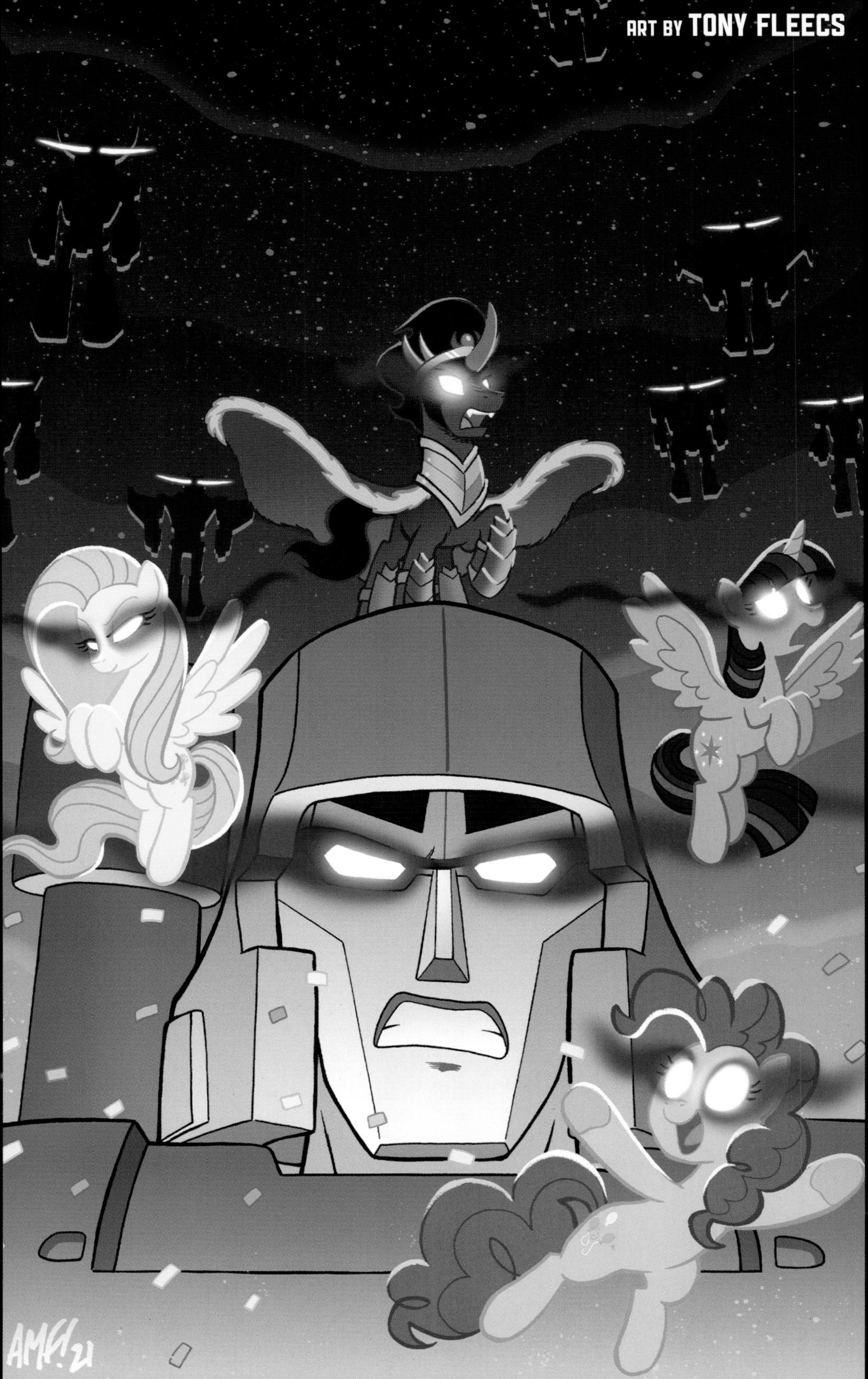
AMF! 21

"THE MIGHTIEST DINOBOT"

WRITTEN BY IAN FLYNN
ART BY CASEY W. COLLER
COLORS BY JOANA LAFUENTE
LETTERS BY JAKE M. WOOD

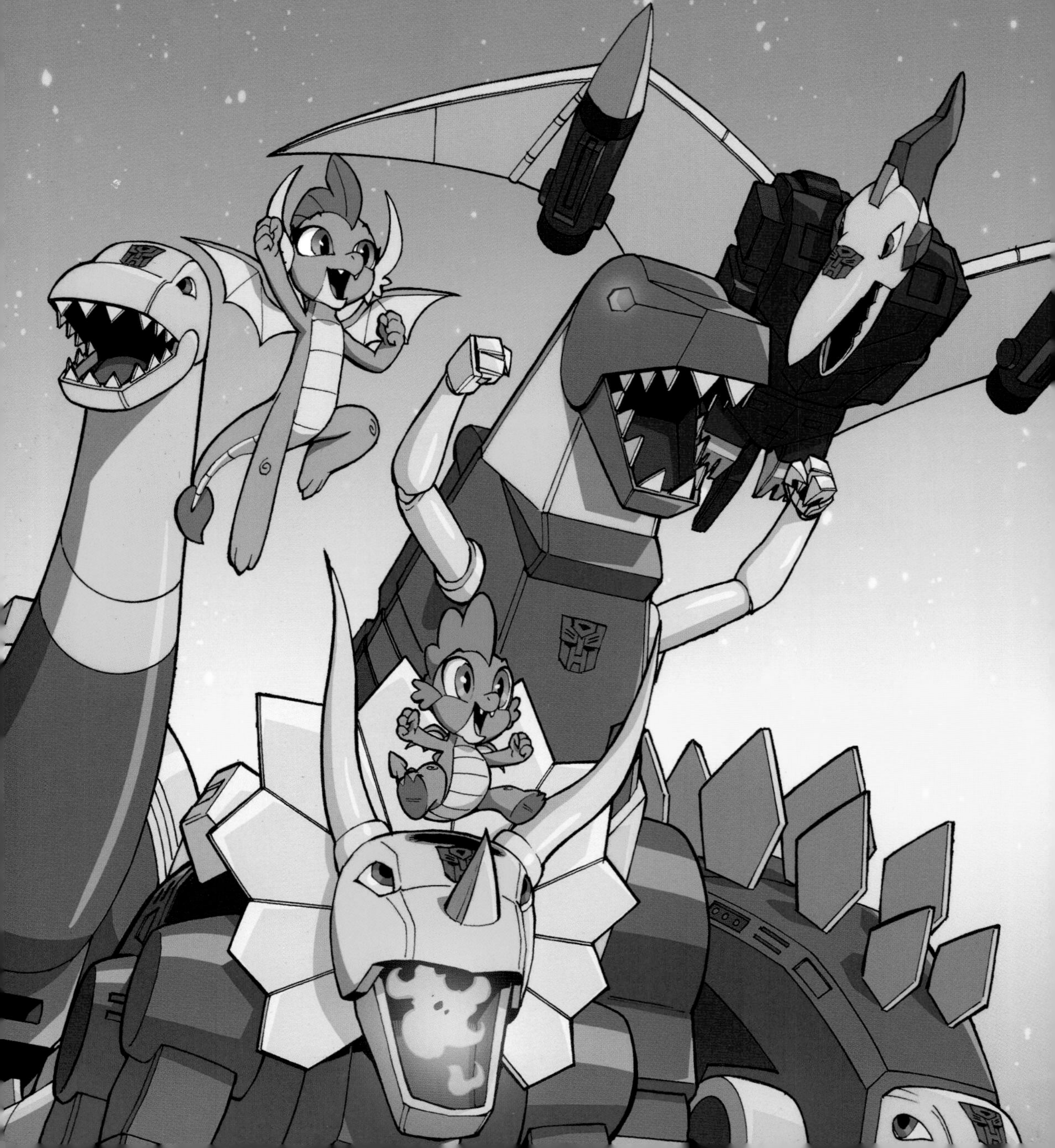

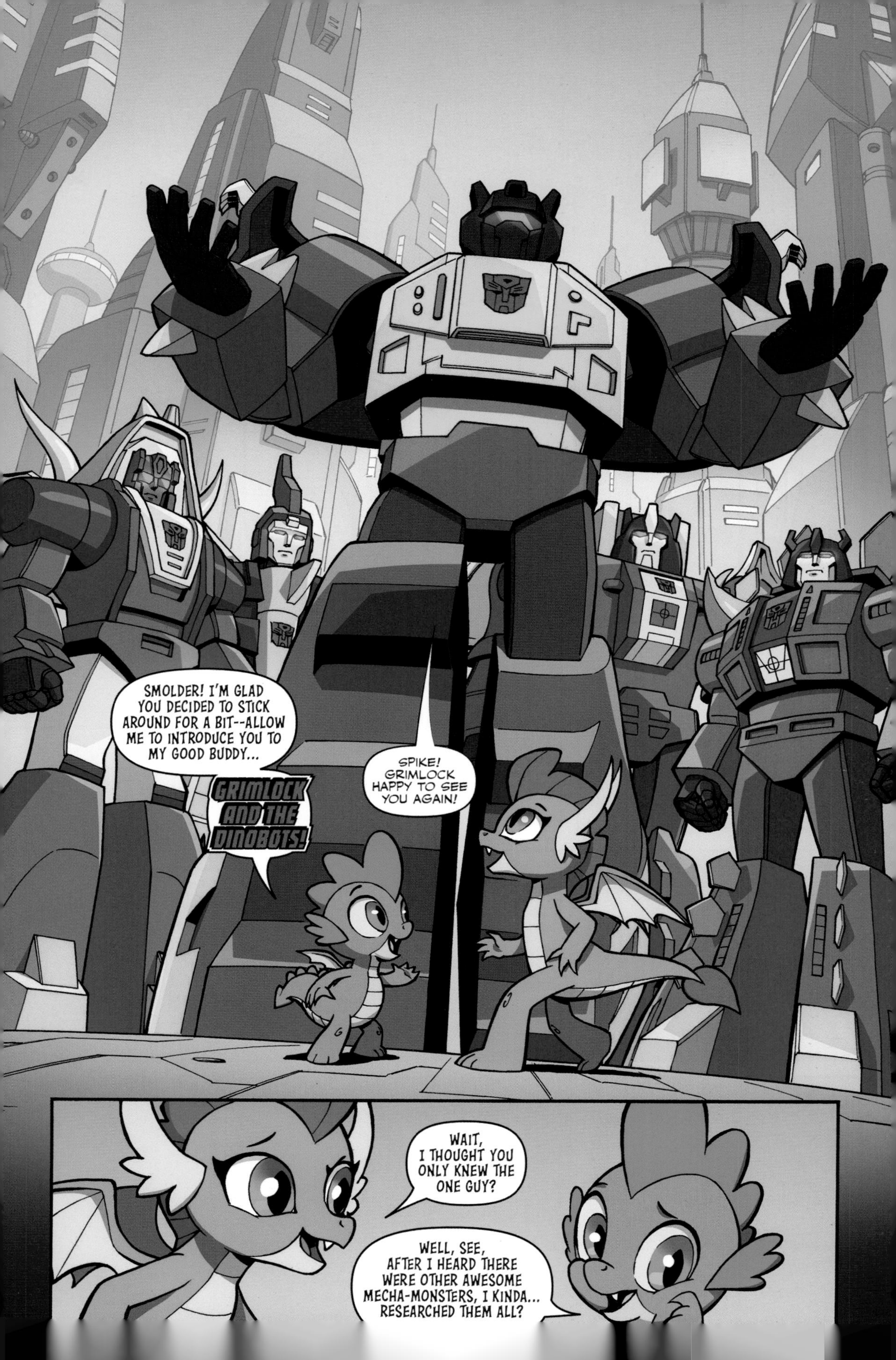
SMOLDER! I'M GLAD YOU DECIDED TO STICK AROUND FOR A BIT--ALLOW ME TO INTRODUCE YOU TO MY GOOD BUDDY...
GRIMLOCK AND THE DINOBOTS!
SPIKE! GRIMLOCK HAPPY TO SEE YOU AGAIN!
WAIT, I THOUGHT YOU ONLY KNEW THE ONE GUY?
WELL, SEE, AFTER I HEARD THERE WERE OTHER AWESOME MECHA-MONSTERS, I KINDA... RESEARCHED THEM ALL?

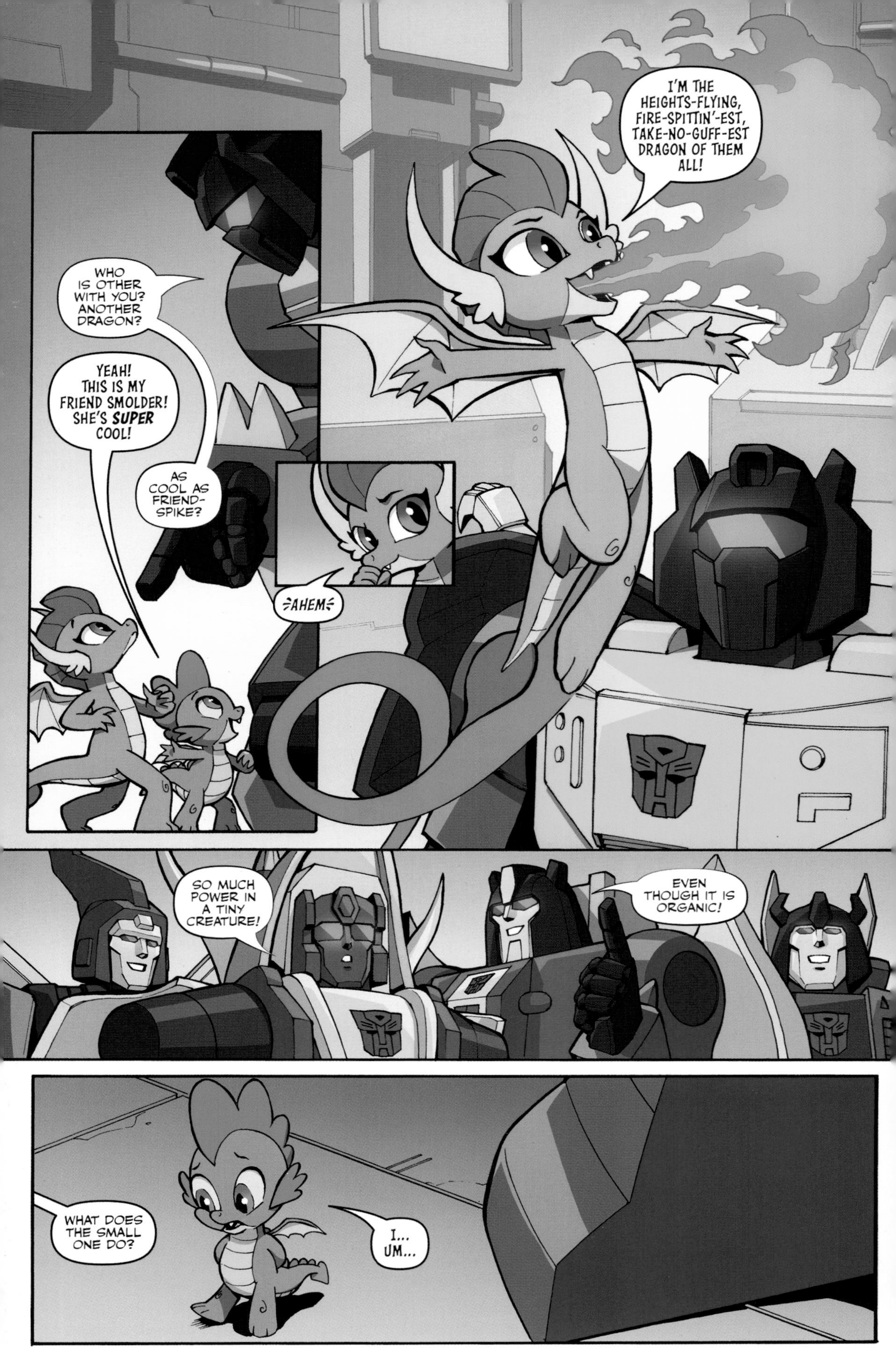
I'M THE HEIGHTS-FLYING, FIRE-SPITTIN'-EST, TAKE-NO-GUFF-EST DRAGON OF THEM ALL!
WHO IS OTHER WITH YOU? ANOTHER DRAGON?
YEAH! THIS IS MY FRIEND SMOLDER! SHE'S SUPER COOL!
AS COOL AS FRIEND-SPIKE?
AHEM
SO MUCH POWER IN A TINY CREATURE!
EVEN THOUGH IT IS ORGANIC!
WHAT DOES THE SMALL ONE DO?
I... UM...

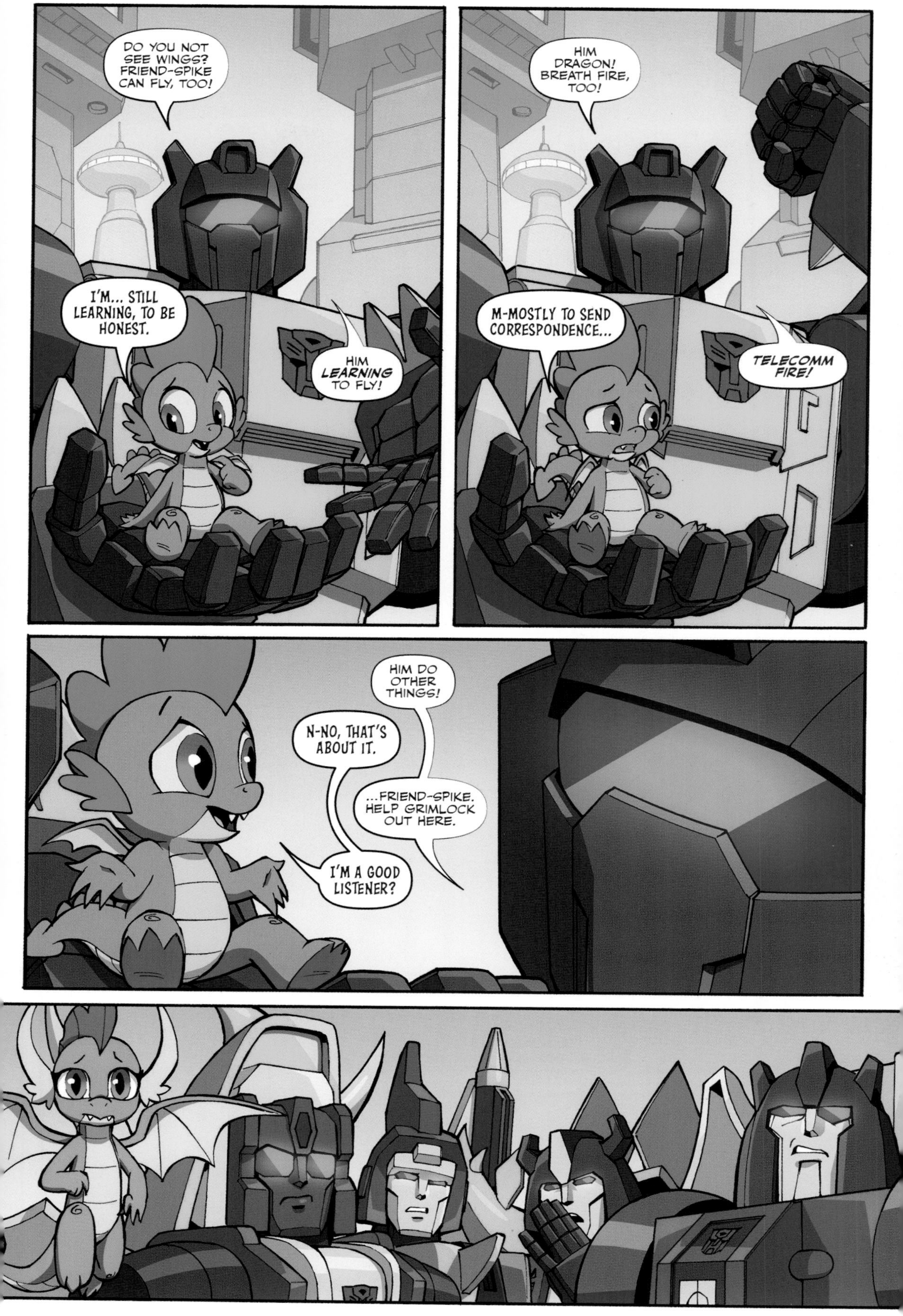
DO YOU NOT SEE WINGS? FRIEND-SPIKE CAN FLY, TOO!
I'M... STILL LEARNING, TO BE HONEST.
HIM LEARNING TO FLY!
HIM DRAGON! BREATH FIRE, TOO!
M-MOSTLY TO SEND CORRESPONDENCE...
TELECOMM FIRE!
HIM DO OTHER THINGS!
N-NO, THAT'S ABOUT IT.
...FRIEND-SPIKE. HELP GRIMLOCK OUT HERE.
I'M A GOOD LISTENER?

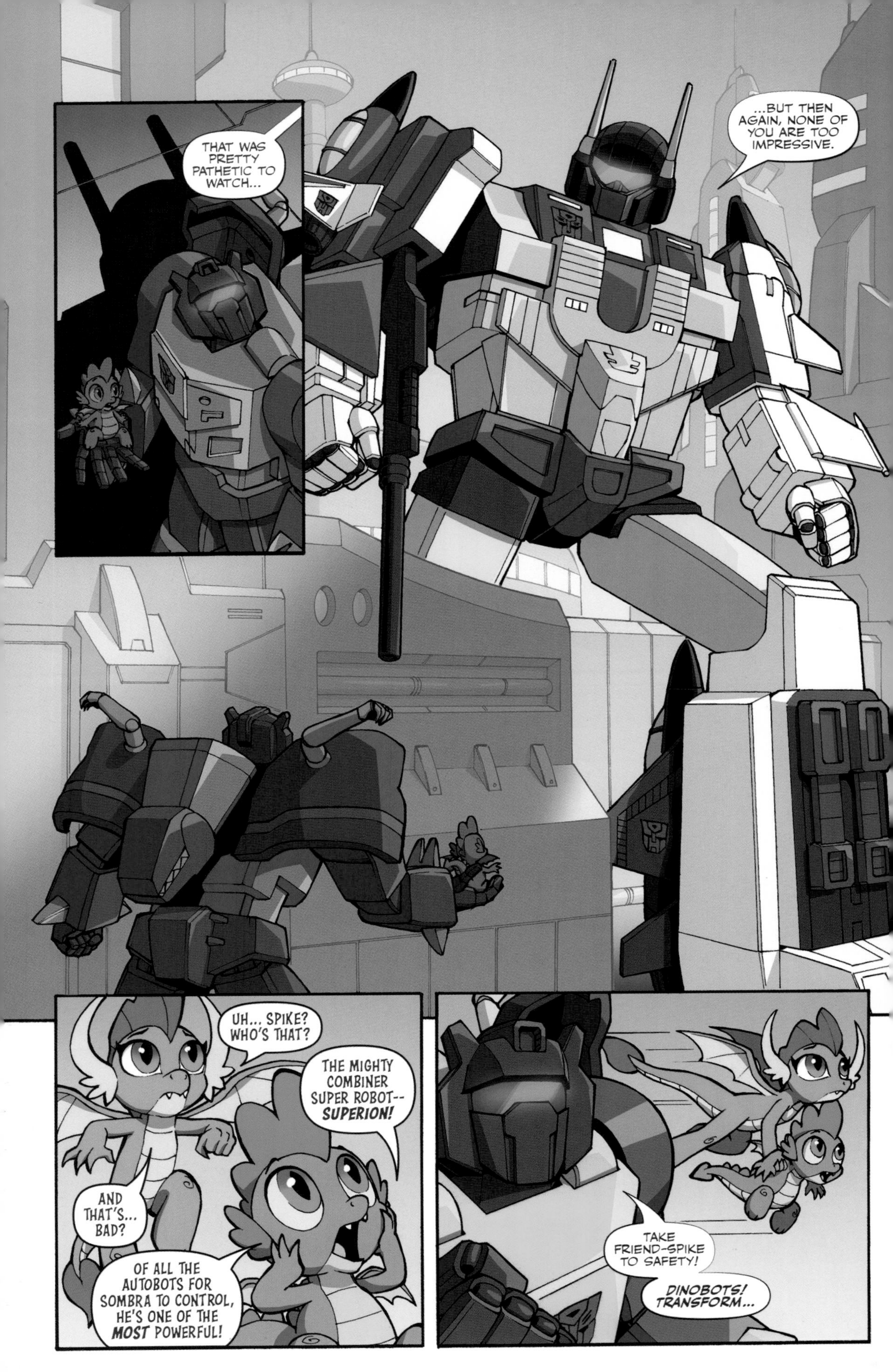
THAT WAS PRETTY PATHETIC TO WATCH...
...BUT THEN AGAIN, NONE OF YOU ARE TOO IMPRESSIVE.
UH... SPIKE? WHO'S THAT?
THE MIGHTY COMBINER SUPER ROBOT-- SUPERION!
AND THAT'S... BAD?
OF ALL THE AUTOBOTS FOR SOMBRA TO CONTROL, HE'S ONE OF THE MOST POWERFUL!
TAKE FRIEND-SPIKE TO SAFETY!
DINOBOTS! TRANSFORM...

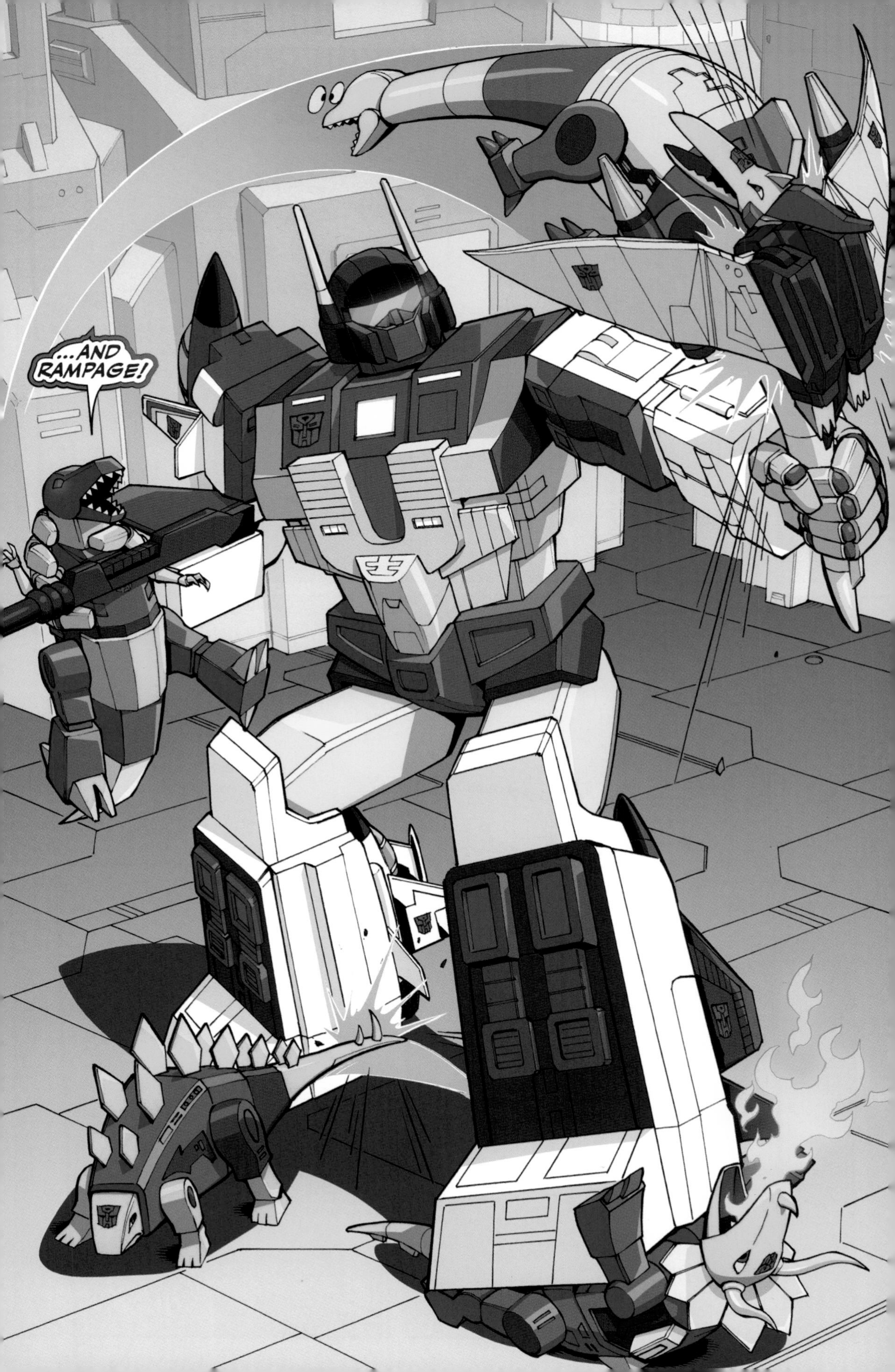
...AND RAMPAGE!

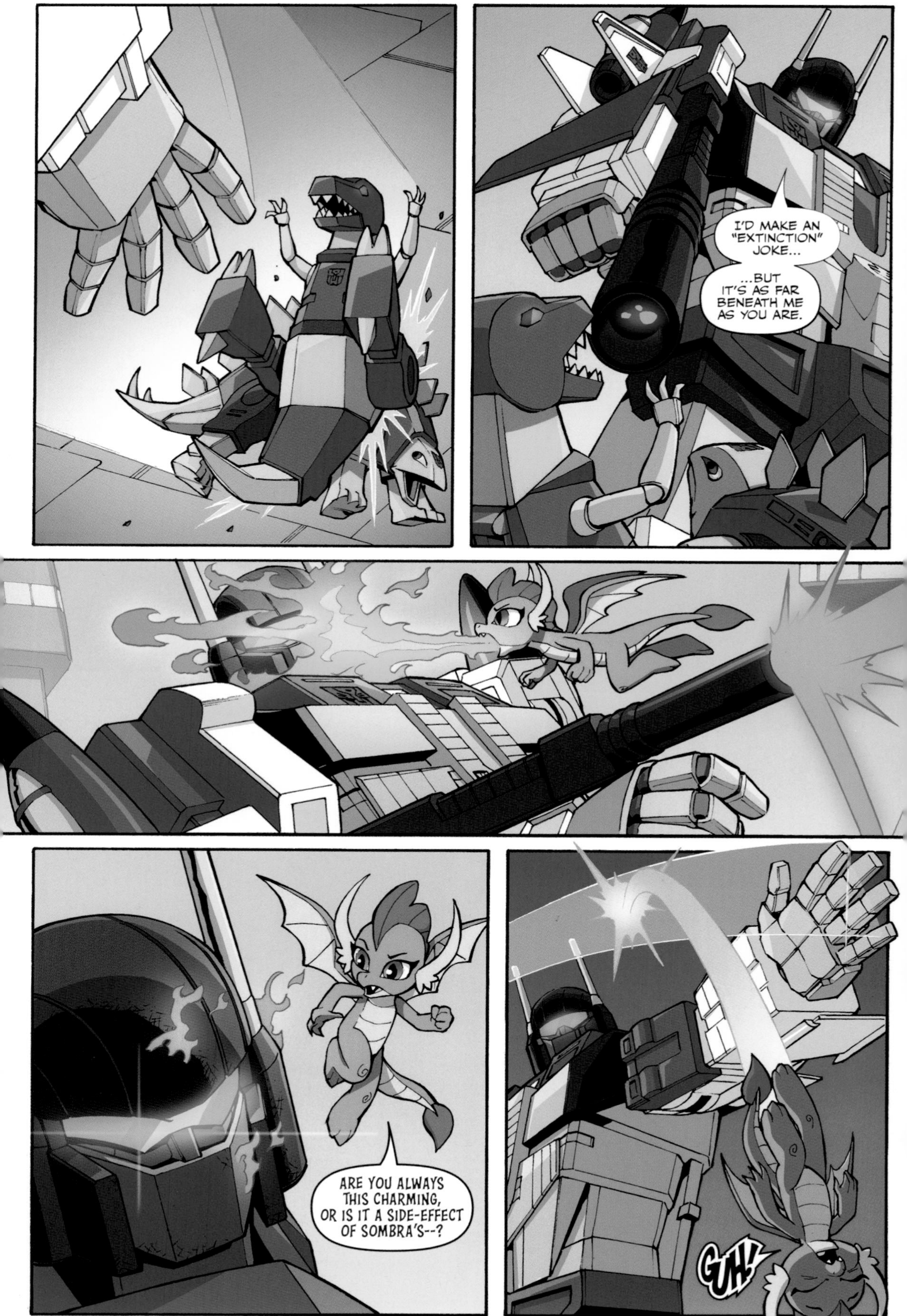
I'D MAKE AN "EXTINCTION" JOKE...
...BUT IT'S AS FAR BENEATH ME AS YOU ARE.
ARE YOU ALWAYS THIS CHARMING, OR IS IT A SIDE-EFFECT OF SOMBRA'S--?
GUH!

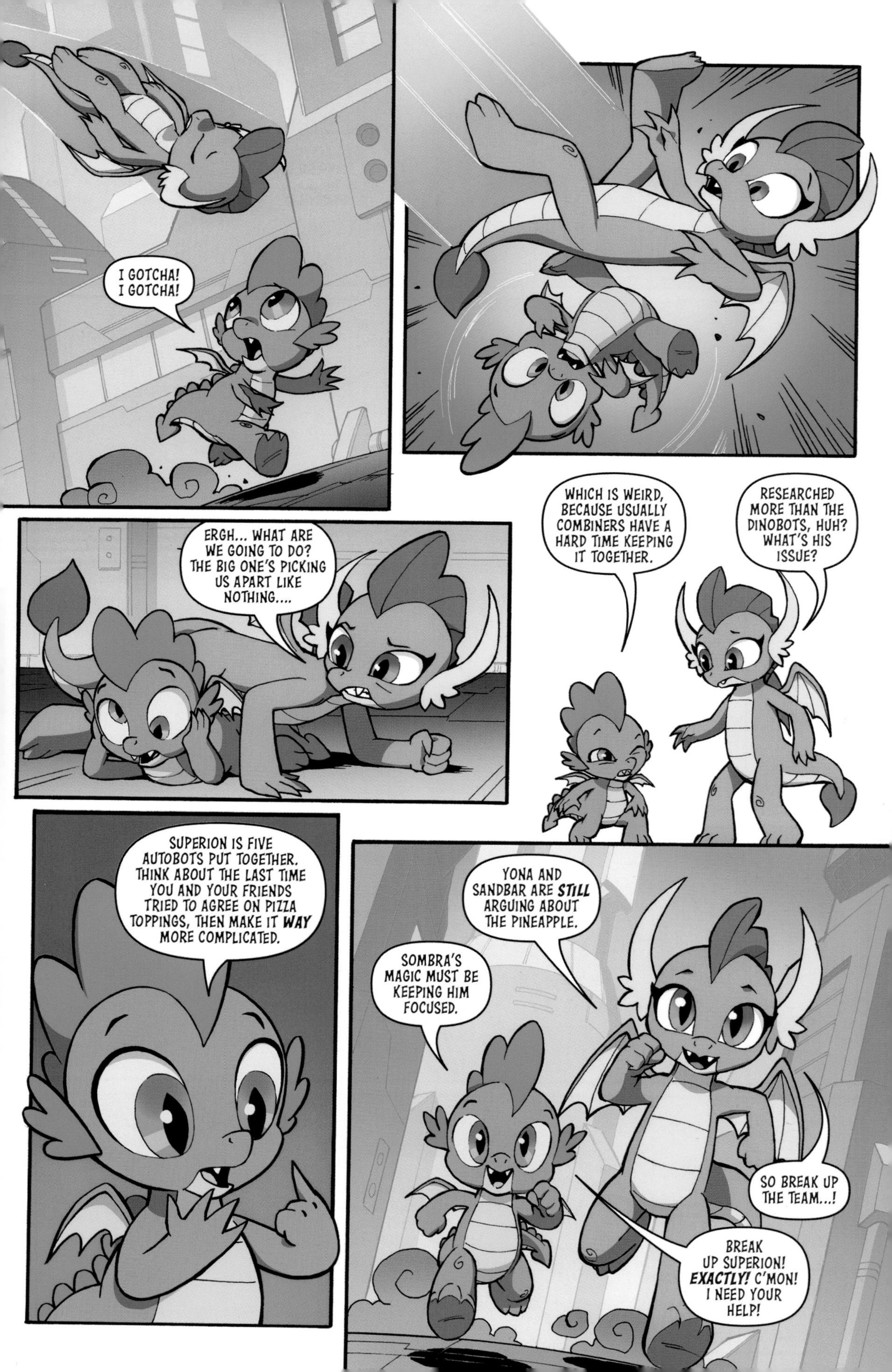

I GOTCHA! I GOTCHA!
ERGH... WHAT ARE WE GOING TO DO? THE BIG ONE'S PICKING US APART LIKE NOTHING....
WHICH IS WEIRD, BECAUSE USUALLY COMBINERS HAVE A HARD TIME KEEPING IT TOGETHER.
RESEARCHED MORE THAN THE DINOBOTS, HUH? WHAT'S HIS ISSUE?
SUPERION IS FIVE AUTOBOTS PUT TOGETHER. THINK ABOUT THE LAST TIME YOU AND YOUR FRIENDS TRIED TO AGREE ON PIZZA TOPPINGS, THEN MAKE IT ***WAY*** MORE COMPLICATED.
YONA AND SANDBAR ARE ***STILL*** ARGUING ABOUT THE PINEAPPLE.
SOMBRA'S MAGIC MUST BE KEEPING HIM FOCUSED.
SO BREAK UP THE TEAM...!
BREAK UP SUPERION! ***EXACTLY!*** C'MON! I NEED YOUR HELP!

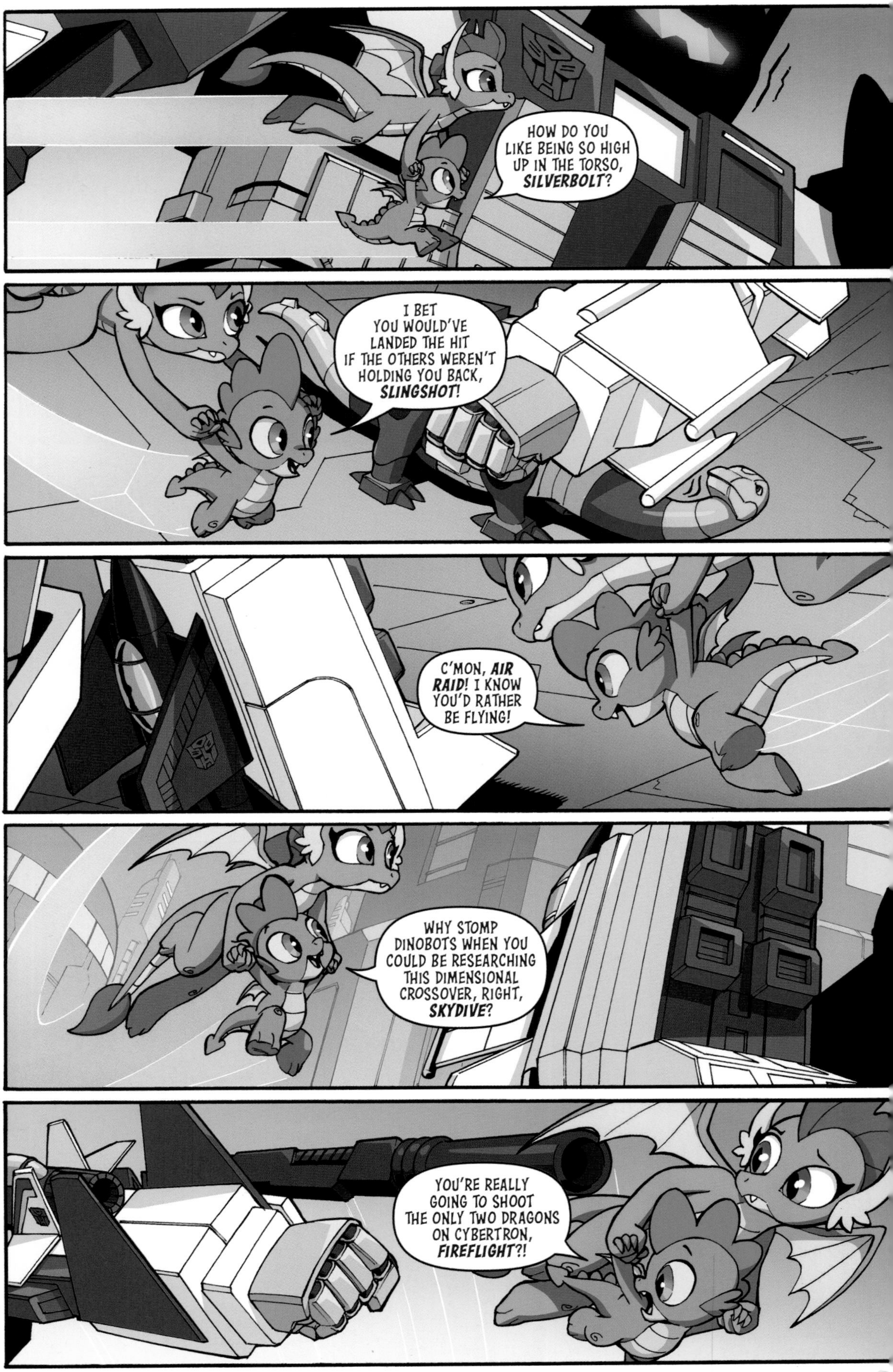

HOW DO YOU LIKE BEING SO HIGH UP IN THE TORSO, **SILVERBOLT**?
I BET YOU WOULD'VE LANDED THE HIT IF THE OTHERS WEREN'T HOLDING YOU BACK, **SLINGSHOT**!
C'MON, **AIR RAID**! I KNOW YOU'D RATHER BE FLYING!
WHY STOMP DINOBOTS WHEN YOU COULD BE RESEARCHING THIS DIMENSIONAL CROSSOVER, RIGHT, **SKYDIVE**?
YOU'RE REALLY GOING TO SHOOT THE ONLY TWO DRAGONS ON CYBERTRON, **FIREFLIGHT**?!

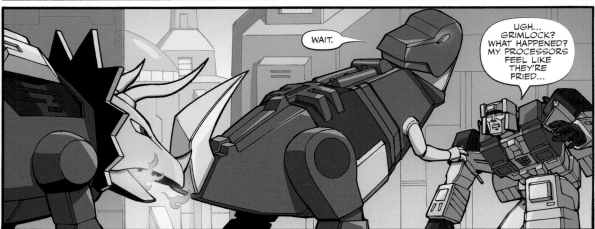

WAIT.

UGH... GRIMLOCK? WHAT HAPPENED? MY PROCESSORS FEEL LIKE THEY'RE FRIED...

LITTLE DRAGON POWERFUL MAGIC?

HAHA--NAH! I JUST FIGURED SOMBRA'S MIND-CONTROL COULDN'T LAST IF WE SPLIT IT FIVE WAYS.

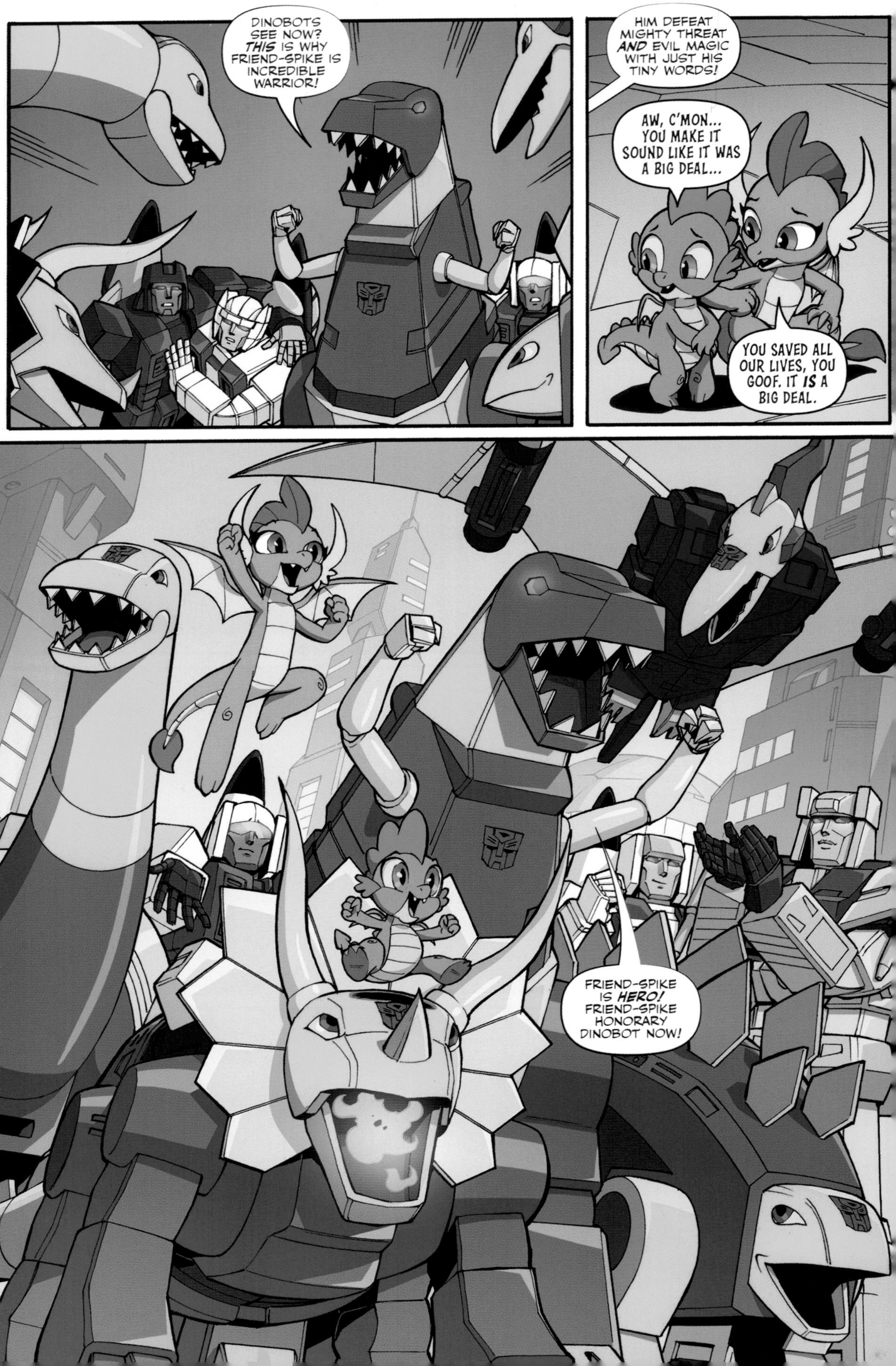
DINOBOTS SEE NOW? THIS IS WHY FRIEND-SPIKE IS INCREDIBLE WARRIOR!
HIM DEFEAT MIGHTY THREAT AND EVIL MAGIC WITH JUST HIS TINY WORDS!
AW, C'MON... YOU MAKE IT SOUND LIKE IT WAS A BIG DEAL...
YOU SAVED ALL OUR LIVES, YOU GOOF. IT IS A BIG DEAL.
FRIEND-SPIKE IS HERO! FRIEND-SPIKE HONORARY DINOBOT NOW!

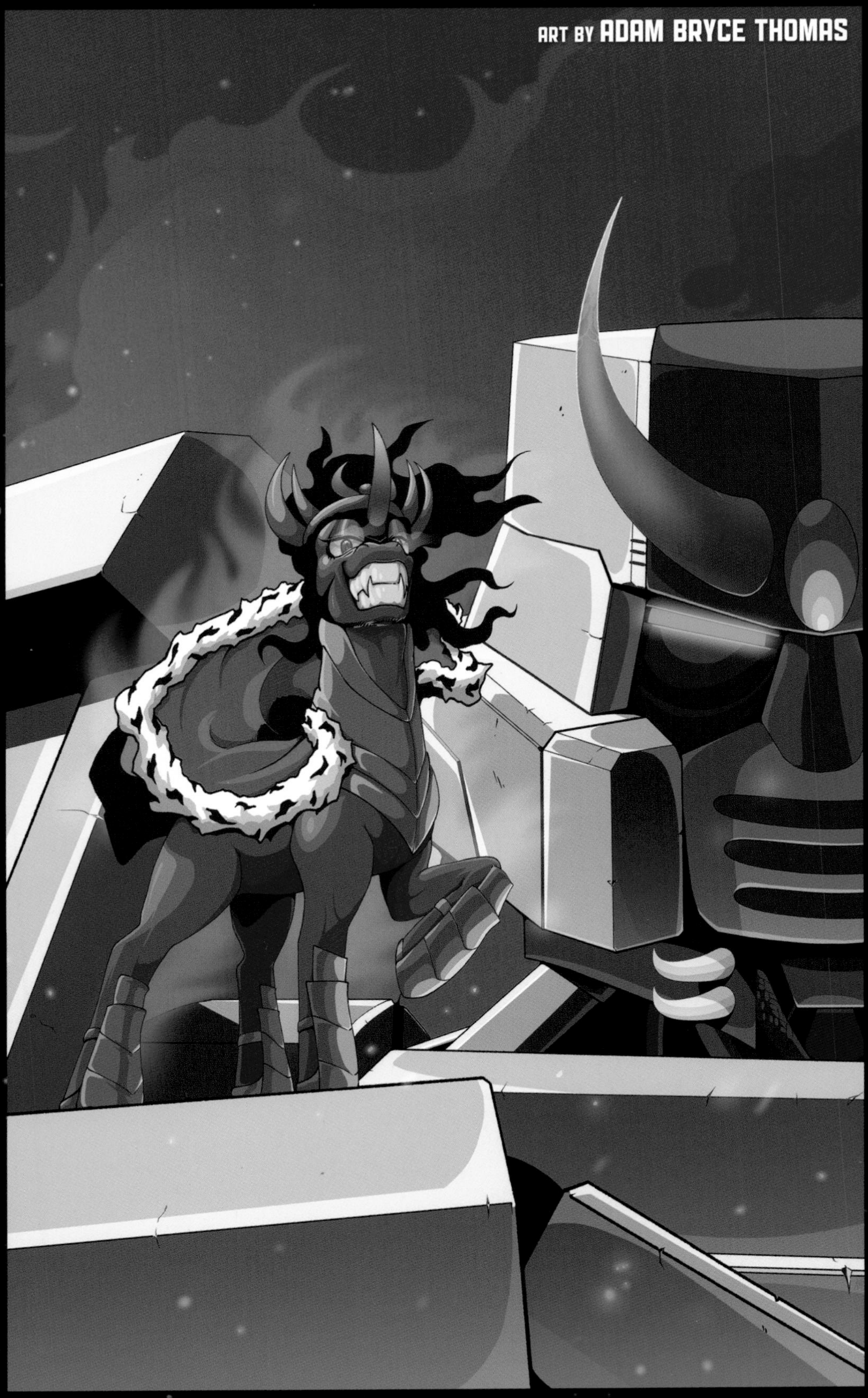
ART BY ADAM BRYCE THOMAS

"FINALE"

WRITTEN BY JAMES ASMUS
ART BY JACK LAWRENCE
COLORS BY LUIS ANTONIO DELGADO
LETTERS BY NEIL UYETAKE

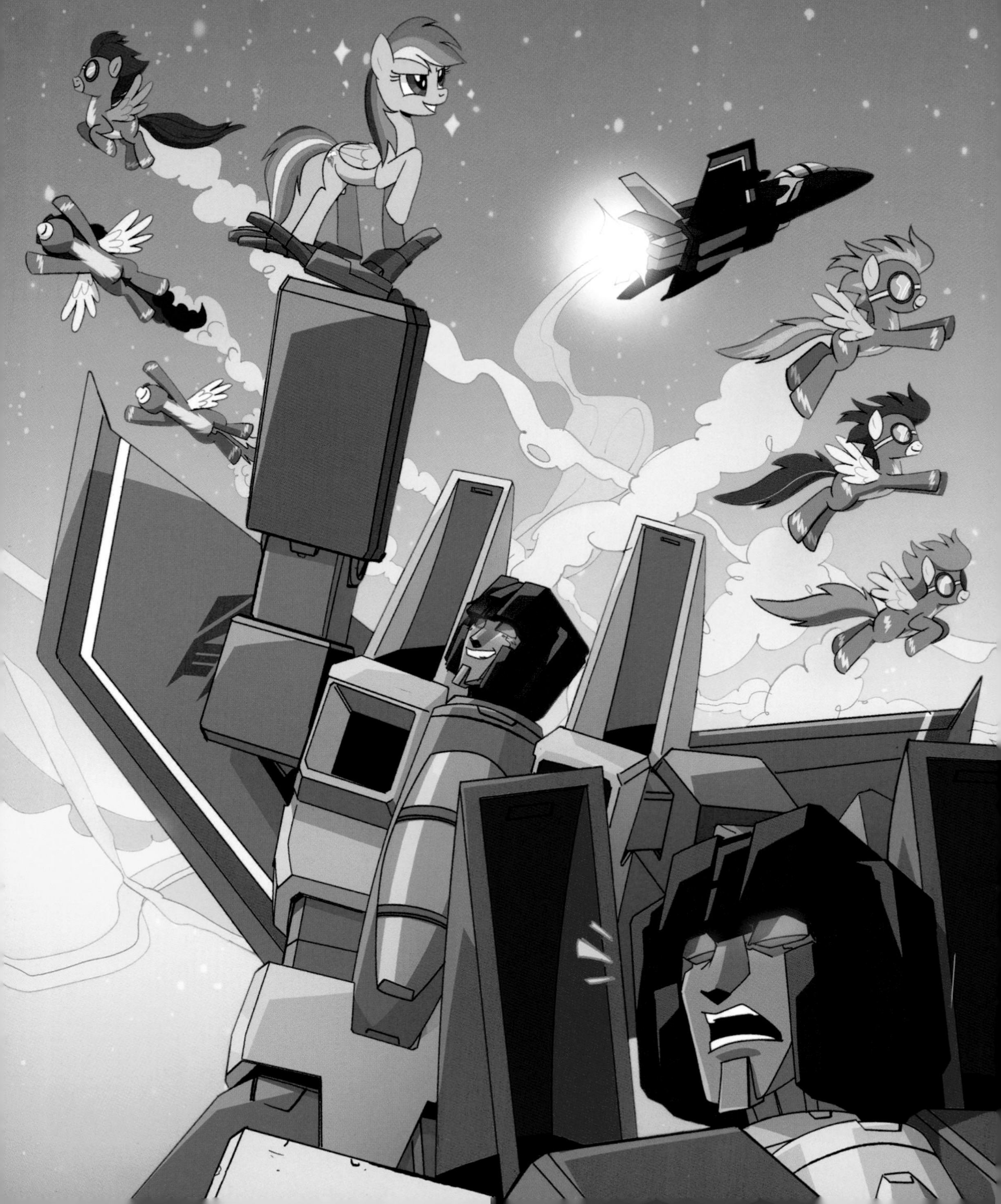

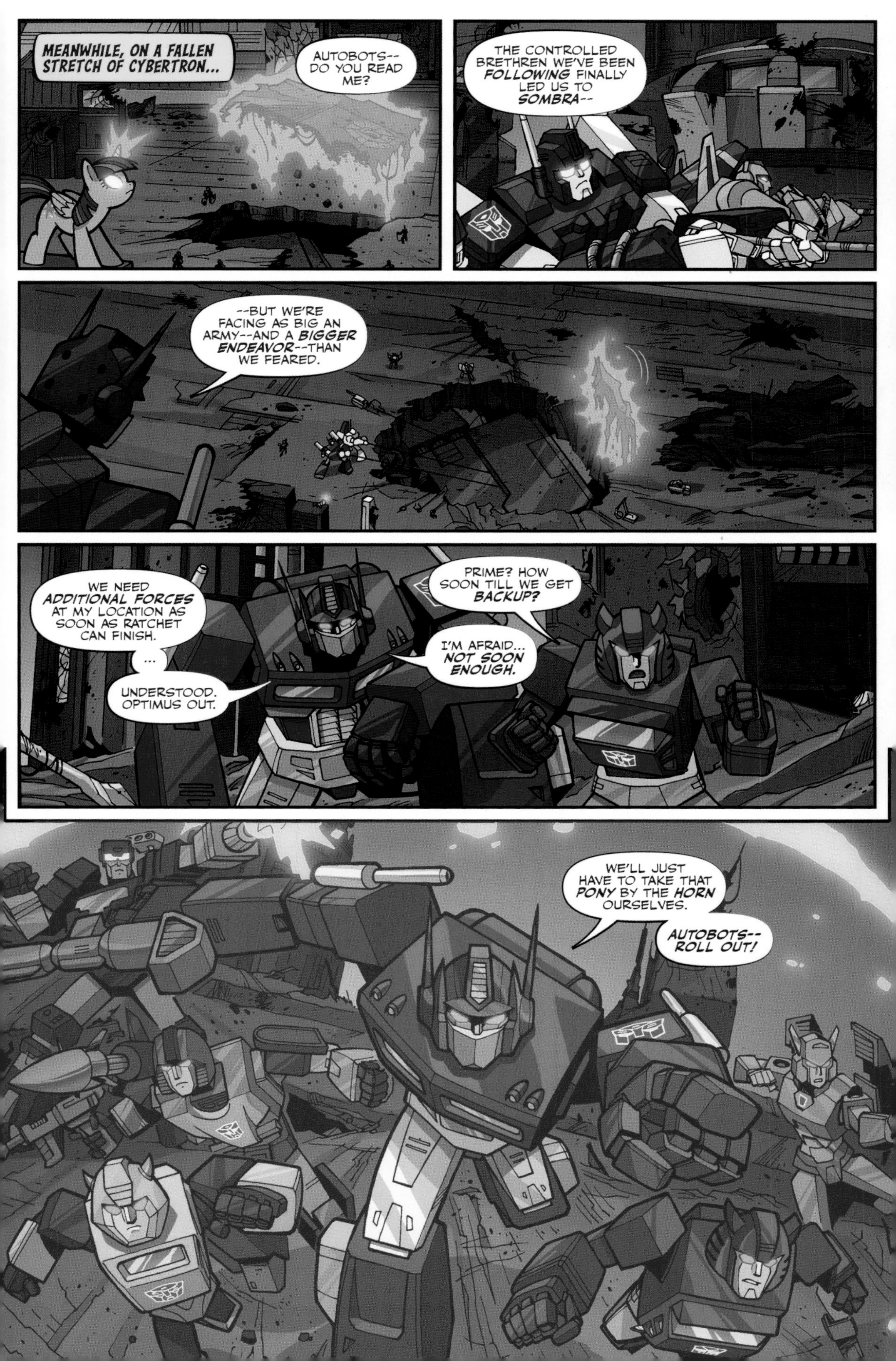
MEANWHILE, ON A FALLEN STRETCH OF CYBERTRON...
AUTOBOTS-- DO YOU READ ME?
THE CONTROLLED BRETHREN WE'VE BEEN FOLLOWING FINALLY LED US TO SOMBRA--
--BUT WE'RE FACING AS BIG AN ARMY--AND A BIGGER ENDEAVOR--THAN WE FEARED.
WE NEED ADDITIONAL FORCES AT MY LOCATION AS SOON AS RATCHET CAN FINISH.
...
UNDERSTOOD. OPTIMUS OUT.
PRIME? HOW SOON TILL WE GET BACKUP?
I'M AFRAID... NOT SOON ENOUGH.
WE'LL JUST HAVE TO TAKE THAT PONY BY THE HORN OURSELVES.
AUTOBOTS-- ROLL OUT!

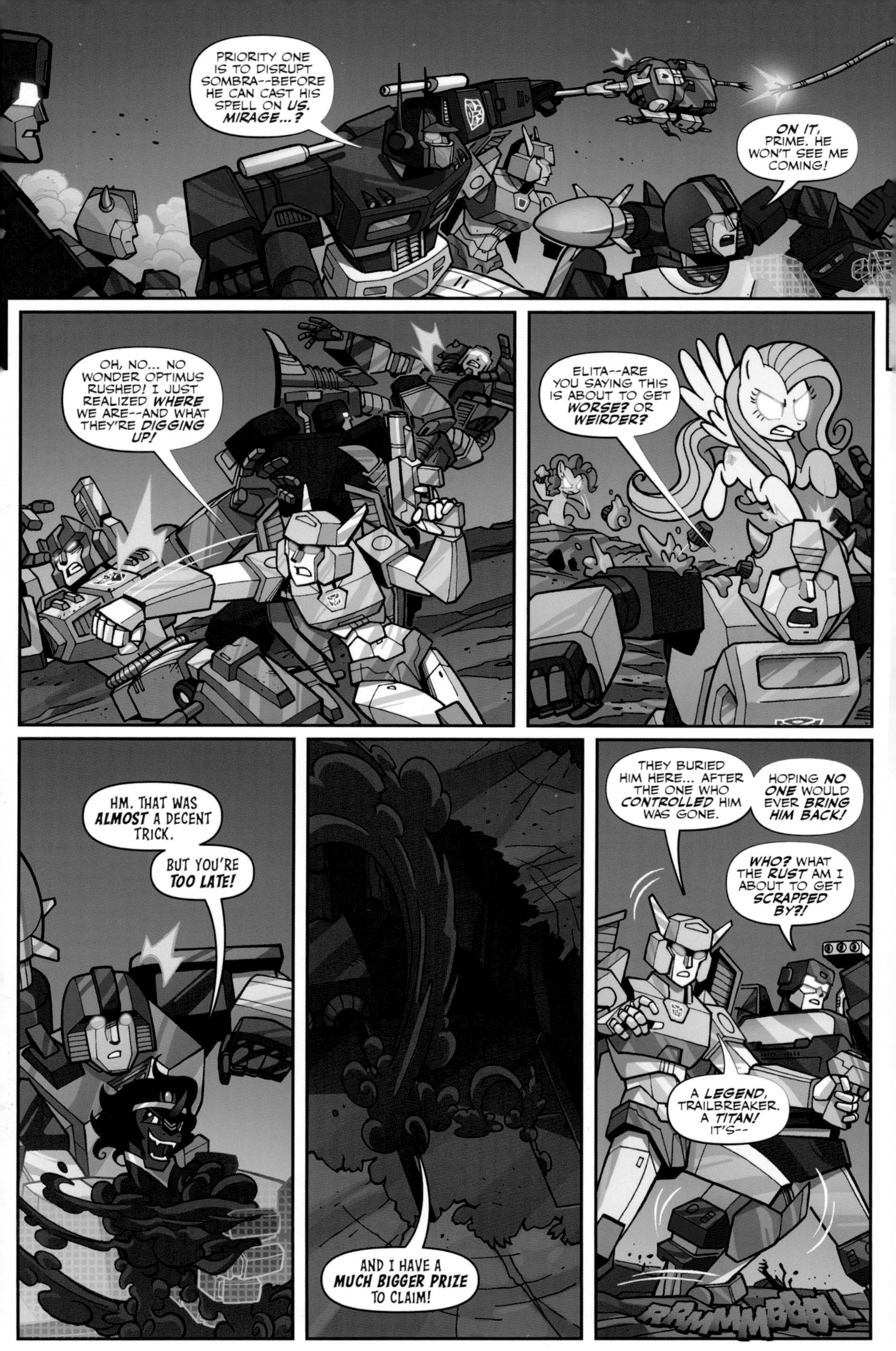
PRIORITY ONE IS TO DISRUPT SOMBRA--BEFORE HE CAN CAST HIS SPELL ON US. MIRAGE...?
ON IT, PRIME. HE WON'T SEE ME COMING!
OH, NO... NO WONDER OPTIMUS RUSHED! I JUST REALIZED WHERE WE ARE--AND WHAT THEY'RE DIGGING UP!
ELITA--ARE YOU SAYING THIS IS ABOUT TO GET WORSE? OR WEIRDER?
HM. THAT WAS ALMOST A DECENT TRICK.
BUT YOU'RE TOO LATE!
AND I HAVE A MUCH BIGGER PRIZE TO CLAIM!
THEY BURIED HIM HERE... AFTER THE ONE WHO CONTROLLED HIM WAS GONE.
HOPING NO ONE WOULD EVER BRING HIM BACK!
WHO? WHAT THE RUST AM I ABOUT TO GET SCRAPPED BY?!
A LEGEND, TRAILBREAKER. A TITAN! IT'S--
RRMMMBBBL

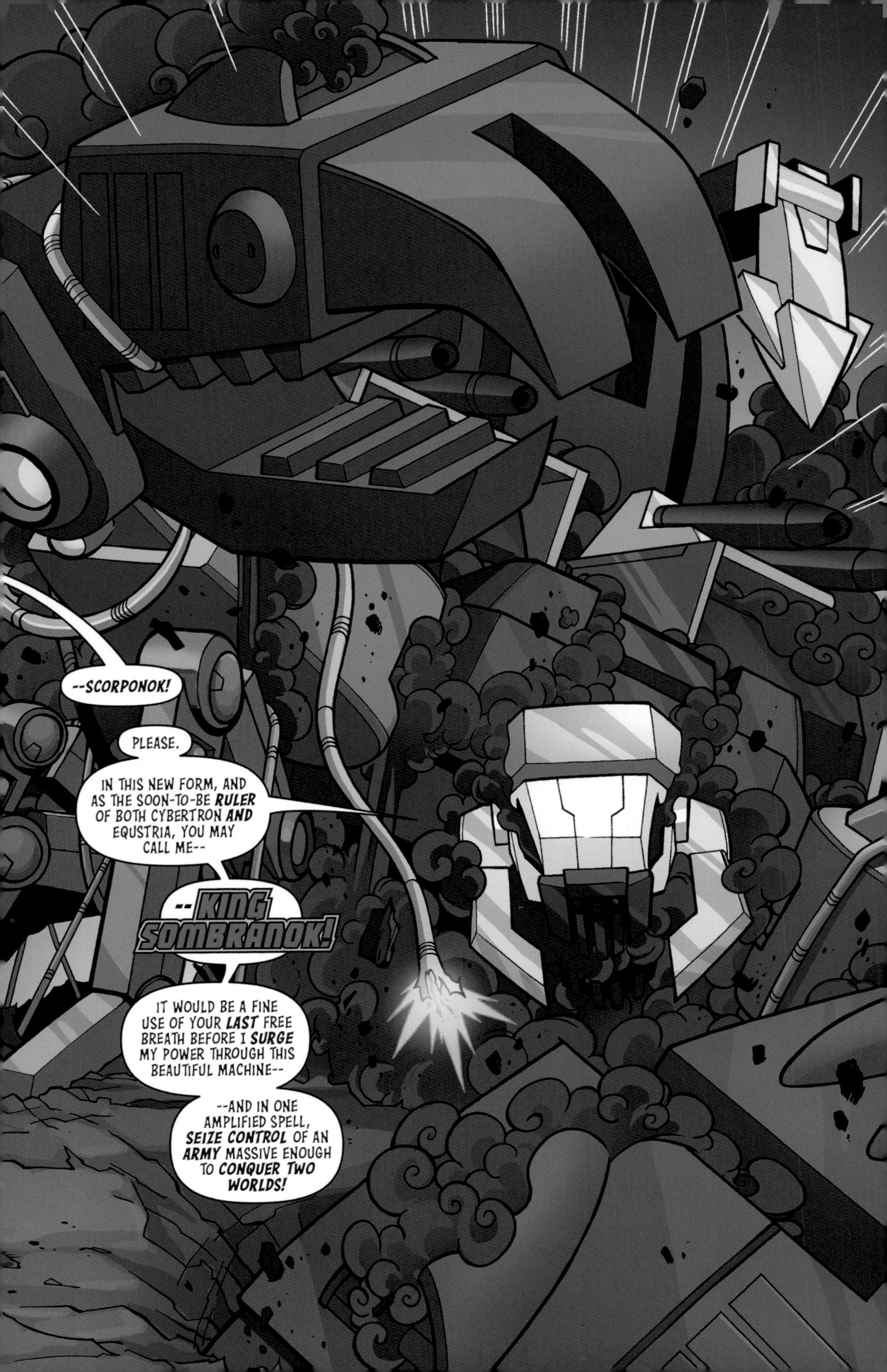
--SCORPONOK!
PLEASE.
IN THIS NEW FORM, AND AS THE SOON-TO-BE RULER OF BOTH CYBERTRON AND EQUSTRIA, YOU MAY CALL ME--
--KING SOMBRANOK!
IT WOULD BE A FINE USE OF YOUR LAST FREE BREATH BEFORE I SURGE MY POWER THROUGH THIS BEAUTIFUL MACHINE--
--AND IN ONE AMPLIFIED SPELL, SEIZE CONTROL OF AN ARMY MASSIVE ENOUGH TO CONQUER TWO WORLDS!

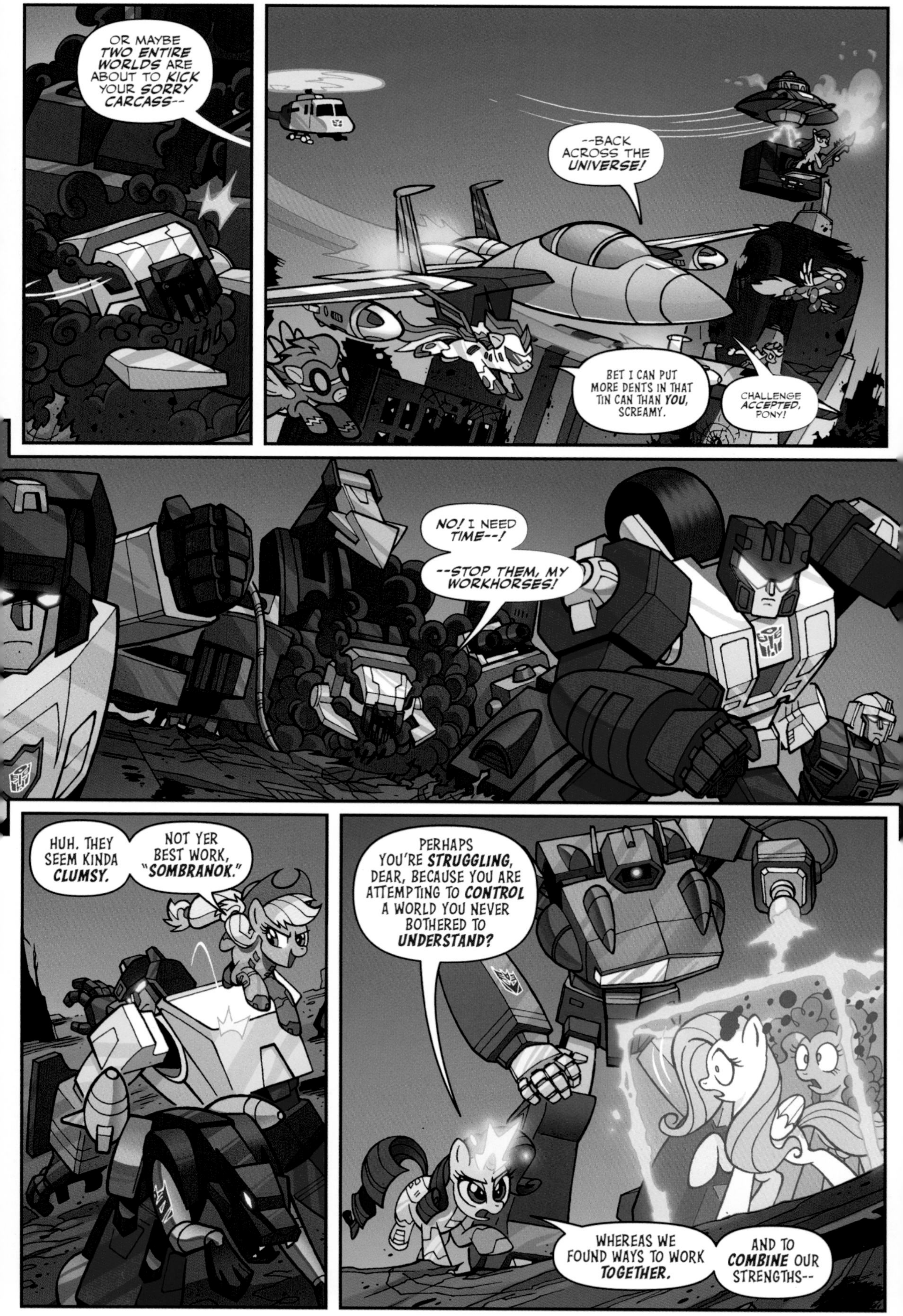
OR MAYBE TWO ENTIRE WORLDS ARE ABOUT TO KICK YOUR SORRY CARCASS--
--BACK ACROSS THE UNIVERSE!
BET I CAN PUT MORE DENTS IN THAT TIN CAN THAN YOU, SCREAMY.
CHALLENGE ACCEPTED, PONY!
NO! I NEED TIME--!
--STOP THEM, MY WORKHORSES!
HUH. THEY SEEM KINDA CLUMSY.
NOT YER BEST WORK, "SOMBRANOK."
PERHAPS YOU'RE STRUGGLING, DEAR, BECAUSE YOU ARE ATTEMPTING TO CONTROL A WORLD YOU NEVER BOTHERED TO UNDERSTAND?
WHEREAS WE FOUND WAYS TO WORK TOGETHER.
AND TO COMBINE OUR STRENGTHS--

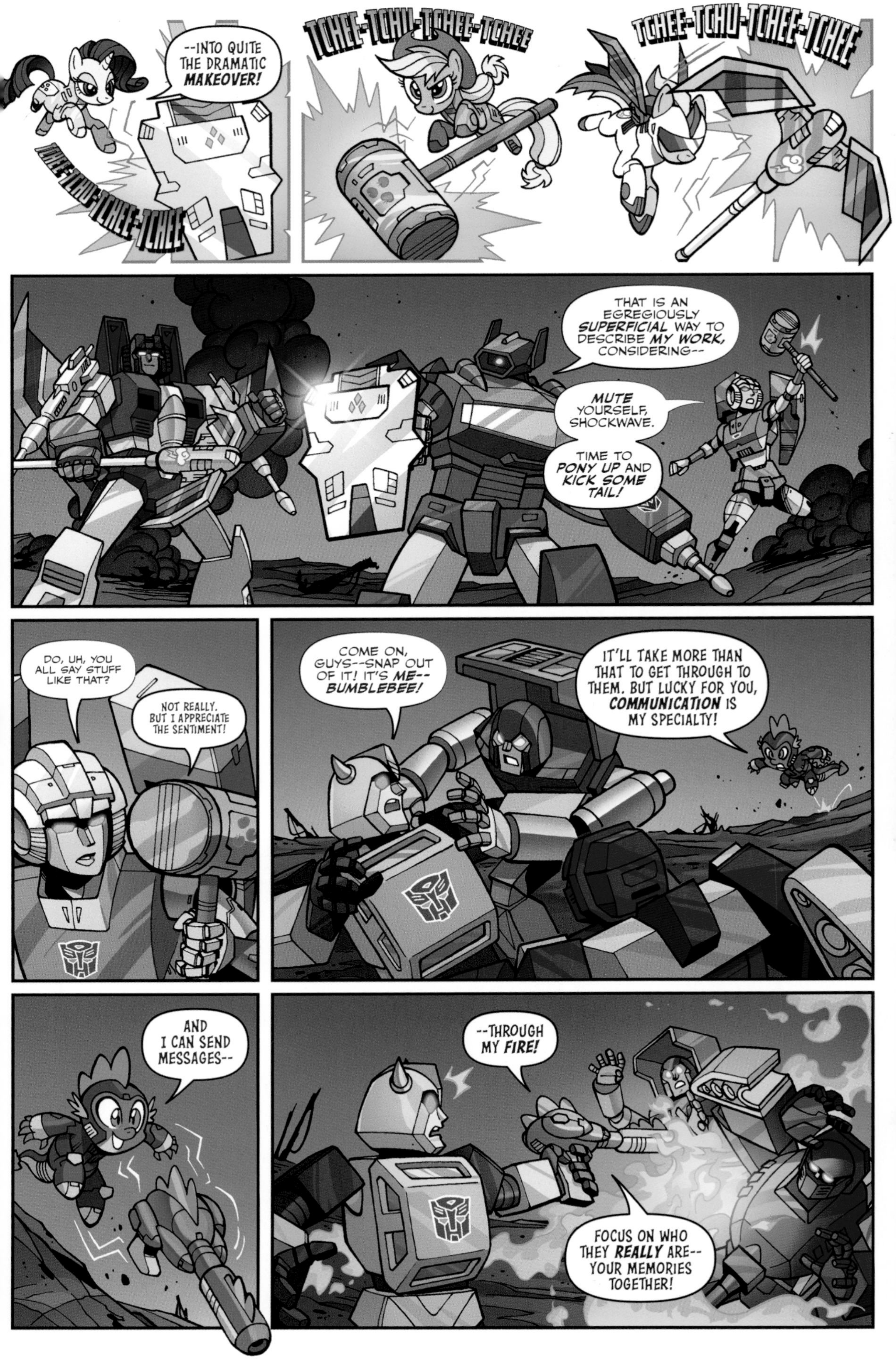
--INTO QUITE THE DRAMATIC MAKEOVER!
TCHEE-TCHU-TCHEE-TCHEE
TCHEE-TCHU-TCHEE-TCHEE
TCHEE-TCHU-TCHEE-TCHEE
THAT IS AN EGREGIOUSLY SUPERFICIAL WAY TO DESCRIBE MY WORK, CONSIDERING--
MUTE YOURSELF, SHOCKWAVE.
TIME TO PONY UP AND KICK SOME TAIL!
DO, UH, YOU ALL SAY STUFF LIKE THAT?
NOT REALLY. BUT I APPRECIATE THE SENTIMENT!
COME ON, GUYS--SNAP OUT OF IT! IT'S ME-- BUMBLEBEE!
IT'LL TAKE MORE THAN THAT TO GET THROUGH TO THEM. BUT LUCKY FOR YOU, COMMUNICATION IS MY SPECIALTY!
AND I CAN SEND MESSAGES--
--THROUGH MY FIRE!
FOCUS ON WHO THEY REALLY ARE-- YOUR MEMORIES TOGETHER!

...AND-- **PRESTO!** WE CAN BREAK SOMBRA'S SPELL!

BEE?! HOW'D I **GET** HERE?

YEAH! I WAS ON THE FIRING RANGE THEN--**WHAM! BLAMMO!**--WE'RE IN A **WAR ZONE?!**

GOT TO ADMIT--I WAS WORRIED THAT WOULDN'T WORK.

NAH... I'VE ALWAYS BEEN ABLE TO **KNOCK SOME SENSE** INTA FOLKS!

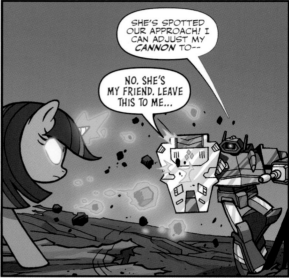

SHE'S SPOTTED OUR APPROACH! I CAN ADJUST MY **CANNON** TO--

NO. SHE'S MY FRIEND. LEAVE THIS TO ME...

MIND CONTROL IS **NOT A GOOD LOOK** ON YOU, DARLING.

R-RARITY? WHOA... HOW LONG WAS I OUT?

ABOUT **TWENTY MINUTES.** BUT I'VE NOTICED THAT THINGS **OFTEN** ESCALATE THAT QUICKLY FOR US.

MEGATRON. THIS MUST BE STOPPED.

NO MATTER THE--

BACK OFF, AUTO-BUTT!

IF **ANYONE** GETS TO BLAST MEGATRON--IT'S GOING TO BE **ME!**

RABODOOOM

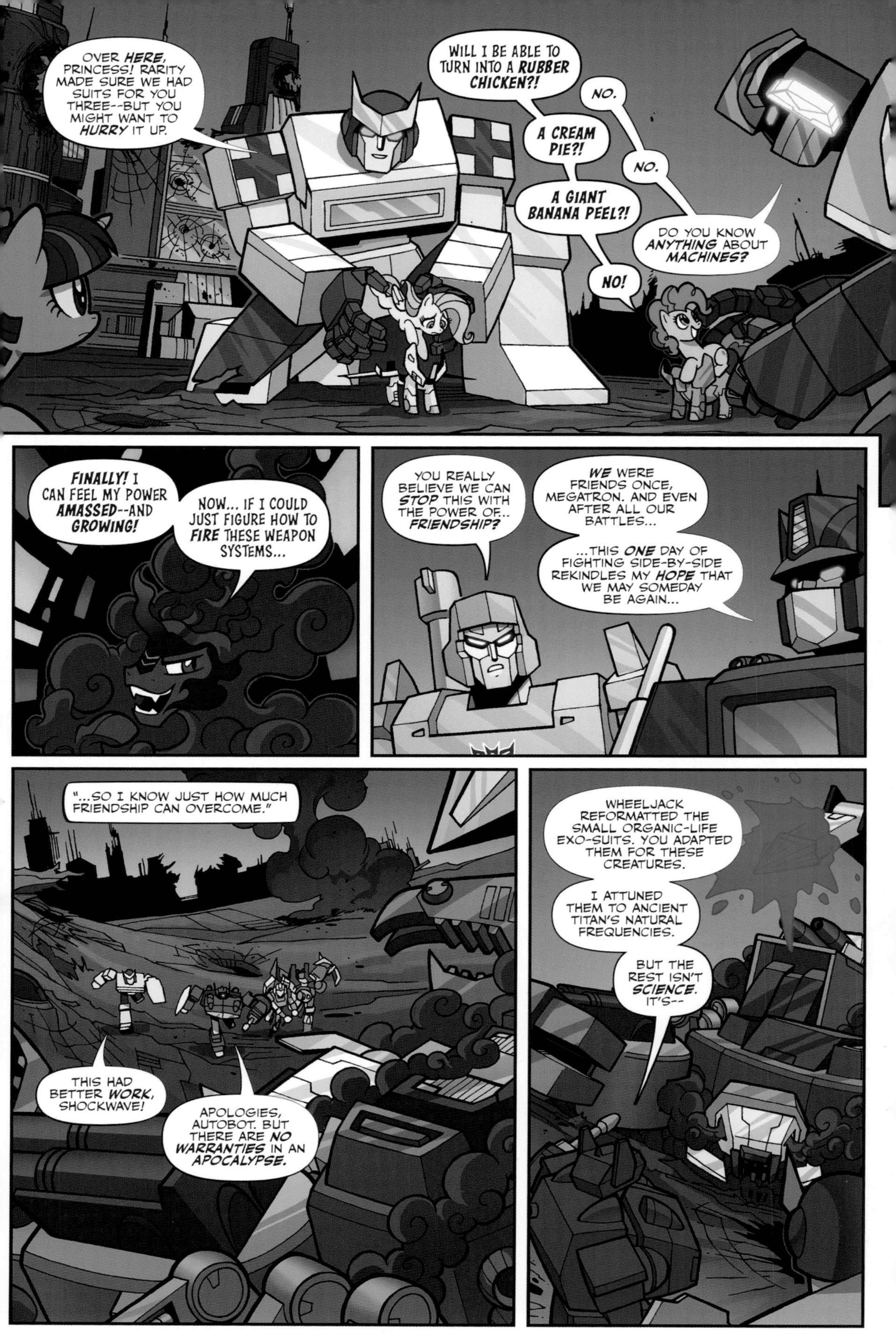
OVER HERE, PRINCESS! RARITY MADE SURE WE HAD SUITS FOR YOU THREE--BUT YOU MIGHT WANT TO HURRY IT UP.
WILL I BE ABLE TO TURN INTO A RUBBER CHICKEN?!
NO.
A CREAM PIE?!
NO.
A GIANT BANANA PEEL?!
NO!
DO YOU KNOW ANYTHING ABOUT MACHINES?
FINALLY! I CAN FEEL MY POWER AMASSED--AND GROWING!
NOW... IF I COULD JUST FIGURE HOW TO FIRE THESE WEAPON SYSTEMS...
YOU REALLY BELIEVE WE CAN STOP THIS WITH THE POWER OF... FRIENDSHIP?
WE WERE FRIENDS ONCE, MEGATRON. AND EVEN AFTER ALL OUR BATTLES...
...THIS ONE DAY OF FIGHTING SIDE-BY-SIDE REKINDLES MY HOPE THAT WE MAY SOMEDAY BE AGAIN...
"...SO I KNOW JUST HOW MUCH FRIENDSHIP CAN OVERCOME."
THIS HAD BETTER WORK, SHOCKWAVE!
APOLOGIES, AUTOBOT. BUT THERE ARE NO WARRANTIES IN AN APOCALYPSE.
WHEELJACK REFORMATTED THE SMALL ORGANIC-LIFE EXO-SUITS. YOU ADAPTED THEM FOR THESE CREATURES.
I ATTUNED THEM TO ANCIENT TITAN'S NATURAL FREQUENCIES.
BUT THE REST ISN'T SCIENCE. IT'S--

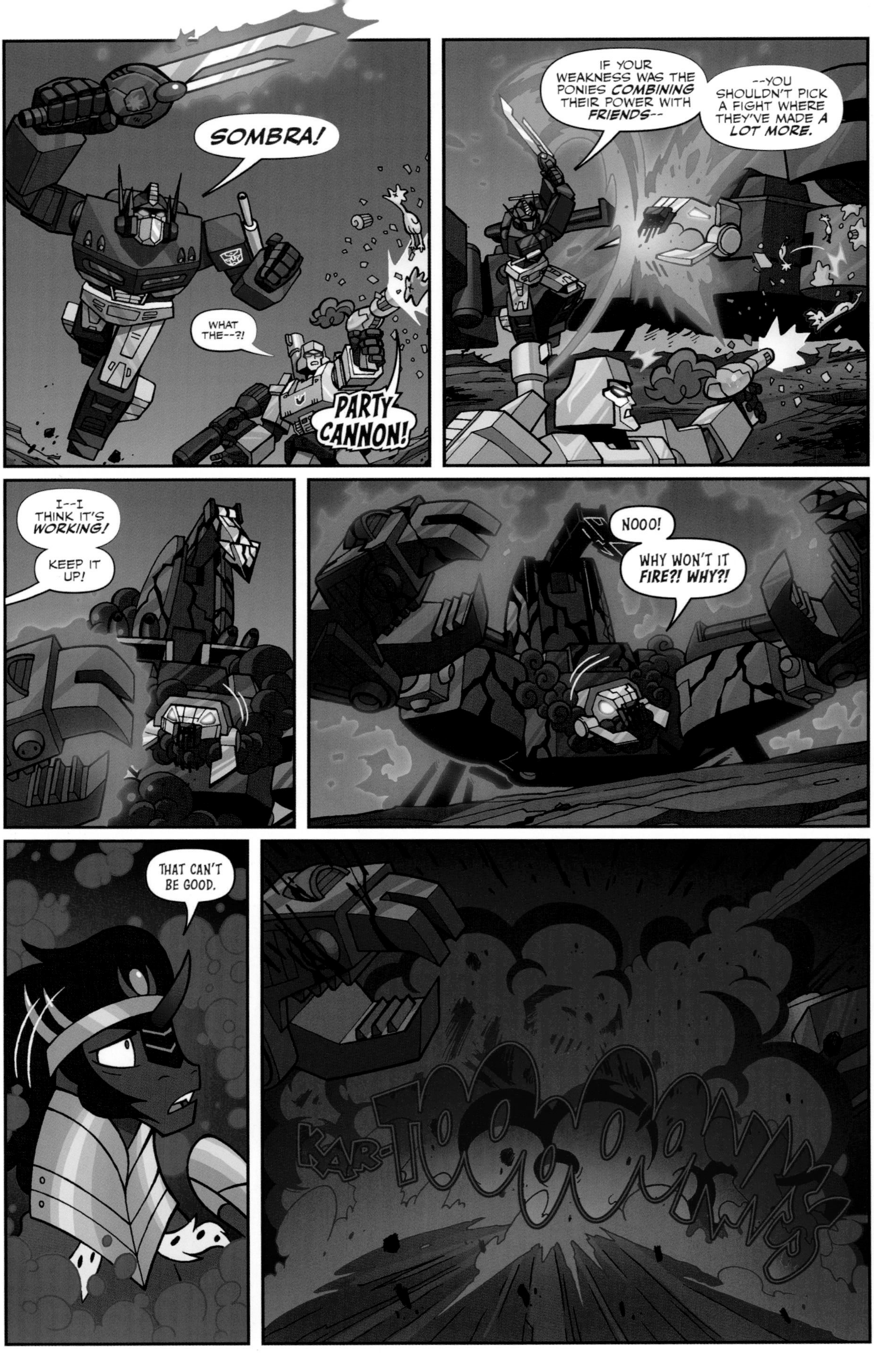
SOMBRA!
WHAT THE--?!
PARTY CANNON!
IF YOUR WEAKNESS WAS THE PONIES COMBINING THEIR POWER WITH FRIENDS--
--YOU SHOULDN'T PICK A FIGHT WHERE THEY'VE MADE A LOT MORE.
I--I THINK IT'S WORKING!
KEEP IT UP!
NOOO!
WHY WON'T IT FIRE?! WHY?!
THAT CAN'T BE GOOD.
KAR-TOOOOOOMMMS

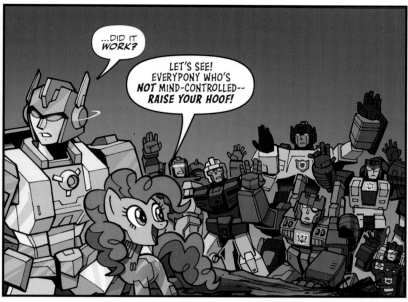

...DID IT **WORK?**

LET'S SEE! EVERYPONY WHO'S **NOT** MIND-CONTROLLED-- **RAISE YOUR HOOF!**

GASP! BUT WHAT IF **I'M** MIND-CONTROLLING THEM NOW?!

THAT'S **ONE THREAT** TAKEN CARE OF. BUT TELL ME, MEGATRON--

--ARE WE ABOUT TO FACE **ANOTHER?**

AS AN **OLD FRIEND** OF MINE OFTEN SAYS--

"**FREEDOM** IS THE RIGHT OF ALL SENTIENT BEINGS."

AND TODAY YOU FOUGHT FOR MY FREEDOM. WHAT MONSTER WOULD I BE IF I DIDN'T ASSURE YOU **YOURS?**

NOW **STARSCREAM,** ON THE OTHER HAND...

THE PONIES' **SPELL** CHANNELS YOUR **THOUGHTS,** FOOL! **INCLUDING** YOUR HOPE THAT A BIT OF **OVERKILL** WOULD "MAGICALLY" TAKE ME **OFFLINE!**

WHAT?! I WAS THE ONE WHO **FREED** YOU!

I--I--

--I'LL **GET** YOU FOR THIS, **MY LITTLE PONIES!**

AND YOUR LITTLE **DRAGON,** TOO!

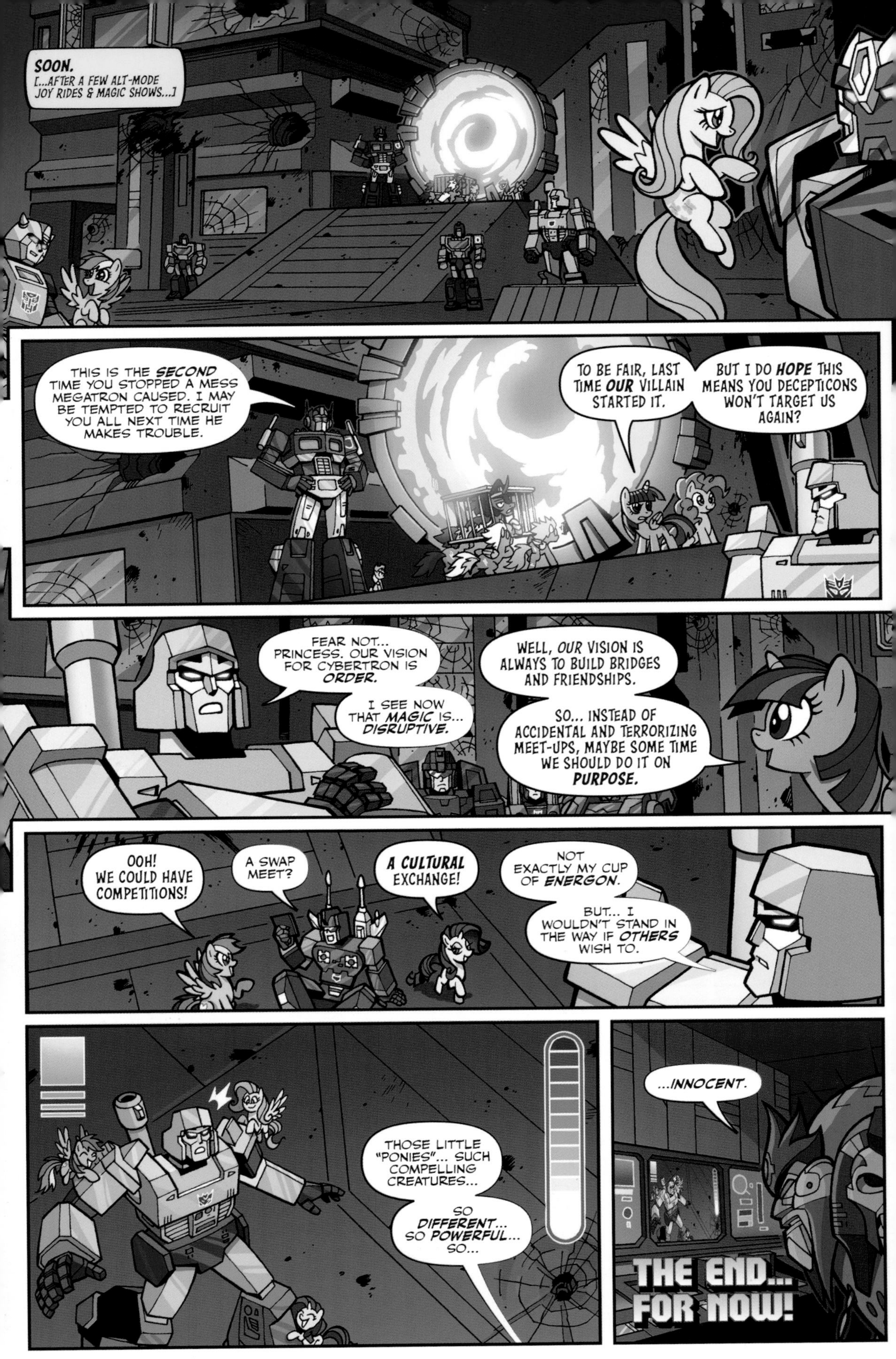
SOON.
[...AFTER A FEW ALT-MODE JOY RIDES & MAGIC SHOWS...]
THIS IS THE SECOND TIME YOU STOPPED A MESS MEGATRON CAUSED. I MAY BE TEMPTED TO RECRUIT YOU ALL NEXT TIME HE MAKES TROUBLE.
TO BE FAIR, LAST TIME OUR VILLAIN STARTED IT.
BUT I DO HOPE THIS MEANS YOU DECEPTICONS WON'T TARGET US AGAIN?
FEAR NOT... PRINCESS. OUR VISION FOR CYBERTRON IS ORDER.
I SEE NOW THAT MAGIC IS... DISRUPTIVE.
WELL, OUR VISION IS ALWAYS TO BUILD BRIDGES AND FRIENDSHIPS.
SO... INSTEAD OF ACCIDENTAL AND TERRORIZING MEET-UPS, MAYBE SOME TIME WE SHOULD DO IT ON PURPOSE.
OOH! WE COULD HAVE COMPETITIONS!
A SWAP MEET?
A CULTURAL EXCHANGE!
NOT EXACTLY MY CUP OF ENERGON.
BUT... I WOULDN'T STAND IN THE WAY IF OTHERS WISH TO.
THOSE LITTLE "PONIES"... SUCH COMPELLING CREATURES...
SO DIFFERENT... SO POWERFUL... SO...
...INNOCENT.
THE END... FOR NOW!

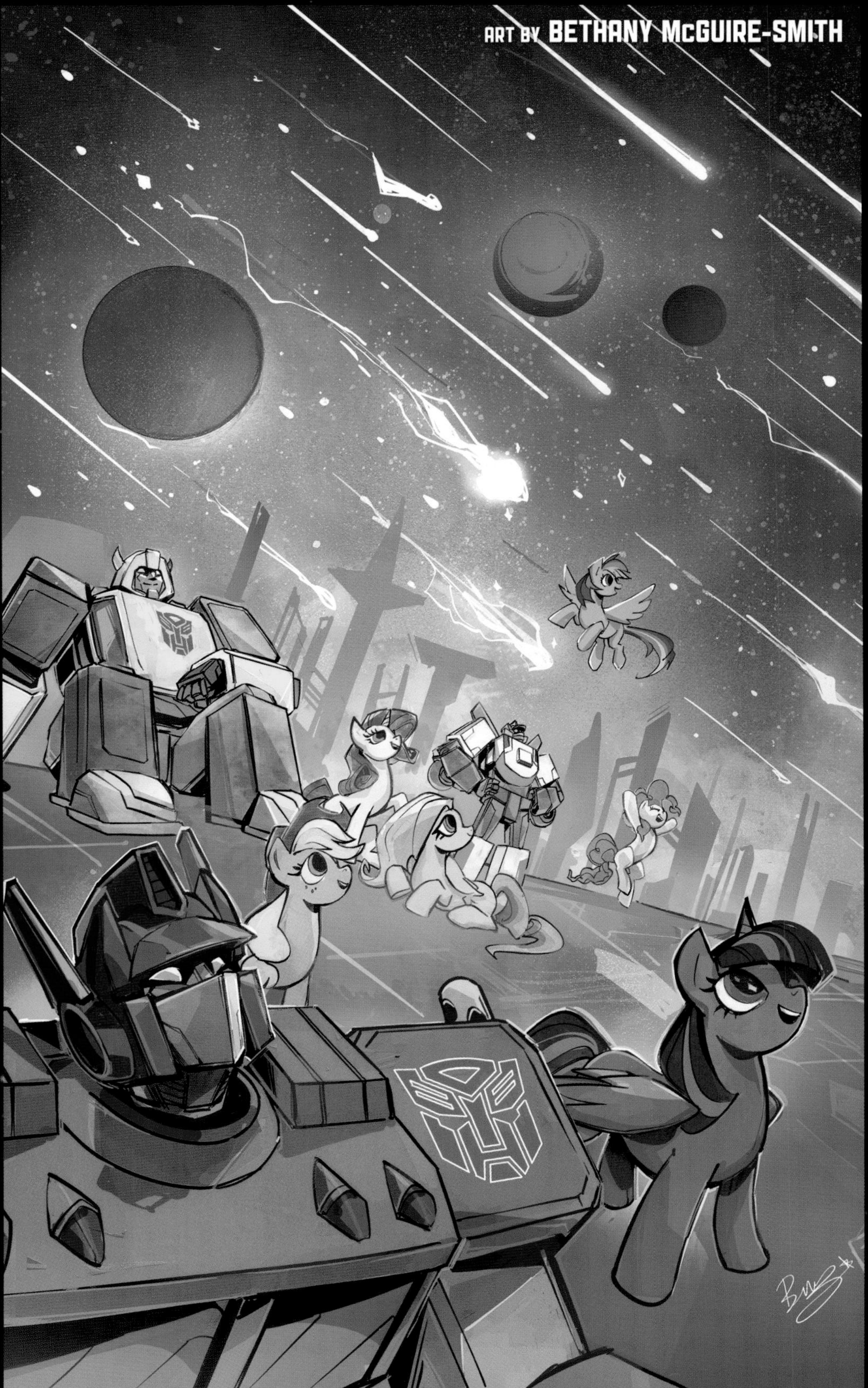
ART BY BETHANY McGUIRE-SMITH

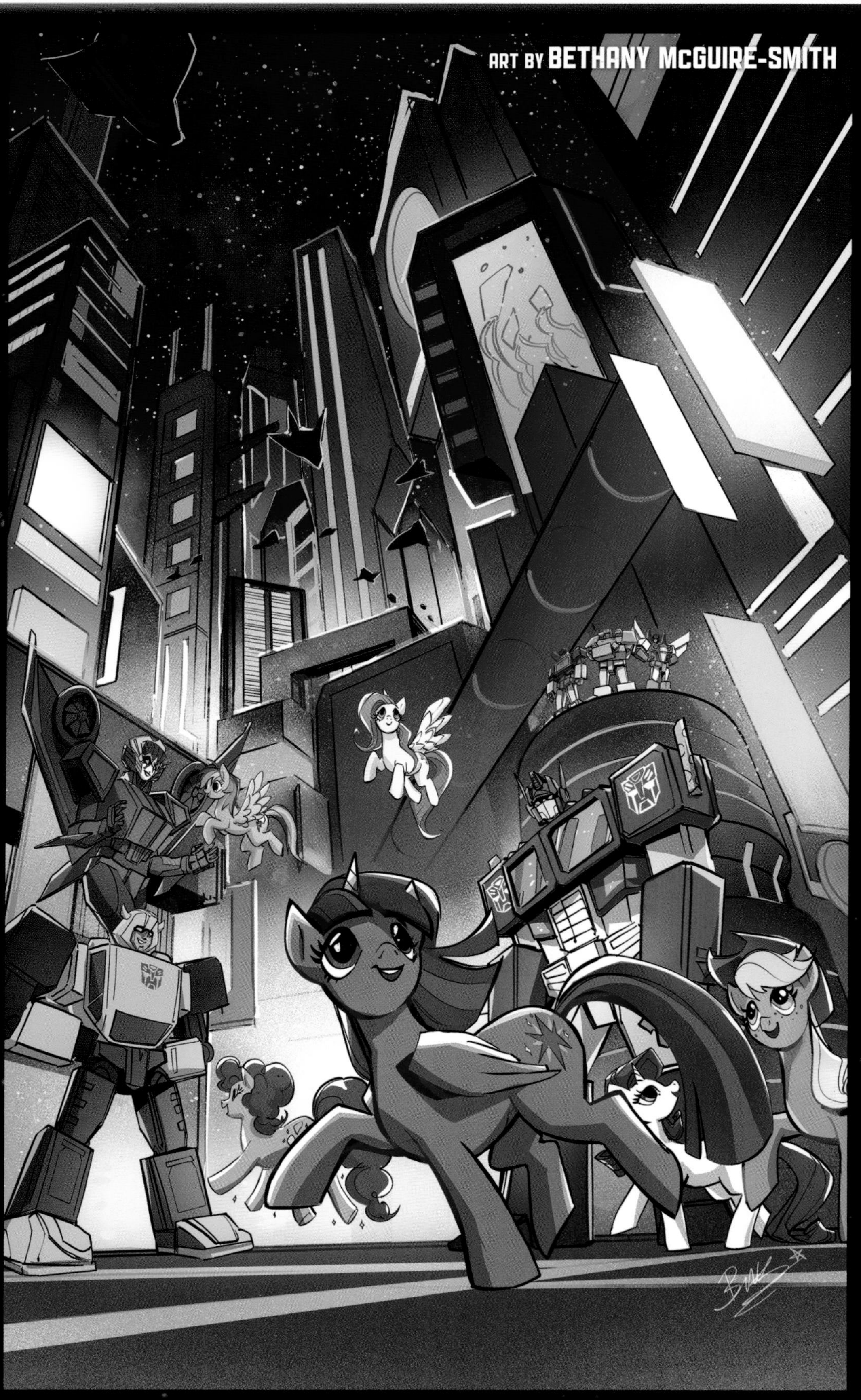

ART BY BETHANY McGUIRE-SMITH

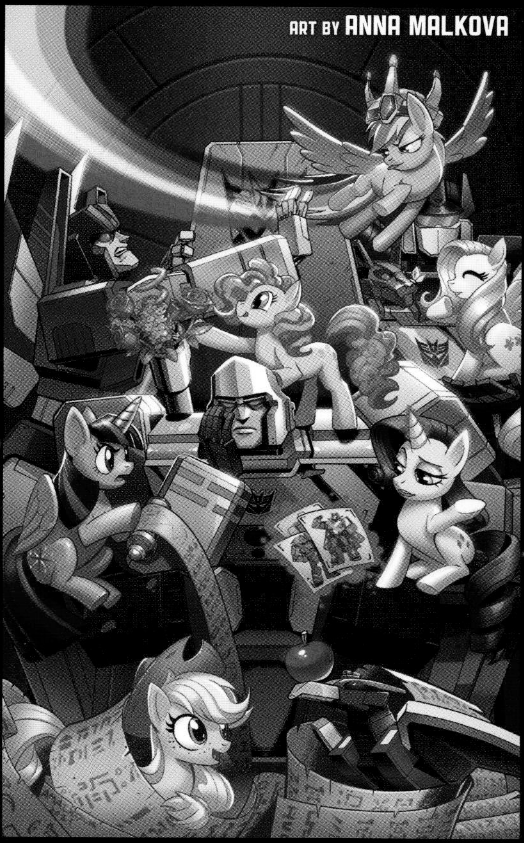
ART BY ANNA MALKOVA

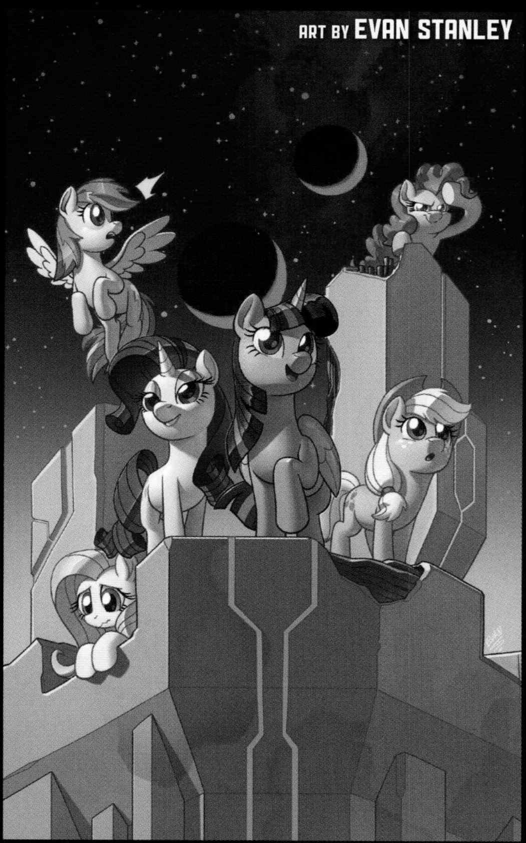
ART BY EVAN STANLEY

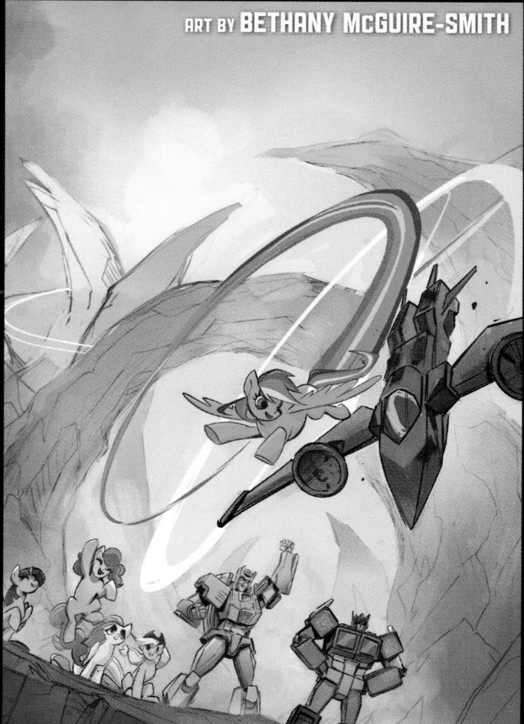
ART BY BETHANY McGUIRE-SMITH

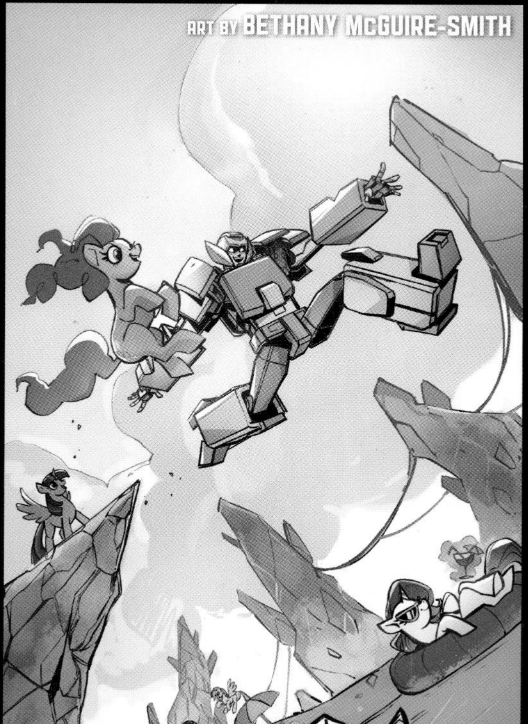
ART BY BETHANY McGUIRE-SMITH

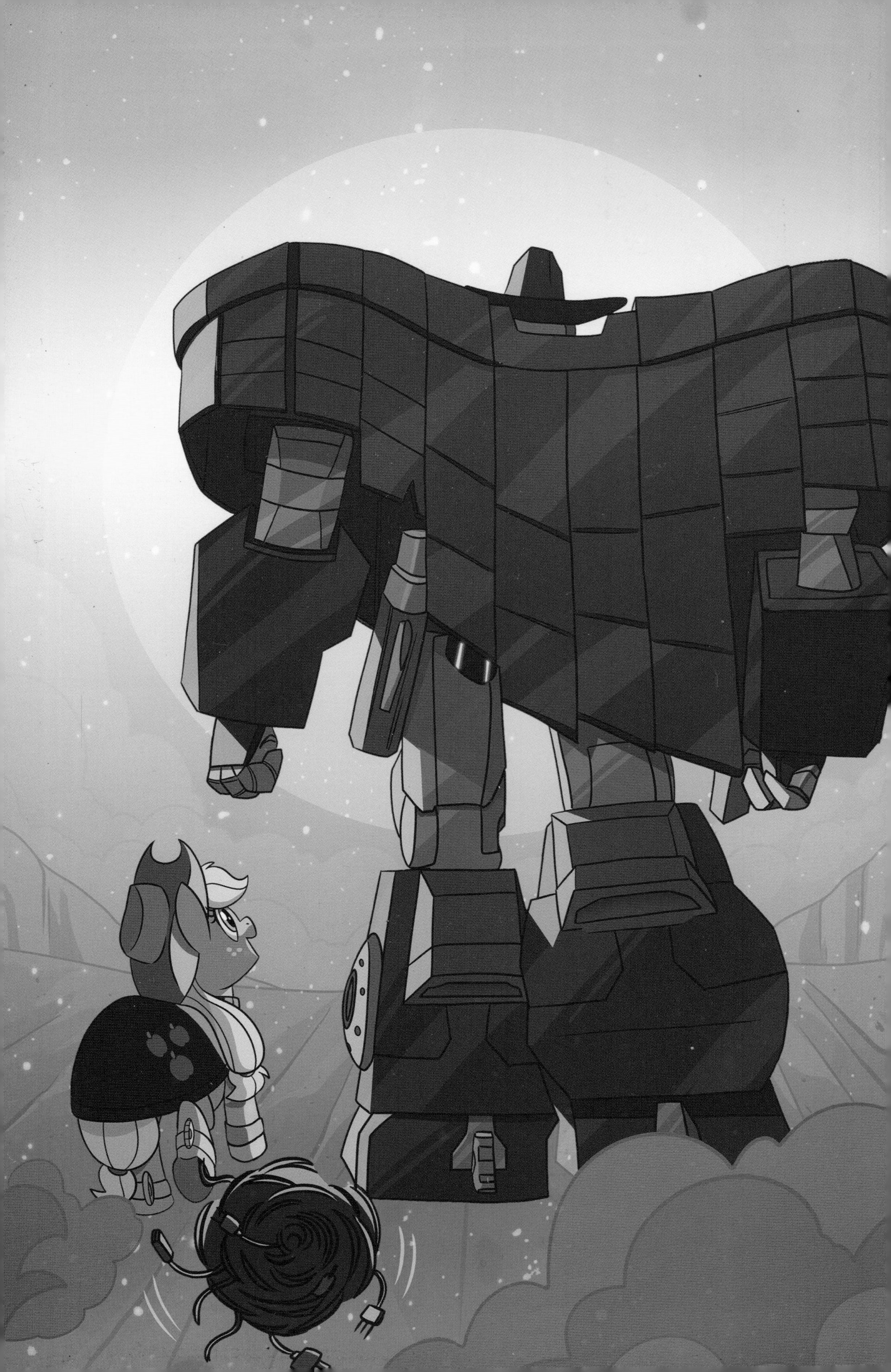